Mike
Kuzara

AuthorHouse™
1663 Liberty Drive
Bloomington, IN 47403
www.authorhouse.com
Phone: 1-800-839-8640

©2012 Mike Kuzara. All rights reserved.

No part of this book may be reproduced, stored in a retrieval system, or transmitted by any means without the written permission of the author.

Published by AuthorHouse   12/07/2012

ISBN: 978-1-4772-6407-2 (sc)
ISBN: 978-1-4772-6406-5 (hc)
ISBN: 978-1-4772-6405-8 (e)

Library of Congress Control Number: 2012915833

Any people depicted in stock imagery provided by Thinkstock are models, and such images are being used for illustrative purposes only. Certain stock imagery © Thinkstock.

This book is printed on acid-free paper.

Because of the dynamic nature of the Internet, any web addresses or links contained in this book may have changed since publication and may no longer be valid. The views expressed in this work are solely those of the author and do not necessarily reflect the views of the publisher, and the publisher hereby disclaims any responsibility for them.

Prologue

Alden Spotted Horse *woke up and shivered in the dawn chill. His blanket had slipped from his naked shoulders and he could see his breath in the golden light that slanted across the sandstone ledge where he had spent the last three days fasting on his vision quest.*

Alden wore the traditional braids of the men of his tribe. They trailed down across the scars left from last year's Sun Dance. The ceremony was an ordeal seldom attempted by one of his advanced years but he had a reputation among his people as a seer and a warrior so he was allowed to add this honor to his title as the last true war chief in his tribe.

The old Indian liked this place the white people called the rim rocks. These sandstone bluffs were composed of the seafloor sediment that had compacted into this soft rock, which then was sculpted into varied shapes by millions of years of wind, rain, and flowing water.

Unimaginable time had passed while the sediment was first grooved and then eroded away leaving these vertical walls. The south side of many of these bluffs held mute testimony to the many human hands that had for thousands of years scratched their enigmatic messages on the yielding sandy surfaces. Much of the meaning could only be guessed.

There was also the smell, a mixture of odors dominated by the Rocky Mountain juniper. Alden often thought that if he tried hard he could make out just a faint touch of the smell of the sea that once covered the area. But as the holder of a doctorate degree, logic told him that it was probably methane seeping from underlying coal seams or perhaps even the natural gas working its way up from the still deeper pools of oil.

Of all the emotions Alden experienced in the US Army, nothing matched the hollow sickness his vision had produced. Alden's black eyes tried to stare at the memory in his mind but it remained an elusive puzzle, a blazing arrow streaking toward a shadowy eagle that sent the bird spiraling to the ground. But before impact, it had become helplessly entangled in a giant web that covered tall dark pine trees. As the bird struggled to get free, a spider with a skeleton face appeared. For some unexplained reason, Alden sensed the spider was a female and she was followed by a pack of wolves. They were strange looking wolves that reminded him of images he had seen in a book once. Suddenly the old warrior remembered; they were called jackals.

Before the spider or her jackals could reach the trapped eagle, a gaunt old grizzly with silver-tipped fur limped up and tore away the entangling webs to free the bird, but the great eagle could not fly. As the jackals came closer to attack the bird, it took refuge on the bear's back. Then the bear limped away turning now and then to snap first one then another jackal in half leaving them writhing on the ground. They were still running when the dream began to fade. Alden could not tell if the riders he saw were in his dream or were they in the misty growing light of the dawn? They were definitely young warriors painted with white and red bands while the ponies sported blue stars. There was a flash of color as the warriors swirled among yellow jackals raising a cloud of dust that obscured everything. The dream melded into reality, for the cloud of dust that he was now staring at was raised by a herd of antelope frightened by an oil company truck.

Although the old warrior's solitude had been broken by modern intrusion, he noted with satisfaction a lone eagle soaring unperturbed by the activity on the earth below. "That should be me," he thought.

Alden Spotted Horse's wrinkled shoe-leather face wrinkled even more as the perplexing memory of the dream whirled through his mind.

He knew he must discuss this vision and its meaning as soon as possible, but right now he needed to get dressed, find something to eat and drink, and get back to his modest home on the reservation. Hunting season would begin soon and his intended audience would be scattered all over the mountains.

CHAPTER ONE
Curiosity

OCT. 1, 3:30 pm, 8,234 feet above sea level, just below a place known locally as Elephant Rock in the Big Horn Mountains of north central Wyoming:

Jerry "Pat" Garrett leaned from his horse and rubbed at the light frost covering the Plexiglas window of an old blue two-horse trailer that had been parked off on the side of what the native population called a *road*.

Actually, *road* was merely a euphemism used to describe the remnants of the old logging trail that paralleled the northerly flowing Big Swampy Creek. The boulder pile about a hundred yards south of the horse trailer, was where larger vehicles had to turn around. Foot traffic, horses, and ATVs could pick their way around to continue on south.

The forest in this area was a good blend of ancient, old- and new-growth timber. The 1890s had seen extensive cutting by hand by that hardy breed of tough men known as "tie hackers." They were gone by 1913. The forest rested and recovered so that by the 1950s one could walk through a forested mountainside that contained burnt snags, 150-year-old stumps with still-visible ax marks, smooth-sawed stumps from selective cutting, trees of every age, and rotting remnants of the wooden flume that carried away the hand-hewed railroad ties. Recent logging left open patches creating "parks" that were slowly relinquishing their openness to young seedling trees providing excellent elk habitat.

There were a few camps further up in parks near the end of the trail under a ridge called "The Arm" supplied by either packhorses or ATVs, but most hunters staged out of a modestly developed campground where this trail met the more improved Boulder River main road.

Big Swampy road, trail, track, (take your pick) turned into a streambed during the first big snow melt. The torrents of rushing water scoured out all of the fine softer material leaving a cobblestone course that tested the best of vehicle suspensions. Scars gouged into the biggest boulders indicated that it was foolish to bring any vehicle without substantial ground clearance this far up, and yet, here sat this horse trailer.

"Well Rosie, guess I'll have to get down for a better look," Pat Garrett told his horse as he stiffly swung down.

Pat tied Rosie to a nearby tree with the lead rope. In his profession as a Wyoming Game Warden, he had learned that anything could happen any time. Having a horse spook without being securely tethered usually meant a long walk. The last and only time Rosie ran off, Pat found her easy enough, but much to his chagrin, his rifle was missing from the scabbard. Someone had found Rosie, tied her to a tree near a main road, and helped himself to Pat's rifle as a reward.

While Rosie shuffled and snuffled nearby, Pat tried peering into the other small windows on the sides of the horse trailer. It was dark inside and mostly Pat was rewarded by seeing himself reflected back from the Plexiglas. What he saw was a forty-year-old handsome face with a thick, black handlebar mustache, brown eyes that looked out of a well-tanned face, framed by a battered black Stetson.

Pat thought he could make out some bedrolls, boxes, and coolers inside, but the Dutch doors on the back were padlocked as was the side access. The combination locks looked pretty new. Pat didn't see any hoof prints, old or new, leading away from the trailer. "Very strange," he thought.

Pat was just about to inform his horse that he thought this trailer was merely storing hunting equipment when he felt warm breath on his left hand, the thumb of which he had hooked in his hip pocket.

Adrenaline caused Pat to leap sideways while turning and clawing for his pepper spray. "Jeez!" Pat yelped as he bounced off the side of the horse trailer, cracking his elbow on one of the tie-down loops welded to the side. The huge black dog that had sniffed at his hand stood calmly confident, watching the discomfited game warden with mildly alert interest.

"Dozer heard your horse." The booming laugh sounded like it came from inside a rain barrel.

"Shit, Ace! I wish you and this packhorse you claim is a dog wouldn't sneak up like that!" Pat gasped as he held his throbbing elbow.

The rain-barrel laugh echoed off the rocks of this narrow canyon. The 140-pound dog remained calmly watching the startled warden.

"I got some coffee and some clean underwear in my tent," chuckled the man Pat had addressed as Ace as he made a small jerking motion with his head to indicate that his tent was somewhere behind him.

Pat could not see more than a few feet into the new growth the forest service had planted about ten years back. The ten- to fifteen-foot trees were so close together, each fighting for sunlight, that Pat could not determine how anyone the size of the man in front of him could possibly fit through what people referred to as a *dog-hair* stand of timber.

Ace looked as much like a bear as did the dog he called Dozer. The man wore heavily greased logger boots that laced clear up to just below the knee. His black soft-wool pants were tucked into the boot tops and a blue-green Woolrich shirt covered a down vest. The wool wouldn't have made the telltale swishing sound against the pine branches that so much other material made. The ensemble had been topped by an Australian rainproof hat but it was now hanging down Ace's back by the stampede string. This left the big man's face unshaded revealing ice-blue eyes behind round granny glasses. The lightly lined face was framed by wild, shoulder-length brown hair that had turned silver at the temples. The bushy, unkempt mustache accented a large hawk nose. The thick eyebrows that slanted up with a little twirl at the end reminded Pat of Spock on Star Trek. Pat correctly guessed the hat had been removed, first to keep it from making noise, and secondly to keep the man from running his face and head into any branches that the brim would have blocked from his vision.

As an enforcer of the law, Pat's training allowed him to automatically take in and make note of as many details as he could quickly process, but it was very difficult to do so since his eyes were continually drawn to the wicked-looking seven-foot spear in Ace's left hand.

Ace seemed consciously cognizant of that distraction since he continually turned the shaft slightly, first one way and then the other, so that the sunlight ran up and down the polished surface of the eighteen-inch blade.

Ace was discreetly aware of Pat noticing the spear, so he grinned and nodded toward the implement in his left hand. "Walkin' stick," he explained.

"Nice!" Pat replied. He also made a mental note of a military-style twelve gauge slung tactical style from the big man's right shoulder. Later, upon getting a closer look at the shotgun, Pat saw a sticker on the butt stock that read, "Polish Bear Spray!"

Pat looked pointedly at the shotgun. "Expecting trouble?" he asked, finally coming down from his adrenaline high.

"Nope," the bear-like man rumbled, "just prepared." Then he continued, "Let's have that coffee. I've got something to talk to you about." As Ace turned to lead the way up the road, he turned back to the game warden, "You better grab your rifle off your horse. Never can tell what kind of dee-linquents we got nowadays ridin' ATVs up and down this road and I don't want you to come up missin' another one!"

Ace explained that his camp wasn't that far off the road, but he and his son had packed everything in along the boulder pile covering the tiny tributary that entered Big Swampy Creek from the east. That way there was no trail into the camp from the road. They then doubled back south and set up camp behind the screen of dog-hair timber just inside the start of the old growth timber. Several hundred yards northeast of the campsite the gentle slope of the terrain ended abruptly in a cliff hundreds of feet high like the blunt prow of a landlocked ship. When the light was right, one could use their imagination to make out the rough outline of an elephant with its trunk curled under.

Dozer patrolled parallel to the two men as they approached a twelve-by fourteen-feet wall tent dyed in blotches of light and dark green. The huge dog suddenly stopped and looked back at Ace who eased forward to gently raise a piece of fish line stretched knee high from tree to tree.

The dog ducked under the line, then the men squatted to get under. "Burglar and bear alarm," Ace explained, then he showed Pat how the line pulled a release on a small wooden contraption attached to one of the ancient stately spruce trees. A weight dropped on a pulley line just like a cuckoo clock, which operated a cog wheel that flipped a wooden clapper. Ace demonstrated the device, which sounded remarkably like a woodpecker drumming on a hollow limb.

"I seen trip lines with empty cans and stuff but I don't want unnatural sounds givin' this place away," the big man explained. "Also, I want the sound to distract who or whatever set off my alarm while I see who it is. That's why it's over there opposite the door."

Pat made note of the elk hanging high up on a meat pole outside the perimeter of the fish line. "Can I see the tag?" he asked knowing it would be there.

The warden checked the tag and license. "No trophy, this one. I didn't know you bow hunted."

"No hunt involved," Ace confessed. "Bulls get stupid during rut. You call 'em in, stick 'em with an arrow and hope you don't have to chase 'em down too far. You're right about no trophy head, but you can't eat the horns, right?"

Pat agreed with that philosophy. Then he observed, "Looks like you used five pounds of black pepper on that meat. Does it really keep the flies off?

"That and the bears," Ace said.

The two men sat on folding chairs next to the stove and drank coffee from tin cups that had to be picked up with a gloved hand.

"Damn! If I sit here much longer catching up on family news and friends, this stove is going to put me to sleep. What else did you want to talk to me about?" Pat asked, knowing from experience that the ritual of discussing family and friends was a time-honored tradition that gave each participant the chance to judge and feel comfortable with each other.

Ace got up without a word and pushed some things out of the way on the tent's only table, a slab of plywood on two sawhorses. He pulled a forest service topographic map from a leather map case, weighted the corners with coffee cups, plates, and a can of peaches, and pointed to a highlighted spot.

"We're here," Ace said, indicating a spot where the elevation lines stacked one on top of the other, representing the cliff behind the camp. "Aaaaaannnnnd riiiiiight, um, here," Ace stabbed the map with a scarred blunt finger, "is some kind of contraption sittin' on this knob up on The Arm. I'm guessin' that it has somethin' to do with these yayhoos down the crik here who have somethin' to do with two other bunches of surly yayhoos here and here!" Ace indicated two more places in adjacent drainages to the one they were presently in.

"I think I've seen those camps," Pat admitted. "One is just down the road here at the Big Swampy Campground kind of off by itself. There's one at Little Swampy and it's all by itself too. Then another is sharing the big campground on Gloomy Creek. They are the only group that has an ATV."

"Did you see their little spy-in-the-sky thing?" Ace asked, clearly agitated. Pat gave Ace a short negative headshake. "I think they're using it to spot elk from the air," Ace continued.

"If that's what they're doing, that's illegal, but I'd have to prove it first. Have you seen this thing?" Pat asked.

"Yep! I watched 'em bring it in one day and I saw it crash once. Me and Dozer been hikin' all around since I got my elk and I just love these mountains. 'Course I sorta make note of where the elk are too, if you know what I mean."

Pat understood that Ace Gronsky would be all too happy to inform his extended family as to the likely whereabouts of elk when they showed up at his camp on the night before rifle season opened, Oct. 15.

Pat looked at his watch, estimated the time until sundown, and asked Ace, "Why don't you tell me all about this. You've really got my curiosity up now."

"Okay, but I'm tellin' you now about a run-in I had with those hard cases downstream just in case the sheriff or anybody asks," Ace said. "I'm sorta surprised they ain't raised a stink, but then too, maybe not!" There was an air of conspiratorial expression to his tone.

Ace described how he had heard a strange sound from above the pine trees as he was on a hike down to the road junction two miles below his camp. It occurred to Ace that he might visit with some of the other hunters in the area who were in the established campgrounds. Maybe he could swap hunting stories with them.

Dozer and Ace had followed the sound to the small campground about fifty yards off road just short of the junction with the Boulder River Road that led eventually out to the main highway. Ace stopped just inside the tree line to observe four rough-looking men craning their necks to watch a small helicopter-like machine with four rotors descend into the clearing under the direction of the man with a remote control box. Ace could see that the screen on the control box, about the size of a small laptop computer, was showing a bird's-eye view of the campground. The man with the control rolled a thumb wheel so that the Minicam on the minicopter panned around the campground. The men were all startled to see Ace and Dozer on the screen watching them from the tree line. As three of them grabbed for holstered automatic pistols, the fourth man, flustered and distracted, allowed the minicopter to flip over in a loop and try to screw itself into the dirt and pine needles. The resulting cloud of dust obscured everything for a moment, and as Ace stepped out of the tree line to apologize for the distraction, one man, a mean-looking cuss with a single eyebrow clear across a low forehead, had advanced with his pistol drawn.

Dozer growled a deep warning rumble and the twelve gauge shotgun slipped off of Ace's right shoulder.

"If he moves, I'll shoot your fuckin' dog!" One-eyebrow screamed.

"And I'll be obliged to cut you in half!" Ace warned. "Now, holster your pistol!" As two of the men started to side step, Ace added, "And the rest of you stay put and gathered together, okay?" One-eyebrow was clearly losing it. His stomach muscles were pumping in and out and his breath was hissing as he hyperventilated. Given a few more seconds he would probably loose control and draw the pistol he had loosely holstered.

"You!" Ace said, as his shotgun barrel pointed to the man wearing a brand new Cabela's cap who stood on One-eyebrow's right. "Take his pistol out with two fingers! Now!" The man on the right was eager to defuse a situation they all saw might escalate, plus this wild-looking man with the nasty-looking shotgun and the wicked-looking spear seemed to be holding all the aces.

"Drop it in the fire!" Ace ordered. Cabela's-cap looked at One-eyebrow with a "what else can I do?" expression. "Everyone keep your arms out! And gather around the fire!" Ace ordered.

The men shuffled to the fire while One-eyebrow was absolutely shaking with rage. "Drop it!" Ace nodded to the man in the Cabella's cap. One-eyebrow's pistol raised a small shower of sparks as it fell into the fire pit. "Now yours!" Ace said to Cabela's cap. "Now you, lefty. *With two fingers!*" Three pistols were in the fire. "Let's get that fourth one in the fire before they all start going off!" Ace didn't need to prod the fourth man, who wore a brand new Lands End checkered shirt.

"Now, I suggest you all dive behind that big log over there until the fireworks are all over!" Ace said, and the four men sprinted toward the protection of the old downed tree on the far side of the campground. Ace and Dozer quickly disappeared into the trees to find a circuitous route back to camp. As they crossed Big Swampy Road and turned to parallel it back up stream, they were cheered by the pop-pop-popping of the pistols destroying themselves in the fire pit.

X X X X X

"Either they fixed that flying machine or they have more than one because I've heard it or one like it flying over on Little Swampy," Ace told Pat who sat there wide-eyed at what he had just heard. The old man went on before Pat could speak. "Since they need a line of sight, near as I can tell, they must bounce a signal off of that little tower they have up on The Arm. It's got solar panels for power and it wasn't there until these guys moved in."

Pat finally got his thoughts collected and asked, "What makes you think they're all connected somehow?"

"Patrick, Patrick, Patrick! What sort of lawmen are they turning out nowadays?" Ace chided with a big wolfish grin. "Didn't you notice there are four men in each camp? They all have brand new clothes and boots. They have brand new black Yukon SUVs, identical cargo trailers, and all the license plates are from Maryland. And the little peek I got through the tent flap showed me they have more than just cots inside. It's all mighty peculiar if you ask me. I don't think this quite falls under the game violations law, but I think the sheriff should be notified don't you? These guys are no more hunters than I'm a ballerina and I'll bet dollars to donuts they're up to no good!"

Pat nodded occasionally as he studied the map and listened to Ace's recitation.

Ace went on, "If you look at the elevation lines here, you'll see that the contraption on The Arm has a nearly unobstructed line of sight to each of those three camps." Pat nodded agreement but merely said, "Hmmm."

Pat looked at his watch, noted the shadows on the tent wall, and told Ace that he would look in on the *hunters,* adding emphasis to the word, hunters. Since he had to get some elevation to check into headquarters, it would give him a good excuse to have a look at the "tower" in the morning. "I'll ask the sheriff if anyone turned in a complaint about your little 'set to' as you call it," Pat grinned. "But I'll be discreet."

Ace thanked Pat for the deference, then agreed it was a good spot for reception since he used the ridge to check in with family every day. His son and other relatives who had day jobs would all be coming up for rifle season in about a week, and that was part of the reason why Ace was babysitting the camp. All the extra provisions, beds, and other equipment were stored in the horse trailer which explained for Pat why it was parked where it was and why Ace's tent was no farther than a hundred yards away behind a thick wall of dog-hair timber. Ace gave Pat his son's cell phone number plus a contact number for Alden Spotted Horse and his grandson Billy Black Stone.

Billy had worked for the forest service and the Indian fire crews, so it was widely known on the reservation that he knew the Big Horns as well as anyone and better than most.

Ace was always glad to have Billy share their camp. Billy said he'd think about it and come up for a couple of days if he didn't get all bunged up from practicing for the Indian relay races.

"Billy told me Alden had a message for me but we've never been near the phone at the same time," Ace told Pat. "It must be pretty important, though, because Billy said he'd get Grandfather to the phone exactly at eleven tomorrow morning and he told me, 'And that ain't Crow time,' so it *must* be pretty important."

Pat made his goodbye, forgot about the trip line, and set off the woodpecker alarm. "Damn it Ace! That's the second time today you made me jump!"

After Pat made his way back out to his horse, Ace and Dozer made a little circle around the area then stopped in a pit made by the rootball of a toppled forest giant. There sat a small Honda generator under a brown plastic tub. "Time to charge up the cell phone and all the batteries, Doze." The dog looked dutifully thoughtful, totally agreeing with his human.

"Whatcha cookin' for supper tonight?" Ace asked his dog. "Ufff!" Dozer woofed softly. "Ufff?" the old man repeated. "We had that last night. Let's go see what Chef Boy ARRRRR! Dee-lightful has in store for us, shall we?" Ace said as he roughed up Dozer's fur.

From the tent, the purr of the little generator could not even be heard. The black extension cord was easy to disguise under a thin layer of needles, sticks and leaves.

Ace cooked supper with a fire of smaller sticks that would be totally burned up, so the stove would be stone cold in two hours. He cut both ends out of the spaghetti can and put the can and both ends in the fire. In the morning, Ace would flatten the metal and put it in a container that would be hauled out when camp was taken down. Trash handled in this manner had no food remnants to attract scavengers. Most everything used in Ace's camp was eaten, burned, or hauled off in a sealed container.

Ace would finish his last cup of coffee while the stove still had a little heat left, then he and Dozer would make one more trip outside. Each would "take care of business," shut off the generator, and retire for the evening. But right now it was time to just sit and listen to the silence that was interrupted by only the tiny furtive sounds one hears in a quiet forest.

Chapter Two
Chicanery

WHILE ACE GRONSKY settled in for the evening, Pat Garrett rode Rosie back down the old logging trail digesting all that he had learned that afternoon. Rosie didn't need any urging since the horse knew that hay, molasses cakes and rest were waiting two miles downstream at the campground. The Game and Fish had set up a camper trailer for Pat along with portable corrals. Putting a horse out to graze was risky and the meadow grass here was not all that good. Although it looked lush and green, it was coarse and had very little real food value for a horse.

The purr of a generator and the subdued light glow through canvas told Pat that the four men Ace had told him about were at home so he turned in, tied Rosie to a tree, and called, "Hello, the tent!"

At the sound of his voice, there was a sudden flurry of activity in the tent as shadows quickly moved back and forth across the backlit canvas.

The tent's door flap was roughly flung aside as two men emerged, one closely followed by the other and both carrying what appeared to be AR-15 assault-type rifles.

"What the hell do you . . .? Oh, sorry, uh, warden," the man with one eyebrow said.

"Just thought I'd stop by and check things out boys," Pat said, trying hard to sound cheerfully casual.

One-eyebrow gave Pat a suspicious look, "What things?"

"I got a report of some trouble here the other day and just wondered if you boys wanted to report anything," Pat explained.

The second man wearing a Cabela's cap started to answer, "Karl, I think he means the thing with that mountain man making us . . . "

Karl's one eyebrow twisted into an intense scowl directed at the other man. "Shut up dickhead!" Then Karl turned the scowl toward Pat. "There's no trouble here. Everything's just fuckin' fine!"

Pat decided it was wise to change the subject. "Well, okay. Um, do you fellas plan to hunt elk with those rifles? They're not legal for big game, you know."

"We got a .308. You wanna *see* it?" One-eyebrow asked sarcastically.

To Pat it sounded almost like a challenge but he decided to let it go. Ace was right. This guy was one mean son of a bitch. Pat also noticed that the man Karl had called "dick head" was wearing an empty pistol holster.

"Well, good night and good hunting!" Pat said as he turned to go. Neither man in front of the tent said a word while they watched the game warden untie his horse, mount, and walk the animal slowly away.

Pat actually felt like spurring the horse into a gallop to see if he could outrun the feeling up his spine that made the hair on the back of his neck bristle.

Pat made a mental note to tell the sheriff to keep an eye on these people. He knew he could call from the ridgetop above camp, but decided to wait until he reached the tower up on The Arm that Ace had told him about. If he was lucky, the tower may be as innocent as something the forest service or USGS had placed there for one reason or another.

While Pat rode back to his camp trailer, other events were shaping up nearly one hundred miles to the northwest over the state line in Montana.

X X X X X

The town of Wesley had been severely depressed for years. It appeared as if it might dry up almost entirely until an outfit called Confedco bought out several run down sugar beet farms. They built a private prison facility they hoped to staff with people from the adjacent Indian reservation while they offered to house prisoners to the highest bidder.

One deal after another fell through while the promoter fought against rumors of scandal.

That was before President Omar Bahktar won his election. In a campaign speech he gave on the reservation, he pledged to enrich "All of my brothers regardless of our skin color, especially the American Indians," he said. Although it meant little or nothing to the national outcome of the election, the reservation voted almost entirely en masse for the US President who now had an honorary membership in the tribe.

To honor another pledge, President Bahktar emptied an offshore prison of terrorist suspects and brought them from their plush living in the balmy Caribbean to a bitter cold windswept plain in Montana.

Now the peace activists, Bahktar, his supporters, the ACLU, and everyone else associated with the move were happy. Even a small group of militia types in the small town of Clayton just over the state line in Wyoming were happy. It was rumored that Confedco had cut corners building the new prison, which was why the state of Montana wouldn't use the facility.

Bobby Joe Bentley was literally licking his lips as he leaned forward to talk in low tones to his friends clustered around a table in the corner of the Clayton coffee shop and cafe.

"It ain't gonna be long 'til some of those rag-head bastards bust out and I'll be here waitin' for 'em!" the weasel-faced wanna-be lawman bragged.

Bobby Joe wore a beard to cover a weak chin, and on the few occasions he removed his signature cowboy hat, a balding head was revealed. What hair was left on his head cascaded past his shoulders in unnaturally kinky curls that appeared to have been the work of a curling iron.

"By God we're with you, Bobby!" said one man in the group wearing a replica Civil War Confederate cap. The rest of the group nodded in agreement.

In spite of the noise in the cafe, and an effort to keep the talk down, some people at the next table stole some uneasy looks toward Bobby Joe's conference table while a couple of them shook their heads in obvious disgust.

Bobby Joe and his "militia" began to brag about all of the weapons they planned to use on the *ragheads* if any of them escaped. Their favorites were the AR-15 equipped with a *bump stock*, an after-market device that turned a semi-auto rifle into a virtual machine gun and, of course, a revolver called the "Judge" which fired either a .45 caliber pistol cartridge or a .410 shotgun load.

Over the summer the group had gone out and "murdered" at least a truckload of four- by eight-feet sheets of strand oriented board (OSB) much to the disgruntlement of the people who tried to keep the range clean at the local Sportsman's Club.

This group gave real sportsmen a bad name with their "toys." The indiscriminate rapid-fire destruction of wooden backboards from no more than a few feet away may have been a boon for the makers of bullets, brass, gun powder and the lumber yards, but did little to improve the image of serious gun owners.

On the other end of the gun rights spectrum, Ace Gronsky possessed a unique business card. It was a photographic reproduction of the ace of spades playing card. The center was graced with five holes, three of which intruded on each other forming a blob while the other two holes were near enough to be covered by an old-fashioned silver dollar.

Alois, or Ace, earned his nickname when he lost a bet that he could hit a playing card at fifty feet using a single action revolver with one hand and do it in less than ten seconds. Ace put five holes in the playing card in eight seconds. When asked why he didn't use six bullets, Ace replied, "Only a fool would use his last bullet!"

Ace decidedly both won and lost his bet. No one doubted that the man could shoot and shoot well. That is why Pat Garrett took some training from Ace. Pat was dissatisfied with the techniques taught at the Law Enforcement Academy in Douglas, Wyoming. Most of the handgun training was two-handed and close quarter. As Ace pointed out one time, "Whatcha gonna do when you're up on a mountainside hangin' onto a tree with one hand or you gotta hang on to your horse?"

"Good point," Pat conceded.

Ace had perforated the playing card at the age of thirty, but now more than forty years later, he was forced to use glasses and sometimes a telescope sight.

So on this October evening while the four men in what Ace called the middle camp fumed about losing their handguns and some of their anonymity, Bobby Joe Bentley and his cohorts plotted imagined mayhem. The Wyoming Game Warden fed his horse and got ready to turn in, and Ace and Dozer settled back next to the Sims wood-burning camp stove in their tent. Ninety miles north, five swarthy Middle Eastern men in a cell in Wesley, Montana, waited for the 130-car coal train to come blaring and rumbling through town to cover the sounds of their escape.

Joey Iron Dog had probably the most boring job in the world.

However, being from a reservation that suffered unemployment four or five times the national average, Joey felt very lucky. This evening he was even more fortunate because someone had left an entire box of sweet rolls in the control room. By eight thirty, they were almost gone and Joey couldn't find his insulin kit anywhere. Joey was going into shock and didn't know it. Like high altitude hypoxia, Joey was in a state of euphoria in which time expanded and everything was just dandy.

The planning and arrangements for smuggling acid in toothpaste tubes, obtaining keys, and escaping in a prison van had all been arranged by shadowy persons who had never exactly identified themselves. Whoever these people were, they had assured the five Jihadists that their mission would be an even greater blow to the Great Satan, the United States, than the heroic events of September 11, 2001. The names Fadil, Zakir, Shadid, Mustapha, and Jameel would be praised in national days of celebration throughout all of Islam.

Shadid discreetly applied the acid to the bars while the others watched in fascination as it quickly dissolved the metal with far less fumes than they imagined. Zakir offered up a silent prayer that even the small amount of fumes would not set off the smoke alarm; it didn't. The bars remained in place with just a small amount of dross holding them in position. Now they waited for the train. The vibration could be felt even before the noise began, and at the first blast of the locomotive horn, Mustapha and Jameel each grabbed a bar and yanked, leaving a man-sized hole in their cage.

Joey Iron Dog was in a diabetic stupor when the prisoners entered the control room with their stolen keys. They quickly found the switches that opened the way to the garage and the prison van. They drove the van serenely through the electrically controlled gate while suspicious gate guards tried to raise the control room for verification. After several wasted, precious minutes, two guards ran to the control room to beat on the locked door.

Joey Iron Dog stared at the faces yelling on the other side of the shatter-proof glass trying to make sense of what was happening. More time was wasted while the guards broke in to discover that the communications system had been disabled. Finally, someone thought of using a cell phone to call the sheriff, but the van was already abandoned in a dark alley in sleeping Wesley, Montana, and a beat-up 1974 Buick had already crossed into the reservation on a frontage road. The old car would soon disappear down one of the many dirt roads that wandered through the reservation like so many random game trails.

Fadil, according to instructions, steered the Buick into the weeds where it had been parked for several weeks next to a faded-brown ten-wide trailer house. Tires on the roof and several pieces of the aluminum siding flapping in the wind completed a picture of poverty-level living quarters. There they found food and water and a change of clothes. The clothes were a good fit and there were even two wigs with black braids. Once dressed, the men looked at each other and laughed. To most people they looked just like almost anyone else on the reservation. Shadid burned the prison clothes in the old wood stove that had been retrofitted into one corner of the living room, and the five escapees settled down to wait as instructed.

X X X X X

In another house on the reservation, Alden Spotted Horse was spending a restless night. Would his old friend Ace think he was crazy? Ace used to kid him lightly about his visions and things he called superstitious nonsense. But that was before the time Alden was contacted by the Medicine Man, Red Fox, over on the Rosebud Sioux Reservation. Red Fox described a particular pictograph and wanted to know if Alden, as a tribal historian, had seen it. Alden told him that the historical society he belonged to had made an exhaustive inventory of all Indian rock art in the area, and such a drawing had never been seen.

The very elderly Medicine Man insisted so strongly that finally he was brought up to Montana and escorted to a place he described from his dream. He also insisted that the pictograph was scratched on a north facing sandstone wall. This was a very unlikely place since weather and wind wore the north faces severely. Almost without exception, all pictographs were carved onto south-facing walls.

Everyone present on the expedition that day was astounded at what they found. The drawing showed an Indian wearing three feathers being stabbed in the back by a soldier.

It was drawn by Crazy Horse more than one hundred years ago before the actual event. It was a matter of record that the great Sioux warrior was killed by a soldier with a bayonet at Fort Robinson, Nebraska!

Alden Spotted Horse had his vision on the south side of this same bluff. This was obviously a place of power but only to people who were *tuned in* to it.

Certain New Age Hippie types claimed an affinity to American Indian spirituality but most Native Americans looked upon these people with the good-hearted acceptance that allowed them to privately shake their heads and mutter, "Whatever!"

While Alden Spotted Horse tossed restlessly in his bed, his grandson, Billy Black Stone, slept the deep sleep of the totally exhausted. Billy had been practicing relay racing with his buddies at the fairgrounds on the outskirts of Crow Agency.

The trees and buildings now occupying the hilltop at the site of the Battle of the Little Big Horn were plainly visible from the fairgrounds. The monument had always been there for the current residents of the area and was just an accepted part of the landscape.

To the tourists who streamed through, it was the "go to" attraction for the area. Although visitation dropped off in the winter, there was still a steady flow of clumsy RVs and other vehicles of every description. For the most part, the parking lot was full of sedans and small or midsized SUVs. A majority of the vehicles found in the monument's parking lot were in sharp contrast to those of the nearby small towns where the predominant means of transport was the ubiquitous pickup truck or a full-size SUV.

Billy Black Stone owned a flatbed pickup set up to pull a goosenecked horse trailer. But in the morning Billy would pull on sweats and running shoes to run several miles along the back roads. As an athlete, that the Indian relay racers were, he needed to stay in top shape the year round.

Billy worked out to keep upper body strength since he also competed in bulldogging events in area rodeos. Like many of the men of his tribe, Billy was quite tall, but unlike too many of his tribesmen, he was lean. He had an extremely good nature and winning ways that kept him out of fights. But his intimidating shape and size probably helped a great deal.

While most everyone rested, getting ready for a new day, Ace Gronsky was finishing a cup of coffee that could be conveniently reached from its perch on the corner of the Sims stove. Dozer snored heavily on the floor while Ace watched a chipmunk skitter about grabbing scattered hunks of dog food from near the sleeping dog's head. The chipmunk would keep the tent area scoured of any food scraps and he would scurry away to pile his treasure in a nest somewhere.

The temperature outside was a nippy twenty degrees, and although the sun had shown all day, the temperature in the shade barely got above freezing. That was a comforting thought for Ace because the elk hanging from the meat pole would still be okay for yet another day, and it looked like some weather was moving in. That would be good for the opening of rifle season if there was some snow for tracking.

The chipmunk came out one last time with its little nose twitching. There was no more dog food visible but the persistent rodent worked closer and closer to the sleeping dog. As Ace watched, he about laughed out loud when the chipmunk lifted Dozer's right ear, snatched the morsel that had lain underneath, dropped the ear and raced off nearly faster than the eye could follow! After the little squirrel had safely hidden itself in the woodpile behind the stove, did Ace allow himself an audible chuckle. One eyebrow twitched on the big dog to acknowledge that he may not have been as asleep as it had appeared.

Ace spoke to his hairy companion, "You big wuss! You let that little guy steal your stuff and didn't move a muscle."

This time one eye opened, the huge dog groaned, rolled on his side, sighed, stretched, and went back to sleep.

"It's hard to believe this big old dog was once a puppy!" Ace thought. He remembered back to the first day he ever saw the pup. He was doing some work at a friend's house near Gillette, Wyoming, that required some hand digging.

"You need a puppy!" Dick Hougen told Ace, not as a question but more of a plea. There were six Saint Bernard and Labrador mix pups milling about as Ace stepped out of his truck.

"What! You want me to get shot so you can move in and take my place?" Ace joked. Dick told Ace to think about it and he could have the pick of the litter. As Ace took his tools around the house, one pup followed clumsily wallowing through the snow.

When Dick came to check on the work progress, Ace was scraping snow out of the way so he could pile dirt without getting snow mixed in with the backfill. As Ace worked, the pup pitched in by pushing snow with his nose.

"Just like a little bulldozer!" Dick laughed, then looked at his watch. "I gotta go check on a pump over on the TR. You'll probably be done by the time I get back so help yourself to coffee or anything else you need. Oh, and I'll get your helper out from under your feet. See ya!" Dick scooped up the pup and disappeared around the house.

Ace finished up, loaded his tools and opened his truck door. The black pup with the white blaze on his chest sat up and looked straight into the man's eyes. "Doggone that rascal, Dick!" Ace laughed. "So he thought he'd just put that little bulldozer in my truck, did he?"

Ace climbed in and shut the truck door ruffling the puppy's floppy ears before starting the engine. "Okay, you can ride with me but don't you go getting sick on me." Dozer rode in Ace's truck ever since, and they had so many memorable adventures together that they were truly best of friends, forever trusting each other unconditionally in a once-in-a-lifetime bond.

There came a day when Dozer could no longer fit comfortably in the truck cab so Ace took out the bench seat, installed a bucket seat for himself and the dog had the rest of the cab.

Ace reminisced about the hot July day down on Powder River. The no-see-ums were biting his ears off, sweat was dribbling into his eyes, but he had to finish his job as the lone line repairman in the fifty-three-hundred square mile area he maintained.

Dozer got hot and wandered to the river to cool off. The twenty-foot cut bank at the job site didn't taper off until about a quarter mile upstream which is where Dozer found his way down to the water.

When Ace got ready to go he put his tools away, he didn't see the dog in the shade of the truck, so he walked over to the edge of the creek bank. There was Dozer looking up at him. "Dang!" Ace thought. Dozer turned to retrace his trail but Ace told him to wait. The dog sat and waited. Ace dragged the extension ladder off of the top of his work truck, extended it, and slid it over the cut bank.

"Can you climb it?" Ace asked. Dozer rose and walked confidently to the ladder and climbed it like it was something he did every day.

At home Dozer pulled the kids around the swimming hole on their inner-tubes until he could barely drag himself out of the water. At family gatherings little kids played "King of the Mountain" climbing all over Dozer's massive bulk.

Ace figured he could probably write a whole book about this remarkable creature and he was confident he would be writing more chapters.

Chapter Three
Confusion

Sunrise seemed a little late since low clouds covered the sky from horizon to horizon. Up in the Big Horn Mountains, the treetops brushed moisture from the lowest clouds and although there was no rain, dew had collected heavily on the drying vegetation. The leaves on the berry bushes had already turned red, and the aspen were beginning to drop some of their golden foliage. A morning like this was almost perfect for the bow hunters since the dampness had taken much of the crunch out of the ground cover and contrast between light and dark was subdued. These conditions meant that odors and smoke would layer out close to the ground rather than drifting upward.

Pat Garrett saddled Rosie in nearly full darkness and swung into the saddle. The regular sodden thump of horse hooves on damp earth lulled Pat into a lethargic state of sleepiness, while the morning chill caused him to tuck his chin down deeper into his coat collar. There was no need to hurry yet.

Pat's plan was to get to a high point by full daylight, pour coffee from his thermos, and scan the country while he made his morning calls.

Other people were up and about too.

In what Ace had begun to refer to as the *middle camp*, Karl scowled at the radio. He had made a full report via satellite phone of everything that had occurred over the last two days and had received his instructions. Now he made plans accordingly. Karl had been out relieving himself when he saw the game warden ride south past the entrance road that led the fifty yards to the clearing for the middle camp. This was now a major concern because the relay tower was on the ridge southwest of the middle camp.

Karl raised the west camp by bouncing his radio signal off that same relay. A sleepy voice crackled in the receiver, "Yeah?"

Karl wasted no time. "Mitch, get on the quad and head up to the relay. I think this goddamn nosy fuckin' game warden is goin' up there."

"So?" Mitch sounded surly. He had probably just got up and hadn't had breakfast yet.

"You heard what happened here yesterday with that mountain man or what the fuck ever he was and then that warden stopped by asking questions. He's suspicious and Omega doesn't like it," Karl said.

"So?" Mitch responded again.

"So Omega is pissed. Real pissed! He says send someone up to the relay and if that warden shows up checkin' it out, make sure he can't report it." There was a pregnant pause, then Karl added, "And hide the evidence, you got that clear?"

"Scratch one game warden then?" Mitch asked.

"Whatever it takes," Karl answered, "but do it quietly. We've already attracted too much attention. Got it?"

"Got it." Mitch's voice sounded dry, emotionless, and businesslike.

Mitch grabbed a doughnut and a can of beer, slung an AR-15 over his shoulder, and tossed a noise suppressor into the cargo carrier on an ATV. He swung onto the seat and started up the jeep trail that would lead southwest, parallel to the same ridge that Pat and Rosie were now climbing from the east.

X X X X X

Although the backbone of the Big Horn range ran not quite north and south, the Black Mountain Arm reached eastward causing four small creeks that drained its north slope to flow northward before intersecting with the Boulder River that flowed easterly through a rugged canyon that opened out to embrace the village of Clayton. The first drainage to the east was Black Mountain Creek. It flowed past the foot of the very prominent Black Mountain upon which perched an old fire lookout.

The next creek to the west was Little Swampy and over the next ridge to the west was Big Swampy. Gloomy Creek was the farthermost west.

The Boulder River Road was a major improved route that cut across the mouths of all four creeks. Each creek in turn had a dead-end road that extended south toward the high ridge officially called the Black Mountain Arm. Locals just called the ridge *The Arm.*

Omega had planned for three camps manned by four men under the command of his lieutenant, Karl. Karl's camp on Big Swampy was camp two. Camp one was on Little Swampy and camp three was located on Gloomy Creek. The men in camp three had set up the relay since the jeep trail up Gloomy Creek penetrated further up to The Arm, allowing them, although it was illegal to do so, to use the ATV to haul the components of the tower to the base of the rock upon which it sat. A trial run showed that the tower had almost total coverage of all four drainage areas.

Two miles up Big Swampy, Ace and Dozer emerged from their tent. How nice it would have been to fire up the Sims stove, but Ace opted to use up some of his precious bottled gas to boil coffee. The atmospheric conditions would have caused smoke from his fire to hover through the dog-hair stand of trees, which would reveal the position of his hidden camp. Ace preferred his privacy even more now considering some of the recent developments.

An old knee injury came back with a vengeance this morning causing Ace to rely more on the spear as a cane rather than a weapon. Most times the limp was barely discernible, but this morning it caused him to be more cautious while he negotiated the boulder field out to the road. From painful experience as a boy, Ace knew better than to trust his footing on the tops of the frosted rocks so he stepped in between as much as possible. And there was always the possibility that had he elected to step on the stones, his boot imprints would be very visible until the surface dried, which might be well after midday today.

Rather than a daypack, Ace had, for years, used an oversized fishing vest that he threw on over the top of any clothes he elected to wear that day. The vest contained all the things a person might need to survive for days if need be out in the wilderness: several types of fire starters, a bosun's pipe whistle, a wire saw, and glow sticks. Reflective tacks, first aid kit, several lengths of parachute cord and some nylon rope, a quilted reflective space blanket, compass, stainless steel mirror, two steel "S" hooks, chemical hand warmers, treated lens cloth, a mini 10 X 25 telescope, two Ziploc bags containing tissue paper, and a water bottle with a built-in charcoal filter that could be filled with any water which would be purified by the filter as the contents were used. The whole vest weighed only four pounds. Adding food enough for two or three days averaged out to nine pounds, which was about equal to the weight of many big game rifles.

One item not included but always present was Ace's concealed-carry pistol. A .38 special, five-shot hammerless revolver resting in an inside-the-pants front holster. Ace wore it as naturally as anyone would wear a wristwatch. The extra cartridges he carried for the pistol were tracer rounds that could be used as emergency flares.

The spear could double as a shooting brace or ridgepole for a lean-to.

Dozer carried his own rations on a special pack that hung on both sides from a harness Ace had made from selected soft leather.

The man and the dog, each wearing their packs, picked their way across Big Swampy Creek and headed southwest and uphill. Their angle would bring them out near the top of the ridge, near the strange tower, and at a good spot to check in with Alden Spotted Horse. Since Ace carried a GPS unit, he planned to get coordinates for the tower and report it to the forest service and the sheriff's department by cell phone.

Traditionally, and today was no exception, Ace carried a small civilian-band two-way radio. The companion unit was left in the tent. The family had discussed contingency plans, and one was that anytime anyone of the group was out alone, they would carry one of six that were all on the same frequency. The unit left in the tent would be for whoever might be looking for them.

Bears were out looking for gut piles so Ace carried his 12-gauge "bear spray" just in case.

Encounters would increase as soon as the rifle season for elk started. The heavy boom of a big bore rifle sounded like a dinner bell for many bears these days.

X X X X X

While Ace was making his way up the slope, Billy Black Stone was just returning from a morning run. Billy was only mildly concerned about the aged Chevy Suburban with a two-wheeled trailer attached parked next to his driveway. The trailer was covered with a bulging green tarp making it look like hundreds of other hunting rigs that were beginning to make their appearance all over this western state.

Billy recognized one of the six people standing next to the Suburban as Lyle Stands. Lyle was one of the many jobless Indians a person could see walking along any road on the reservation.

"Lyle!" Billy said by way of greeting. Lyle shuffled forward to meet Billy and jerked his head back to indicate the five men behind him. "They need a guide for the Big Horns and I told 'em about you."

"Can't," Billy said shortly. Lyle shrugged for everyone's benefit.

Billy noticed the questioning look from the rather odd-looking bunch behind Lyle. "I can't guide you. I got other stuff to do," Billy said loudly.

Lyle began to see opportunity slip from his grasp. "Hey, they said they would pay good and I could, like, maybe help or something."

Before Lyle could offer any more persuasion or Billy could react, one of the men stepped quickly forward, drew a pistol from under his shirt and stuck it in Billy's ribs. The man's name, Billy would learn, was Mustapha.

Mustapha nodded at the wide-eyed Lyle and spat, "Kill him!"

Zakir advanced with a wicked-looking knife just as a pickup popped up over the rise not a hundred yards away. The knife and pistol were quickly hidden from view from the approaching vehicle. There were five people in the cab and six in the back. Lyle, much to his credit, surprised everyone by quickly stepping into the road with his thumb out. The pickup did not stop but slowed enough for Lyle to grab the tailgate and flip himself into the pile of humanity crammed in the pickup bed.

Billy and the five escaped prisoners stared after the retreating pickup while at least eleven pair of eyes stared back at them.

As the beat-up old pickup disappeared over the next rise, there was a babble of excited conversation amongst the escapees that Billy could not understand.

It was obvious to the men that they could not stand in the road holding an Indian boy at gunpoint, so they herded Billy into the third seat in the Suburban. While Mustapha climbed in beside him, Billy took stock of his options. There were few indeed.

The only ways out were to crawl over the men filling the first two seats or over the back seat to the rear doors, which may or may not open from the inside. He was stuck with people he didn't know for reasons he could not fathom.

After the Suburban began to move, Jameel handed Mustapha a map. "We have instructions to go to a place called Black Mountain. Is this the place?" Mustapha's finger hovered over a spot on the map that Billy recognized as, indeed, Black Mountain.

Billy nodded his head. "Good!" Mustapha said triumphantly, "I was right!"

Jameel had apparently had an argument with Mustapha about reading the map but saved his dignity by sneering, "Yes, you found it, but we still do not know the best way to get there." Then he made a sour face, "Especially in *this!*"

Billy realized Jameel was probably right. The Suburban was only a two-wheel drive pile of junk.

Mustapha looked meaningfully at Billy. "We need to be at this place by early afternoon tomorrow. We expect you to show us the best roads and if you do not, Zakir will be most happy to show you what he can do with his knife." As that message was delivered, Zakir leered at Billy from the front seat.

The five kidnappers hadn't had much rest. They had just started to doze off in the old trailer house last night when a man wearing a hooded sweater drove the Suburban with the trailer up to their hiding place. It was about two hours until dawn and all they could see was that the vehicle they were to use had been followed by another that remained about twenty yards behind while they were given their map by the hooded man. "Everything you need is there," he said as he gestured at the Suburban. "You need to leave now." He turned and walked back to the waiting vehicle which they could see was a new, dark, full-sized SUV. The SUV spun around on the road and disappeared into the night.

The fugitives had found food and a variety of weapons inside the Suburban. After trying to decide how to get to their destination, they were getting desperate from taking roads that led nowhere. The only one with much experience driving, Fadil, wasted a lot of time trying to back the trailer so they could turn around. It was on one such foray that the fugitive five found Lyle Stands looking for a ride.

Billy Black Stone was quick to recover his common sense, which was to convey a sense of compliance while he attempted to sort out the strange situation in which he now found himself.

He first gained some sense of confidence from his captors that he knew his way around by guiding them out to roads that appeared to be more properly maintained than the ones they had started out on. He also had the driver, Fadil, verify that the Suburban had two gas tanks and that both were full. Billy explained that they could stay off the highways by taking the Jones Creek Road to reach the backbone of the Big Horns.

Mustapha allayed his suspicious nature by checking the map against the sparse road signs they passed and checking the progress on the map.

By nine o'clock that morning the Suburban had gained the top and after turning south, Fadil turned into a small campground. Everyone dismounted the vehicle to consume some of the food packed in a cooler, break out some bottled water for everyone, and relieve themselves one at a time in the forest service outhouse.

Mustapha proved to be clever in one respect. He insisted that Billy use the facility first. This would preclude Billy trying to scratch a message on the wall to possibly be discovered. While Billy was behind the closed door, he quickly pulled out his cell phone that hung from a cord around his neck and turned it off. All the time they were driving here, he prayed that no one would call. Now he could save the battery for any opportunity that might present itself. He thanked his Spirit Helper that his kidnappers had not spotted the phone under his bulky sweater.

As Billy emerged from the outhouse, he saw that Zakir and Shadid had pulled the canvas on the trailer back and were examining the contents. When they heard the outhouse door bang shut, they quickly pulled the tarp down but not before Billy saw the gleam of some long metallic objects surrounded by some olive-drab framework.

X X X X X

While the escapees were loading back up in their Suburban on one part of the Big Horns, Pat had finished tying Rosie to a tree inside the tree line at the edge of the park below the suspicious tower. It wasn't so much of a tower as he had imagined. In fact the non-reflective paint caused the thing to blend in pretty well with the surrounding background. Pat could see that this strange structure would stand out sky lighted only when a person got to within about a hundred yards.

Normally, Pat would be skirting a park just inside the tree line, but today he looked at his watch and began a beeline to the tower.

As Pat swished through the wet grass, which made his boots shine with moisture, he thought he heard the sputter of an ATV motor drifting over from the west. He knew there was a well-traveled jeep trail there so he filed that away as an item of little consequence. The sound of the ATV faded or stopped and the only sounds now were sounds of nature as Pat climbed the outcrop that held the tower.

There were several solar panels, a compartment for batteries and electronics and several antennas. The four legs had been secured with explosive bolts and the whole thing was a compact six feet in height. It certainly appeared more military than civilian, but all identification had been ground off and spray painted over.

"Might as well call from here," Pat thought.

He pulled out a small thermos from a fanny pack, poured a cup of coffee that he held in his left hand, took a couple of sips, and raised the field glasses attached to a special harness on his chest.

Pat was doing a sweep, adjusting the range with the focus wheel, when the hair on the back of his neck began to tingle. He'd felt that before. He was certain he was being watched. He let the glasses ease back to their harness, then bent down and set his coffee on the rock.

Pat turned around and pulled his radio out of his pack, turned it on, selected the frequency for the county sheriff, held it to his left ear and pressed the transmit switch.

"Warden Garrett for Sheriff Harper, over." He was told to wait so he started a three-sixty scan with the binoculars when Harper's voice, made even more tinny and irritating by the radio's small speaker said, "Garrett! You find Billy the Kid yet?" It was a stupid joke but Harper said it every time. "Sheriff, I'm up on The Arm at the head of Big Swampy and I'm looking at some sort of communications thing here that I think is related to some ill . . . " Pat stopped in midword. From the corner of his eye Pat saw what appeared to be a fat-looking gun barrel poking its way over a log at the edge of the park. With the radio still pressed to his left ear, Pat started to turn and at the same time his right arm crooked back. His right thumb flipped the snap loose on his hip holster, and he began to pull his .45 caliber, model 1911, semi-auto Springfield from its holster. Pat's wristwatch read 11:16.

Ace was making good time after his knee loosened up. He had stopped twice to remove one layer of clothing, which required him to take off his survival vest and hang it from a convenient branch. He had cut a trail of fresh hoofprints, which he supposed belonged to Rosie. There were other hunters in the area but they would be using their horses to get further into more roadless areas.

At his second stop Ace was shrugging into his vest. He had just checked his watch. It read 11:16 and he thought he heard two pistol shots in quick succession. Pistol shots had a flat sound that didn't carry very far and it was often difficult to determine from which direction they came.

Looking back, Ace wished he had hurried, but it was not uncommon for someone to shoot a pistol in the mountains, maybe at a porcupine or some such thing, who knows?

By the growing amount of daylight filtering through the trees, the man and his dog could tell they were getting close to an open area or a park as the locals called them.

Still following the horse tracks, the pair were mildly surprised to find Rosie tied to a tree just inside the tree line.

Ace patted the horse and as if she could answer asked, "Now where in the world did that Pat get off to, Rosie?" The horse nickered softly and stomped the ground impatiently.

Dozer stood at attention staring out across the park. Ace got down on his knees, laid the spear down in the grass, and got down on his elbows to look out over the top of the grass. From this angle he could just make out twin grooves Pat had left making a pretty straight line toward the rock that held the odd-looking tower.

The shotgun shifted awkwardly on his back as Ace lifted the spear, blade first, then planted the butt cap in the soft soil to assist rising from the ground and literally climbed up the shaft. At the sound of his voice, Dozer looked at his human with that typical head tilt so common to the species. "Y'know, Doze, if it wasn't for this here spear I would have to crawl to the nearest tree to get on my feet. Well, let's see where that young Patrick of ours has got to, shall we?"

The man and the dog followed the dim trace across the park. As they approached the rock, Dozer changed his gait from an easy trot to a stiff-legged stalk. A strange sound issued from his throat. It was a mixture of growl and whine that caused Ace to pull the sling strap over his head to bring the shotgun around to tactical ready. Ace stared at the scene for only a few seconds while a wave of sickness swelled in his belly and made his mouth go dry.

Pat's coffee cup sat on top of the rock. There were two fresh, white bullet scars on the granite. One empty .45 casing glinted from the moss-covered shelf in the rock to his right. But worse was the bloody smear down the front of the rock face.

Dozer started off around the left side of the rock with a sharp bark looking back to urge Ace to follow. Ace didn't need the dog to lead him. Someone had dragged something around to the east side of the outcrop.

Following the trail on rubbery legs, Ace was almost overwhelmed by a terrible feeling. He was repeating "No, no, no!" with every step. Rather than his mind going numb Ace went into a state of acute awareness. His eyes took in every detail now and his ears strained to pick up any sound.

Dozer continued around the outcrop to the top of a rockslide. Some convulsion long ago had heaved and cleaved this part of the mountain to create a jumbled mass of boulders that spilled for five hundred yards down the slope. Dozer was following the blood smears to the middle of the jumble where he stopped and looked down, then back at Ace.

There, fifteen feet down in a gap in the boulders, lay the crumpled heap that was Jerry "Pat" Garrett of the Wyoming Game and Fish Department.

The starch went out of Ace as he sat and began to sob.

CHAPTER FOUR
Collusion and Retribution

11:22 AM MOUNTAIN Standard Time:

Dozer padded up to Ace and laid his head over the man's shoulder. Ace wrapped his arms around the huge dog while hot tears rolled down his cheeks. After a few minutes the expediency of things that needed to be resolved moved the man into action, so he removed his survival vest and pulled out a length of nylon rope.

11:22 AM Mountain Standard Time:

Mitch rolled into camp three on Gloomy Creek and dismounted from the ATV. There was blood on the front of his pants and on the sleeves of his coat. Fortunately, he hadn't met anyone on the jeep trail coming back from his ambush of the nosy game warden. Mitch was forced to do a sloppy job because the warden had pulled his pistol at the same moment the high velocity .223 bullet entered his side just below the arm pit. The bullet tore through the top of his heart, exited the left front of his chest, and hit the left arm causing it to throw the two-way radio away somewhere off the outcrop. The two shots from the warden's heavy pistol were the result of an involuntary muscle reflex he guessed. The bullets ricocheted harmlessly off the granite but the sound might have been noted by someone in the area.

Mitch disposed of the body in the rock jumble, then looked briefly for the radio but couldn't find it. He quickly gathered his *trophies*, the warden's badge, billfold, pistol and binoculars and trotted back across the park to the path that led to his ATV.

11:22 AM Mountain Standard Time:

The nondescript Suburban carrying five escaped prisoners and a kidnapped Indian boy turned onto the only stretch of highway they were forced to use to reach their destination.

The reception of the local AM radio station faded in and out, but the announcer's voice cutting through the static and engine noise informed the passengers that the fugitives' getaway van had been found in Wesley, Montana. A second suspected getaway vehicle had been located on the reservation, but nothing was said about the possible kidnapping of an Indian boy.

The Grant County Sheriff offered no speculation as to which direction the fugitives had gone except that the State Patrols of Wyoming and Montana were keeping a sharp lookout on all major highways.

11:22 AM Mountain Standard Time:

Sheriff Glenn Harper of Grant County, Wyoming, folded up the paper printout of a photograph of a two-story white-walled house surrounded with tropical vegetation, dropped it into his private desk drawer, locked the drawer, and slipped the key into his pants pocket. "Life is good," was the satisfied look he telegraphed on his ruggedly handsome face.

The picture the sheriff had slipped into the drawer was of a house in Belize. In a short while it would be his permanently. "What a deal," he thought to himself. At last he could get out of a marriage gone sour and a county that still had not accepted him even at face value.

At first Sheriff Harper's wife Gloria, an uptight devout Catholic, had accompanied him on his frequent trips to Deadwood, South Dakota, to gamble. But after a while she made excuses to stay home because the whole casino thing was too boring.

Then Glenn met Angelita. The slightly built Philippina with dark almond eyes could do things with him that he'd only heard about.

However, Glenn was in more trouble than he could handle. His gambling debts were piling up and one of his deputies had him in a real bind. Deputy Delbert "Del" Fulton had confiscated a box of kiddie porn tapes which he squirreled away for private viewing. Glenn had found them and got hooked on watching them and then that damned Del found out about it!

Now the two were locked into a Mexican standoff that Del was milking for all it was worth. The ill-conceived favoritism shown to the obscenely fat deputy was the talk of the department.

Meanwhile, Angelita introduced Glenn to someone who offered to give him a way out of all of his problems if he would merely do his job as usual and wait for special instructions. To show good faith, his benefactor paid his gambling debts, and on one three-day gambling trip, flew Glenn and Angelita to Belize in a private Lear jet from Rapid City. They were shown the house in the photo that would be his when his "service" was over.

Sheriff Harper was thinking about these things when the cell phone he had been given, the one that had never rung until now, rang.

10:22 AM Pacific Standard Time:

The former speaker of the house, Monica Farizzi, stared out the window at the rain that obscured Mount Olympus. She was not pleased at the distorted reflection that looked back at her. Her thin mouth and sunken cheeks only accented a face that resembled a death's-head skull. She tried a smile. That made it worse. "Shit!" she said out loud.

There was a timid tap on her door. "Come!" she snapped.

"He's here. Shall I see him in now?" rasped a bent old man with thinning gray hair.

"Yes, yes!" Monica said impatiently.

Two men entered the room and the elderly butler very quietly closed the door. No one spoke as the taller of the two men walked to Farizzi's massive desk.

The tall, younger man, dressed in a well-tailored gray suit, placed a small case on the desk. He opened the case and removed a device that displayed several LED lights. The young man carefully walked about the room holding the device first one way, then the other. "Clean!" he said when he was done. He touched a button and set the device on the sill of the room's only window. He turned and said, "Secure, sir!"

The older man had lined heavy features with a distinctly Mediterranean look. He nodded toward the device on the windowsill. "It sets up vibrations on the glass to defeat remote listening apparatus. Now we can talk."

"Does anyone know you're here?" asked Monica Farizzi.

"My private plane comes and goes as I please. No questions asked," the older man stated it as matter of fact. "Even though the whole world knows the face of Pavel Santorini, I have ways of staying unseen."

"I see," said Monica.

"No you don't!" Santorini said abruptly, putting her in her place. His tone and his look implied she should dispense with trying to make conversation and listen.

Getting right down to business, Pavel began. "I am here in person because I want no record of what I am about to say. All other means of communication are subject to discovery no matter how well they are encrypted or by what means they are sent. Eric will give you a special phone and a list of times that you must turn it on. That way you can find a secure place to receive our messages. You cannot make calls on it and it must be thoroughly destroyed, not just disposed of, when we tell you to. Understood?"

Monica nodded silently.

Pavel went on. "We have set a multifaceted plan in motion. I'm sure you have heard of the prison break in Montana? Good! *He* is meeting with environmental groups in Jackson Hole, Wyoming, and we know the route Air Force One will be taking back to Washington. We worked very hard to get that route planned. All of the teams are in place and the coordination has been tested. We have two plans to make sure that once the escapees have done their job they will not survive. Major law enforcement for the area has been bought and paid for. We don't anticipate any problems but if some develop, all of the players are expendable. There was considerable discussion within our group about this decision and we came to the conclusion that this president is more valuable to our cause as a martyr. Kennedy was nearly elevated to sainthood and we gained much traction from that. This will put us over the top regardless of who wins the next election." Santorini continued, "You will have a 95 percent chance of getting your old job back after we manipulate public opinion with the aid of the internet conspiracy mill. Every right-wing group, terrorist organization, and religious cult will be suspect."

Monica felt a chill when she considered the enormity of the undertaking, but at her age, time was running out to accomplish all the things that would guarantee her place in history books, street names, and on statues.

Pavel nodded to Eric who picked up the case they had brought. "You may keep the device. Tell anyone who asks that the Chinese gave it to you."

Santorini did not even say goodbye. He and Eric turned and let themselves out while Monica's trembling knees let her flop unceremoniously into the huge throne-like chair behind her desk.

X X X X X

By the time the meeting in Seattle was over, Ace had completed the grim task of retrieving Pat's body from the boulder pile. Dozer looked on sadly feeling his human's pain. Ace laid the warden next to the outcrop. The sky was overcast as if even the heavens were in mourning. There was still a modicum of shadow and coolness there, which would slow the process of rigor mortise. A tinny voice from the grass near the base of the rock caught the attention of Ace and Dozer. It was Pat's radio! Ace picked it up and not sure of two-way protocol, pushed transmit and said, "Yeah?"

Dispatch on the other end asked, "Pat?"

Not knowing what else to say, Ace said, "No. Pat's dead."

The radio squawked, "What?"

"I said this is Ace Gronsky and I'm using Warden Garrett's radio." There was no response so Ace pushed transmit again, "Hello?"

"This is Sheriff Harper. Who is this and what the hell's going on?"

Ace repeated, "This is Ace Gronsky. I just found Pat Garrett shot and killed up here on The Arm."

Harper sounded highly irritated and a bit incredulous. "I just talked to Pat not over thirty minutes ago!"

"Well, since then somebody shot him and I'm sure it's no accident," Ace replied.

"What makes you think it's a murder?" the sheriff asked.

"It's a long story and I ain't got time to waste. You need to come up and look at the scene," Ace told the lawman.

"Uh, just exactly where is this you say?" The sheriff didn't seem overly concerned about Pat's death and neglected all of the other questions law enforcement usually asked. Actually he seemed to be more interested in Ace's involvement.

Ace pulled out his GPS. "Here's the exact coordinates of the crime scene. You ready to write this down?"

The radio came alive again. "Yeah, I'm ready."

Ace read the coordinates into the radio and the sheriff read them back.

"Okay, got it. You sit tight and we'll have someone up there in a couple or three hours, maybe longer," Harper said.

Ace looked at the radio for a minute then made up his mind. "Pat was a friend of mine. A good friend. I'm bringin' him down to the Big Swampy Campground!"

"Look here, Gronsky. You move the body or interfere with a crime investigation and I'll slap you . . . " Ace shut the radio and the sheriff off.

As Ace and Dozer set off across the park following Dozer's nose and the faint marks in the grass, Ace remembered to turn his phone on. It rang almost immediately. Ace said hello and was genuinely glad to hear Alden Spotted Horse greet him with, "Ka Hey, old grizzly!"

Ordinarily they would trade insults before getting down to business but Ace briefed the old Indian about the recent events. His voice almost quit him when he got to telling about Pat.

"Ace, I grieve with you and will say a prayer for your friend. I know your heart is heavy and I also know the hurt may make you crazy." There was a respectful pause. "You should know I had a vision." And Alden told Ace about his dream. "I realize now it was you in my vision. I want you to keep a clear head because I fear this is far from over. There must be some very powerful evil for me to see it from here in a dream." Alden paused then asked, "Have you heard the news?"

Ace allowed as how he had not turned the AM radio on because it would not pick up any stations until the ionosphere settled down late at night.

Alden informed Ace of the prison break. "The five guys are supposed to be terrorists and the law is looking in all the wrong places. On top of that, they kidnapped Billy but that didn't make the news. Probably because it was just an Indian," Alden said acidly.

The old man passed along Lyle's account of Billy's abduction, then he added, "The Indian telegraph works pretty good up here so the word is that they went up Jones Creek and are heading your way. Maybe to Black Mountain."

"That doesn't make sense," Ace said. He had been walking during the phone call and now he was at the edge of the timber. "That's a dead-end road!"

"I know," Alden said, "but Lyle said they asked him first about how to get there and he told them they better get Billy to show 'em. Then they were going to slit Lyle's throat 'til the White Bears came along. Ace, I hope you can get him outta there 'cause that's a real mean bunch!"

"Don't worry too much Grandfather (It was a term of endearment rather than an expression of relationship), the mountain seems to be swarming with meanness but I'll do the best I can. Right now I have to take care of another friend," Ace said with more conviction than he felt.

"Yes, you do what you have to do. I will stay by my phone now to be your message center. Good luck and may the Great Spirit guide your hands, your feet and your aim."

Ace closed and shut off the phone to save on the battery and followed the assassin's tracks into the trees.

X X X X X

As Ace and Dozer followed the trail, Deputy Del Fulton slouched down in an unmarked Ford Bronco just off the main highway near the Boulder River Road junction. He had eaten a double order of greasy French fries and just finished a third cup of coffee when the urge to urinate grew too great to ignore. Del stood beside the open door with his back to the traffic getting a good stream going when the song of tires on the pavement signaled an approaching vehicle.

Del kept the stream going and muttered, "Maybe this'll be a busload of cheerleaders come to see somethin' they ain't seen before!"

Instead of continuing past, the vehicle turned onto the Boulder River Road. That put the Suburban pulling a small trailer on the other side of Del's Bronco from the deputy. Del looked up across the top of his vehicle. "Shit! That's the rig I was told to watch for!"

Del got the sheriff on his cell phone. "Okay, I seen 'em! They turned off on the Boulder River Road."

Harper instructed the deputy to follow at a discreet distance and if they turned off on the Black Mountain Road, find a place with cell phone coverage to report back in.

Del was congratulating himself on his good fortune. "Got the sheriff in my pocket. No papers to serve, no domestic fights to break up, no checkin' out dead people, cows or horses, just sit around watchin' folks. What a job!"

X X X X X

While Del was patting himself on the back, Ace was examining the ATV tracks on the jeep trail near the headwaters of Gloomy Creek. One traction cleat on a left rear tire had been torn half off leaving a gap of evenly spaced marks in every revolution. "Good enough for me!" Ace told Dozer as he turned and trotted back across the park to where Rosie was more than eager to be untethered from her tree. The horse was unsettled by the smell of her former rider, which made getting Pat's body loaded even more grimly difficult.

Ace began to cry again as he lashed his friend to the horse which made this trip Pat's last ride home to camp.

It was mid-afternoon and the sky was still overcast. People in the campground were lingering over beers, barbecues, and campfires when the look on one person's face caused others to look in the same direction. All talk stopped. Even the wind seemed to pause out of respect.

As the apparition drew closer the observers could see a grizzled face that housed haunted red-rimmed eyes under a broad Australian hat. The man used a tall spear like a walking stick while a huge black dog paced along beside him. The horse that most of them recognized as Rosie bore the pitiful remains of her former rider. Almost in unison everyone in the campground silently removed their hats.

Several men in the campground detached themselves from the onlookers to follow Ace to the game warden's camper trailer. Ace leaned his spear against a tree; without a word, the men helped him undo the lashings to ease Pat's body onto a nearby picnic table.

"We need a blanket," said one of the campers.

Ace dug into Pat's pockets and came up with a key. "I think this will let you into the camper. I need someone to go out to the main road to direct the county coroner here."

"I'll go!" one man said eagerly as he turned and started for one of the four-wheel-drive pickups parked nearby

"The sheriff knows about this and I gave them the location of the crime scene. But just in case they can't figure it out, it's up at the end of the jeep trail on Gloomy Creek. Can I count on some of you staying here with Pat?"

"You bet!" said one of the campers and two others nodded in agreement. The man who spoke asked, "Uh, just in case the sheriff asks, who do we say brought, uh, you know . . . , uh . . ." The man was clearly uncomfortable with the situation and the look on Ace's face.

"Tell 'em it was Ace. I'm gonna leave my dog here. I got some business to take care of. He'll be no bother. Dozer!" Ace said sternly. "Stay by Pat!" The huge dog padded over to stand at attention by the picnic table.

One of the campers had wiped the blood from Rosie's saddle and as Ace swung into the saddle, he said, "Thanks. I'll be back shortly."

As he rode past, Ace snatched up the spear he had left leaning against Pat's camper trailer and spurred Rosie into a gallop west up the Boulder River Road.

As the campers watched the departing horseman, one turned to the others and let out a held breath with only one word that summed up their feelings, "Jesus!"

It was a ten-minute gallop to the Gloomy Creek junction with the Boulder River Road. The campground was up the side road only a hundred yards from the main road. Ace slowed Rosie to a walk and steered the horse onto the pine duff on the road's edge. When he saw the large white wall tent with an ATV parked nearby, Ace stopped the horse inside the tree line, dismounted, and tied her to a tree. "Good girl," Ace whispered to the horse as he patted her neck and studied the layout.

Four folding chairs sat around the fire pit. A thin curl of smoke indicated there was still some fire left.

There was one other small wall tent across the campground, three camper trailers, and a half dozen nylon pup tents. Unlike the last campground, there were no loiterers to be seen. Ace thought he could detect voices coming from the big wall tent. "Sounds like a card game goin' on in there, and everybody else is fishin' or hikin'. Good!" Ace said to himself as he unslung the 12 gauge and walked toward the ATV.

Ace looked at the back tires but failed to see the telltale flaw on any of the exposed cleats.

He laid the shotgun on the cargo carrier and worked the shift lever into neutral then went around to the rear of the machine.

The sun coming from the wrong angle made inspecting the tires difficult for his old eyes, so Ace used his spear to help lower himself to hands and knees for a better look. He pushed against the machine to make it roll ahead. Was that the flaw on the cleat? Had he found the machine he had been looking for? Just to be sure, Ace pushed the machine a little more for a better look. He did not expect the ATV to roll so easily but it did! It rolled ahead and crashed into one of the folding chairs. The low murmuring in the tent stopped abruptly.

When the machine rolled, it put Ace off balance and he rolled onto his right side.

Time went into slow-motion mode.

Mitch, still wearing bloody clothing, burst out of the tent drawing his pistol. He was closely followed by a larger man who grabbed his arm with a warning that gunshots would bring other campers running. As Ace was rolling back up to hands and knees, Mitch jammed his pistol back into his holster and jerked an ax from the nearby chopping block while he began his run towards the old hunter on the ground.

The events described here took place in roughly four or five seconds.

Mitch, with the ax raised high overhead and sprinting full tilt, was only fifteen feet away as Ace, strictly out of long habit, picked up the spear, point first, to help raise himself from the ground. Mitch was in mid-stride when the spear point came up to contact the rushing man right under the sternum. The eighteen-inch blade did not stop until the point contacted the backbone severing Mitch's spinal cord. The spear's butt cap skittered only a foot before it contacted a root and stopped. Mitch was suspended in midair at the end of the six-foot shaft for probably half a second before he toppled sideways writhing like a harpooned fish.

The larger man who had stopped Mitch from using his sidearm and two others who followed from inside the tent stood in shocked immobility at what they had just witnessed.

Adrenaline overrode stiff joints and a bad knee allowing Ace to move quickly to retrieve his 12 gauge from the ATV and insert a deadly charge into the chamber with a "Ka-choonk!" that sent a clear message to anyone who could hear it. The three men slowly raised their hands without even being told.

Ace opened the cargo carrier of the ATV with one hand while Mitch gurgled his last on the ground. In the cargo carrier was Pat's badge, binoculars, billfold and pistol, and the suppressor Mitch had used in the ambush. Ace shifted his position to better cover the trio by the tent.

"I want one of you to go back inside and get this fella's gun and a plastic bag," Ace ordered, then added, "and whoever comes out better be carrying the rifle in one hand by the end of the barrel. If not, I'm gonna let a whole fist full of number-two shot find a new home and I guarantee you ain't gonna like the visit!" Ace stayed positioned so that the two men outside were lined up with the tent flap. The third pushed the tent flap carefully aside with his hand holding the AR-15 by the barrel. The other hand was held high holding a white plastic grocery sack.

Ace backed away to keep the men all in a line while he ordered the man with the rifle to lean it against the ATV and drop the plastic sack on the seat. When that was done, Ace ordered the men to stand by the fire pit while he worked with one hand to put Pat's belongings and the suppressor in the sack. Next, he yanked the spear from the body on the ground. The sound it made caused one of the men he held at gunpoint to visibly shudder. "Good!" thought Ace.

The old man leaned the spear on the ATV by the rifle, then leaned over to pluck Mitch's pistol from its holster. As he walked toward the men they shifted nervously but made sure they kept their hands high. The muzzle of the black 12 gauge probably looked like the end of a road culvert to these guys, Ace smiled to himself. He casually dropped Mitch's pistol into the hot coals in the fire pit. "You! Likewise! Pull it out with two fingers and drop it in the pit!" Ace ordered. "And now you, and now you!"

All four pistols were now in the fire pit.

"When and if the sheriff ever shows up, you boys better have a real good story cooked up for what happened here. But right now I think you better dive over yonder creek bank and keep your heads down!"

The three men needed no urging since the plastic grips on the pistols were already starting to burn and flare.

Ace quickly gathered the spear, the rifle, and the sack and headed for the tethered horse. He had to tie the AR-15 on behind the saddle because Pat's rifle was still in the scabbard. He slung the shotgun across his back, crawled into the saddle, and swung Rosie around so he could grab his spear from where he had leaned it against a tree.

Ace and Rosie were several hundred yards down the road when, for the second day in a row, four handguns destroyed themselves in a fire pit.

Ace rode up to receive more than a few curious looks from the men he'd left at the Big Swampy Campground. Ace untied the AR-15 from the back of the saddle and handed it and the plastic sack to the nearest man. "Evidence," he said.

CHAPTER FIVE
Coincidence

"YOU DON'T SUPPOSE I could get one of you guys to clean up my spear do you?" Ace asked as he handed the imposing weapon to one of the men waiting by the table that held the game warden's body.

The man looked at the gore on the blade and back at Ace with a question in his eyes.

"I take it personal when someone kills our game wardens and I take *personal* to the extreme when it's a friend," Ace proclaimed. "I believe the coroner will find a fella up at the Gloomy Creek Campground who did not fail to take my point lightly, if you get my drift." Ace looked toward the main road. "Takin' their own sweet time ain't they?"

"Yeah," one of the men agreed, "ever since that pretty boy from the *left* coast took over, the Grant County Sheriff's Office looks more like the Keystone Kops every day."

"Well tell the chief cop when he gets here there's one more body for him to 'investigate,' " Ace said sourly. "Right now I got some more business over to Black Mountain, but I'll appreciate it if you keep that information to yourselves. I'm gonna borrow Pat's horse one more time. Come on Dozer, we gotta go find us an Indian."

This time the horse went off at a slow lope making it easy for the big dog to keep up. Partway down the Boulder River Road, Ace guided Rosie up a game trail that would cut about three miles off and bring them out of the timber a couple of miles up the Black Mountain Road. It would serve two purposes, namely saving time and energy, and the chance of meeting the sheriff on the Boulder River Road would be cut in half.

X X X X X

While Ace was on his way through the trees, the fugitives in the Suburban were facing a small dilemma. The Black Mountain Road was a dirt track full of ruts and mud holes. Although Billy could not understand the language, he sensed his captors were discussing the wisdom of keeping him around. While getting a bottle of water from the rear cargo space, Billy discreetly tried the rear door handle and discovered that it could be opened from the inside. But before he could formulate a plan of action, fate tossed a wrench into the fugitive's gears.

Fadil had eased the front of the Suburban into the edge of a very long puddle in the road caused by a seep that filled the ruts. Traffic had pushed the water further and further. Four-wheel-drive vehicles chewed this piece of road into a bog that the two-wheel-drive Suburban had no chance of negotiating. Here was Billy's chance!

"I'll check it out for you," Billy volunteered. Mustapha was not sure what he meant. Billy began to remove his shoes. "I'll go out there and you can see how deep it is. Maybe we can find a way across."

The men discussed this briefly and Mustapha let Billy ease past him to the passenger door. "We will be watching you so do not try to run," he warned. "Not if I get a chance," Billy thought. He tied the laces together and hung his shoes around his neck. "Damn! This water is cold!" he said to himself as he waded out into the water-filled ruts. In the middle, the water was past his knees. It didn't look good.

Billy pointed to the west. "People have been driving around up there," he called. "Want me to check it out?"

More discussion. Mustapha nodded affirmatively. This park they were in was perhaps four-hundred-yards long and about one-hundred-yards wide. The road cut through the middle. As Billy worked his way west, he also angled away from the main seep so that it appeared the ground was more stable closer to the trees. Another thought bloomed. "Look!" He pointed to the very prominent peak to the east. "If we get stuck maybe the people in the fire lookout will see us and send help!"

The Jihadists were really distracted now. They hadn't even noticed the lookout tower. Fadil was getting conflicting directions from Shadid and Jameel who were trying to help him back the trailer up, a task the driver had not yet mastered.

Billy was weighing his chances. It was still thirty yards to the tree line and Mustapha had an M-16. The man was not taking his eyes off of the Indian, and neither was Zakir who had a boxy looking automatic weapon hanging from a strap around his neck. Probably a 9-mm, Billy thought.

Everyone in the park was startled by the thuddity-thud-thud of hoof beats. Ace had taken this all in from the trees seventy yards away. "Rosie," Ace muttered, "I'm gonna cut loose with this shotgun in a minute and I'm gonna take a calculated bet that Pat had a chance to get you used to gunfire." Rosie only twitched her ears then went back to pointing them at the action in the park. "You ready Doze?" The dog was also intent on the scene before them. "Okay, then, let's go!"

Mustapha and his crew were initially too stunned to react as the horseman bore down upon them. They had never considered they were actually under any threat from anyone out here in the middle of nowhere. By the time they realized that this was indeed an attack it was too late. Ace angled Rosie quartering to Mustapha and cut loose with a charge of number two shot from twenty feet away. Most of the shot missed to the right but Mustapha caught one BB in the right eye and a half dozen more in the shoulder and neck. He dropped his M-16.

"Get him, Doze!" Zakir was scrabbling to get his machine gun up and working when Dozer launched himself squarely into the man from a full run. The momentum carried them both out into the muddy ruts in front of the Suburban. Zakir's weapon flew out and disappeared in the muddy water. Dozer's weight pushed the terrorist completely under the muck.

Mustapha was staggering around screaming while Fadil was reaching over the seat for one of the other weapons that were probably on the seat or on the floor. He came up with a pistol just as Ace poked the 12 gauge through the passenger window. Fadil got the whole load in the midsection, which released a good portion of his intestines right into his lap. Unarmed, Jameel and Sahdid stood helplessly by the back of the Suburban. Dozer guarded Zakir by baring his teeth in the man's face every time he lifted his head from the muck.

Billy trotted up. "Good to see you, Uncle," he grinned. "What took you so long?"

"Business," Ace said. "Pick up that M-16 would you. I always wanted one. And now I suppose you want to ride or are you gonna run barefoot like your ancestors?"

"I think we better get the hell out of here, Uncle." and the boy lithely vaulted up behind Ace. "Sorry Rosie!" he said to the overloaded horse.

"Come on Dozer!" and they headed for the safety of the trees

Once they were well inside the timber they stopped, and Billy slid off the horse and began putting his shoes on.

"Do you realize how humiliating this is?" Billy asked. Before Ace could answer Billy said, "My people will never live this down if it gets out. An Indian rescued by the cavalry!"

They rested for a few minutes while Ace filled Billy in on everything that had happened the last two days.

"Damn, I'm really sorry to hear about Pat," Billy said. "You know when you came riding up I never even noticed it was his horse. Those are some pretty bad dudes. You know they were gonna cut Lyle Stands's throat until the White Bears came along. What the hell is going on?"

"Your grandfather had a dream about this too. Maybe we can put it all together," Ace said thoughtfully. "But right now if you don't mind walking up to my camp, I'll take Rosie back where she belongs and then meet you there. Take the M-16, you never know what you might run into."

"I just hope I can get in and out of the campground without running into that dip shit sheriff." Ace said.

Billy took off on a lope through the trees. Ace watched him go and thought to himself, "I used to be able to do that but now all I want to do is go to bed. Come on Doze, let's go."

While Ace was taking Rosie back through the short cut, Jameel and Shadid had the unpleasant task of pulling Fadil's remains from the Suburban's driver's seat. They called to Zakir for assistance since Mustapha was no help to anyone now. The wounded man had sat down in the grass rocking back and forth in pain, blubbering to no one in particular. Zakir was fishing for his machine gun when he heard a rumble up the road from the south. He shouted a quick command to Jameel and Shadid who frantically dragged Fadil's body back to the trailer and unceremoniously stuffed his leaking corpse under the tarp.

What appeared to be a mobile ball of mud roared toward the Suburban as Zakir, still covered with muck from the puddle, slid into the driver's seat hoping the muddy slop would cover the blood and gore.

Tommy Thompson and his mud-bogging buddy Travis Olson slid their jacked-up three-quarter-ton four-wheel-drive perched atop huge tires to a stop at the far end of the bog. Tommy leaned out the window. "Hey! You guys want us to pull your rig on across?" Then he glanced at Travis with a wicked grin and winked.

Zakir stayed in the Suburban but hollered back, "Yes! Yes! We have had some accident. We . . . uh . . . have to go that way!" Zakir pointed south with a muddy left arm. With his right hand, he motioned frantically for Shadid and Jameel to get Mustapha loaded into the second passenger seat. Thankfully, the man had shut up and wiped most of the blood off of his face.

Tommy gleefully spun his truck around and backed toward the Suburban spraying water and muck everywhere.

Travis swung out of the cab and around into the pickup box without getting down. He picked up a beat-up tow strap they had found in the road, leaned over the tailgate, and dropped the loop of one end over the trailer ball on the back bumper.

"I ain't getting' *my* boots muddy, mister!" Travis threw the other end toward the Suburban.

Zakir gave Travis a withering look. "If I had my machine gun you infidel son of a donkey," he thought to himself, but, nevertheless, stepped out into the mud, retrieved the tow strap end, and found a place to attach the large steel hook.

Travis swung around the edge of the pickup cab and bounced into the passenger seat. Tommy eased the big pickup forward to tighten the tow strap. "We are SO gonna cover up those Ki-Yi's!" He giggled.

Travis replied, "I don't think those guys are Indians. That one talked like an Arab or some fuckin' thing!"

"Whatever," Tommy said. "This is gonna be so cool!"

"Ready?" Tommy asked. "Do it man, do it!" Travis urged.

All four directional traction tires on the big pickup truck churned through the bog as Tommy pressed the accelerator flat down on the floor. The Suburban was totally lost to sight in a veritable blizzard of muddy water and Black Mountain muck.

The fugitives in the Suburban frantically rolled up the side windows while Zakir tried to figure out how to turn the windshield wipers on. The boys in the pickup hadn't even given them a chance to start the engine. The escapees could see absolutely nothing, but realized they were not in the bog anymore and were picking up speed every second.

Zakir stomped hard on the brakes and had the satisfaction of snapping the tow strap.

When the strap broke, Tommy and Travis let out a long "Yee-haw!" as they peeled around and roared past the dripping mess that contained a seething Zakir and his companions.

"I need a gun. Any gun!" Zakir barked as he flung open the driver's door. Jameel and Shadid scrambled to come up with something and found the pistol Fadil had tried to use. Zakir snatched the weapon, jumped out, pointed the gun at the fleeing pickup and pulled the trigger.

Nothing! In a blind rage he savagely pulled the slide back ripping the web of skin between his right thumb and forefinger. By the time he brought the pistol to bear again, the pickup had disappeared into the trees at the north end of the park. Zakir emptied the magazine anyway.

X X X X X

While Tommy and Travis were laughing themselves silly and making plans to regale their friends about the great prank they had pulled on some foreign asshole hunters, Ace noted the passage of the coroner's box van headed toward the Big Swampy Campground. He had heard it coming and turned off the road into the timber, then stayed inside the trees to see if the sheriff's distinctly painted SUV would be trailing the coroner but all he saw was a nondescript Bronco.

"Might as well take it easy now," Ace thought to himself. Then out loud he said, "You and Rosie were magnificent today." Ace aimed the comment at Dozer who gave a satisfied glance up at the man in the saddle. Ace went on. "I know that look. You're thinkin' 'Yeah, I know.' I've seen that look before, you big lug. You sure took care of that mean lookin' son of a bitch in the mud hole. It's proud of you, I am!"

The coroner was just finished loading Pat's body when Ace got to the campground. "So that's who was in that Bronco," Ace thought as he watched the fat deputy take off west ahead of the coroner's van. He eased Rosie out of the trees toward Pat's trailer and her corral.

X X X X X

"This might be gravy train duty," Deputy Del Fulton told himself, "but it sure is boring." After Del reported to Sheriff Harper that the

Suburban he was told to watch for had indeed turned into the Black Mountain road, he was instructed to drive on to the Big Swampy Campground to meet the coroner.

Del had heard some radio chatter about the game warden being shot, but for some reason Harper had said to question the people at the campground, take notes, and follow the coroner back to Grant City, the County Seat.

The sheriff hadn't said anything about a second body, probably because there was no radio coverage from the campground, Del reasoned.

"Sheriff didn't say anything about evidence," Del told one of the campers when the man handed him a plastic bag containing the warden's badge, billfold, binoculars and pistol and the noise suppressor.

"Ace Gronsky said he found this stuff in the cargo box of an ATV up at the Gloomy Creek Campground," the man told Del. "Then the owner tried to brain Ace with an ax. I guess you could say he didn't get the job done 'cause that's who the coroner is supposed to pick up next."

"Shit!" Del said as he climbed into his Bronco. Del led the way to the Gloomy Creek Campground mostly because he didn't want to eat the dust kicked up by the coroner's box van.

The ATV and Mitch's body were right where Ace had left them. Three men sat in camp chairs around the fire pit, but only one got up when the deputy got out and walked toward them. "Good afternoon. I'm Deputy Sheriff Del Fulton of the Grant County Sheriff's Office," Del said officiously while he stuck out his right hand. The tall, lean, and muscular man standing in front of the short, fat deputy made a sharp contrast in human shape. The man merely stood silently ignoring the deputy's outstretched hand.

Del nervously pulled out a small notepad and pen. "Uh, you mind telling me what happened here?"

"Yes I mind!" The man said it as a challenge.

Del was ever mindful that he was beginning to live up to his reputation as the "Barney Fife" of Grant County so he countered, "Now see here . . . ," he paused waiting for a name, but none was offered, "If you won't tell me what happened, I'm sure you'll be talking to Sheriff Harper. And he won't be easy on you when I tell him how uncooperative you were." Fulton was pouting now.

"You do that, *deputy*," the man spat back over his shoulder as he spun around on his heel. His obvious contempt for the law fairly dripped from the way he said "deputy", then, dismissed the lawman and went back to the fire pit. Neither of the other men bothered to even look up.

Del felt obligated to order somebody around so he instructed the coroner to take photos of the *crime scene*.

After the photos were taken, the coroner and his helper laid the corpse out on a zippered bag and were ready to close it up as Del walked by. The coroner looked up. "You gonna check this guy for ID and stuff?"

Del puffed out an exasperated sigh, "Yeah, I guess I'd better. You want to inventory the pocket contents for me?" He tossed the notebook to the helper. Del and the coroner dug through all the pockets. "Huh," Del snorted, "clean as a whistle." He looked back over his shoulder at the three men around the fire pit. Then he looked at the coroner. "You gonna ask them if they have a name for this guy or anything?" The coroner shook his head and started to zip the bag. "You ask if you want to. I just want to get outta here. Those are some scary guys!"

Del let all pride slip away by agreeing. "Yeah, me too. We'll let Harper handle 'em."

On their way back through the Big Swampy Campground, Del noticed that the game warden's horse was back in her portable corral munching on a couple of pats of weed-free hay. "Good!" Del thought to himself. "I won't have to mess with that Ace character." Del led the way back out to the main road happy to be heading for town. It was past supper time. McDonald's would be selling a double order of everything tonight.

X X X X X

While Del was on his way out, one of the men seated around the fire pit on Gloomy Creek looked at the tall man, "Sergei, you should be ashamed of yourself," he sneered. "I thought that deputy was going to piss his pants!" They all laughed. None seemed to be the least concerned about the fate of their camp mate, Mitch.

"Do you think we have to be concerned about this sheriff?" asked the first man.

Sergei snorted. "Don't worry your pretty head my little babushka!" Sergei liked to tease Kelly, the smallest of the group. When told who the team members would be, Sergei hoped "Kelly" would be female. Instead, Kelly turned out to be a former tunnel rat for the IRA.

"Karl told me that Omega has taken care of the sheriff. And speaking of Karl," Sergei looked at his watch in the dimming light, "it's time to check in. Tomorrow is a big, big day."

X X X X X

"Comin' in!" Ace called as he approached the tent.

"Your woodpecker scared the crap out of me," Billy said as Ace and Dozer pushed through the flap.

"Yeah, I forgot to tell you about that." Ace laughed at the thought. With everything that happened today even *he* was jumpy.

"Huh! Dough gods, Spam, stewed tomatoes and coffee," Ace observed. "That's quite a supper!"

Billy sat back in a folding camp chair with his feet up on a cooler; he affected a serious scowl and proclaimed, "Old Crow saying says, 'if white man complain too much, he can cook his own fuckin' supper!'"

"Your point is well taken, oh wise and powerful no-feather chief," Ace said as he picked a dough god from a bowl on the table and tossed another to Dozer who swallowed it in one gulp.

"I was ready to set your supper out for the bears," Billy said, "what took you so long?"

Ace explained that he had slipped in behind Karl's tent to eavesdrop for a while. He pulled out a small plastic device from his pocket called a Game Ear. "It is truly amazing what you can hear when you turn one of these gadgets up to full power," Ace explained. "I'll tell you what I heard later." The two friends traded a few more insults, threw dough gods to the dog, and went through a second pot of coffee while they discussed recent events.

"I found out those guys who kidnapped me escaped from the prison up at Wesley. Funny thing about it is they don't seem concerned about getting away. I mean why would they be so dead set on going up Black Mountain Road? It just dead ends in that little campground in the bottom of that box canyon. You look at it a certain way, it's almost like someone sent them into a trap or something," Billy mused.

Ace agreed and expressed his suspicion that all of this business with the tower, the three camps, and the Jihadists was all tied together somehow.

"Well, tomorrow I gotta get up there on the ridge and call Grandfather and tell him I'm okay," Billy said. He thought of something else to pass along. "We got a good team worked up this year for the Indian relay races and we been practicin' against those guys from Lame Deer. It's a blast!" Billy was naming all of the young men who were into the relay racing but stopped at the sound of a loud snore.

Ace was sound asleep in his chair by the warm stove.

"Poor old guy," Billy thought. "This much activity must be pretty hard on somebody over seventy."

Then Billy thought about the rescue and the old hunter galloping full tilt across the meadow just like John Wayne, only for real. Firing that 12 gauge with one hand? "I sure as hell hope I can do as well when I'm that old," Billy said to Dozer, who opened one eye at the sound of a voice.

Billy crawled into the top bunk knowing that when the stove cooled off, Ace would wake up, make one last nature call, and turn in.

CHAPTER SIX
Coalescence

THE RED GLOW of first light faded quickly into a dull gray overcast, a repeat of the previous day's weather.

Ace built a small fire of pencil-sized sticks in the Sims stove and stepped outside to watch the smoke trail straight up, then spread quickly to dissipate into the tops of the tallest trees.

"Looks like we can still cook with wood without giving away our location. How do you like your elk steak?" Ace addressed Billy who was just returning from a nature call.

"Are we really going to take time for a big breakfast?" Billy asked, watching the smoke which had now turned into a translucent haze as the fire burned hotter.

"Do young bucks answer questions with another question these days, or is that an old Indian trick?" Ace grinned.

Billy quickly shot back, "No. We learned to speak with forked tongue from you white guys!" Then he continued, "Well done. If my steak has any resident parasites, I want 'em fried good and dead."

"Good. I got some taters and onions to go with it," Ace replied. "Might be a long time 'til supper. I have this feeling up the middle of my back that this will be a long, busy day."

"You took quite a chance listening in on those guys down the creek," Billy commented. "Does your *feeling* have anything to do with what you overheard?"

"Well, it sorta cleared up a few things, like these three camps have some sort of coordinated activity that they plan for this afternoon. They have to wait for something else to happen over there on Black Mountain

Creek first," Ace mused, "but they don't have any direct connection except through this Omega outfit, who the hell ever that is."

"I can't figure out that Karl fella either. Just from what they were talkin' about, he knew a couple of the other people, like that Sergei, over at the Gloomy Creek Campground and one he called Shamus at the Little Swampy Creek Campground. It sure sounded like they used to work for some security outfit over in the Middle East. I'm thinkin' these guys were all hired in from a lot of places." Ace was turning the steaks over and stirring the potatoes and onions in the huge frying pan.

"It almost looks like one of those big bank robbery operations you see in the movies except this is up in the mountains with nothing around but a few early season elk hunters," Billy offered. "It just doesn't make sense. But then a lot of stuff white people do doesn't make sense." Billy grinned, poking Ace with a stick of wood he was about to add to the fire.

"Watch it kid, or I'll drop your steak on the ground!" Ace warned.

"I won't encourage you to make any improvements," Billy countered, "you'd better just leave it in the pan!"

Ace relished playing the part of the grumpy old man while Billy enjoyed countering with witty barbs fired from the perspective of the smart-aleck youngster. They both feigned wounded indignation with practiced ease much to the consternation of any "uninitiated" onlookers who expected to see them at each others throats any second. It was a game played well.

Billy had obviously been ruminating over something for he suddenly broke the silence of their breakfast. "Now I remember what these guys remind me of," he said around a mouth full of steak.

"You mean these so-called *hunters*?" Ace prompted.

"Yeah. I was just a kid, but you remember those thugs the security company hired during the coal mine strike?" Billy asked. Ace allowed as how he had, by nodding his head. Billy continued his thought train, "They struck me as a bunch of Soldier-of-Fortune-type wanna-be's, walking around like they were Green Berets or Navy Seals or something."

Ace agreed. "That's the impression I got. Not really skilled or trained to any extent, just criminals that aren't in jail yet." Then he added, "But double dangerous because they have some idea of being on a *mission*."

The pair finished their breakfast and burned the paper plates. Ace wiped out the big frying pan with a paper shop towel and burned that too. The extra coffee pot held boiling water which he poured over their utensils that had been deposited in the big frying pan. A few drops of dish soap and a soft bristled brush made short work of breakfast dishes. Ace poured the dishwater into a pail by the stove, then poured more hot water into the pan, added a dash of bleach, swished it around and poured that into the pail. One more hot water rinse eliminated any cooking odor or grease, and Dozer made short work of leftovers.

Ace and Billy packed the food coolers out beyond the trip line to a spot between two tall pines located on the opposite side of the camp from the meat pole. Here was another pole high off the ground from which dangled several poly ropes. They attached the coolers to the ropes, hoisted them to about twelve feet and tied them off.

"That's the best we can do for keepin' the camp from smellin' like a grocery store, but I seen bears tear hell outta stuff just for the hell of it anyway," Ace said, then he added, "The elk hangin' from the meat pole will be enough of a distraction where we shouldn't have to worry much."

Billy agreed. "Using that all-steel horse trailer for a storage locker is a pretty clever way of keeping the clutter down."

"Only one drawback that I can see," Ace commented. "If it snows, we ain't gonna stay hid much, are we?"

Again Billy agreed. "Under any other circumstances I'd say it's not a big deal, but right now the more we stay out of sight, the better."

"Yeah," Ace said, "all I wanted was some privacy before the whole mountain started crawlin' with hunters. After the family and friends get up here it wouldn't have made any difference, but that's all changed now, huh, Doze?" Ace asked the dog as he ruffled his head, but the question was aimed at Billy.

Back at the tent, Ace pulled a .50-caliber ammo can from a row of similar cans under the bunk bed. The lid opened with a pop and he lifted out two small two-way radios from a cache of six.

"This is yours," Ace said as he handed one to Billy. "It has a call button, but I prefer not use it. Too noisy. Push the transmit button once, wait, then push it twice. That's our signal to pick up and it don't wake up the whole neighborhood if you know what I mean. If you have trouble but can't talk, push transmit three times, wait, and then three more times. There's extra batteries in that can. Better put some in your pocket."

Ace shrugged into his day-pack vest, slung the 12 gauge over his shoulder, and grabbed the spear from its roost by the tent flap which got Dozer's full attention. "We'll forego your pack old buddy. I think I have enough for both of us. I just want another look at that tower on the ridge. And we better stop by the horse trailer to see if we can outfit this Indian with something besides a sweat suit and running shoes so he can go call his grandpappy."

Ace found Billy some clothes that fit from the stash the family planned to use during the rifle season and even a pair of boots that worked as long as Billy wore two pairs of socks. Before he closed the trailer door, Ace pulled out a metal case and popped the twin latches. "You better strap this on," he said as he handed Billy a leather gun belt and holster rig. The holster was a military style full flap that completely covered an early model Ruger single-six .357 Magnum revolver. "Bought this the first year they made 'em and I had Ernst Saddlery custom build the belt and holster."

Billy undid the snap, pulled out the heavy pistol, and rotated the cylinder. "Six rounds?"

"I sent it back to the company when they said they would install a transfer bar at no charge. Now you can safely keep 'six pills in the bottle,'" Ace explained. "That so-called *gunfighter* who accidentally shot himself during the Johnson County invasion probably wished he'd kept an empty chamber under the hammer."

"Gee, thanks Ace for trusting me with this, but I still got this," Billy said as he held up the M-16.

Ace reminded Billy, "The only ammo we have for that thing is in the magazine. You have a whole belt full for the pistol. I might warn you that it has a competition trigger that's smooth as silk and the sights are adjusted for six o'clock on a two-inch bull at fifty feet. Keep in mind that the trajectory crosses your sight line and drops back in at about a hundred yards."

"Pretty hot then, huh?" Billy asked.

"Yeah. You'll know it when it goes off!" Ace laughed.

"You gonna use that game trail that angles away from the creek and passes through those old cabins?" Billy asked.

"Yeah. Us old timers need to take the easiest way we can these days. Too bad we can't stay out on the road but those assholes still have one of those spy-copters. So keep a sharp look out, stay out of sight, and let me know what your grandpappy says."

Billy said he would be careful. They made a radio check and both hikers disappeared into the trees on the west side of Big Swampy Creek.

X X X X X

While Ace and Billy were setting off on their errands, the men in the three camps had received their instructions from Karl who had received his instructions via satellite from Omega. Each group opened their cargo trailers and removed three white PVC cylinders marked with large black block letters that read "U.S. GEOPHYSICAL SURVEY." Thus burdened with the cylinders, large square backpacks, telescoping tripods, and their weapons, the three teams trudged into the forest from their respective camps.

The team from the Gloomy Creek Camp were having more difficulty than they could handle being one man short. After some consultation with Karl over their radio link, they decided to leave one cylinder at camp and continue with only two.

On Black Mountain Creek, Mustapha had spent a sleepless night and kept the others awake with his constant complaining. His injured eye was draining pus down his cheek and the man looked positively miserable.

Zakir was in a black and murderous mood. They had had trouble trying to set up their tent, and the only other camper at the box canyon campground who offered to help them was rudely rebuffed for his efforts. In fact, the strange-acting men made the camper, Ned Sturmer, so nervous that he forgot about his plans to fish, quickly struck his tent, and headed back out to civilization.

Mustapha had trouble reading their instructions but got help from Jameel, who seemed to be the only one showing any amount of sympathy for the injured man. Together, their meager command of written English allowed them to assemble the gear that took up a great deal of the space inside the tent. Zakir and Shadid wrapped up Fadil's remains in a scrap of canvas, thankful that any witnesses had vacated the area, unceremoniously dropped his corpse into a shallow washout, and covered it with just enough pine duff and dirt to hide it from casual view.

When the satellite phone was powered up, Mustapha called the number on his instructions, called out the checklist to Jameel, who assured him that all was in readiness, and now all they had to do was wait for the signal that would propel them all to everlasting world fame and the adulation of generations of Jihadists.

Shadid had boiled water and they all sat back to sip their tea and gaze at the beautiful, deadly missile poised to rip through the top of their tent.

X X X X X

While the Jihadists were sipping their tea, Deputy Del Fulton was at the foot of the mountain spending a great deal of his on-duty time in one eating place and then another. He had overheard the mud boggers, Tommy Thompson and Travis Olson, loudly bragging about the "stunt" they pulled on a bunch of "furrin" hunters. Del was on hand at the cafe in Clayton when Ned Sturmer also overheard the same story.

Ned approached Tommy. "I'll bet that's the same bunch I ran into. There was one mean-lookin' son-of-a-bitch with a wicked-lookin' knife in his belt. I offered to help 'em set up their tent, but he plumb spooked me so I got the hell out of there!"

Tommy laughed loudly. "Well, unless someone pulls them back through that bog hole, they'll be there 'til it freezes up!"

Del got up and waddled out to his Bronco. He slid into the food-stained driver's seat and punched in some numbers on his cell phone. Sheriff Harper answered immediately. Del noticed that he seemed uncharacteristically edgy.

"'Member them guys you told me to watch?" Del asked.

"Yeah, are they still up there on Black Mountain Creek?" Harper wanted to know.

"Hah!" Del laughed. "Some mud boggers pulled them through a big puddle up there, and a fisherman said they're as good as stuck at the Box Canyon Campground. They got a tent set up and everything. Fisherman said there ain't nobody else up there after they run him off. He said they scared the shit out of him. Who the hell are these people?"

The sheriff still sounded nervous. "Never mind who they are. You'll find out soon enough. I want you to hang around Clayton and I'll tell you what to do when the time is right." Harper didn't say goodbye. The deputy stared at the phone for a minute, shrugged his shoulders, and went back to his stool in the Cafe.

X X X X X

While Deputy Fulton ordered another doughnut in Clayton, Wyoming, a historic conference in Jackson Hole was coming to a close. Fawning environmental types were besieging President Omar Bahktar with questions during a Q&A that was nothing short of an extended campaign speech.

"I'm so happy to be here in this splendid place. The backdrop could not be more magnificent! Let me be clear. I will not allow greed to destroy this pristine example of our most precious environment. We must preserve at all costs our natural heritage, and if that means rising energy costs then so be it! Under my leadership this country will demonstrate that we can have a vibrant and productive economy and . . . (pause for effect amid wild cheering), and I will take personal responsibility to see that we wean ourselves off of dirty fossil fuels while creating green jobs for Americans (more wild cheering).

"Mr. President, Mr. President. What about the Arabs?"

"My friends in Saudi Arabia have assured me they are doing everything they can to put down extremism while seeing to it that the price of oil is kept as low as possible."

"Mr. President, are we going to go to war with Iran?"

"We'll let the Israelis do that! Ha! Ha! Just kidding! I still believe that when I'm re-elected I can get Iran to come to the table to talk about peace. I have a plan to lift all sanctions to show good faith, and I believe that the reasonable thing for them to do will be to reciprocate."

The people in charge of the gathering were pointing to their watches. There was a plan to take the president on a tour to see wolves in the wild before it was time to board Air Force One, which was scheduled to leave the Jackson Hole Airport at 2 pm.

While the environmentalists were having orgasms in Jackson Hole, Wyoming, Monica Farizzi ordered an early lunch brought to her office and left word that she was not to be disturbed all afternoon. She looked out her window toward the Pacific Ocean. A slow-moving storm had been predicted, but visibility under the overcast stretched clear to the horizon. She checked the phone in her suit-coat pocket and stared at the soft glow indicating that it was fully charged. The minutes ticked by and the knot in her stomach tightened. She had some nagging doubts about what she knew was about to happen but consoled herself that the reward was worth the risk. She told herself she would merely be seen as a bystander whisked into her place in history by tragic events that would be forever pinned to a handfull of wretched Islamic Extremists.

X X X X X,

Billy Black Stone found a good strong cell signal at the top of an outcrop, which gave him a good view of the country below the ridge that people called The Arm. He dialed a number, listened to four of five rings, and was about to leave a message when his Grandfather answered.

"Billy! I'm so glad to hear your voice." Alden Spotted Horse's normally taciturn voice sounded abundantly joyful.

"I was about to give up on you, Grandfather. Did you leave the phone in the outhouse again?" Billy laughed. It was a joke they shared about the time the phone had fallen from Alden's clothes at the outdoor toilet. Even though they got a new phone to replace it, many of Alden's friends had heard about the misadventure. They would say things like, "You sound pretty shitty today!"

"No. I took it to bed with me in case you called and I couldn't find it in the blankets. You got away from those guys okay?"

Billy told Alden about his rescue by Ace and some of the things that were happening on the mountain.

"Word got around here, you know how it goes, and Jefferson Iron Bird came around to tell me they thought those guys who grabbed you were from the prison and they went up in the Big Horns. Looks like our own police know more than anyone else," Alden said.

"Grandfather, I have a new rifle and Ace let me wear his old pistol. There are more really mean people up here than I ever knew existed, but they don't know how to find us, so as long as I stay with Ace, I'll be alright," Billy assured his Grandfather.

"Billy," Alden warned, "you do everything Ace tells you. His heart is good and his mind is clear. My dream tells me there will be more trouble of some kind, but you will be protected because you also have a good heart. I will keep the phone by me and I will tell Jefferson to let the rest of the police know that you are okay. My vision said to watch the sky, but you watch where you put your feet!"

Billy said his goodbye and closed the phone. It was getting close to noon so he clicked the two-way radio transmit once, waited, and did two more. Ace answered. It sounded like he might be pretty close.

"You know that point at the end of The Arm that overlooks Gloomy Creek?" Ace asked. Billy allowed as how he did.

"I'll wait for you here and see if you know what to make of this contraption on the rock," Ace said. "And I'll start a little fire so we can have some coffee and share some lunch."

Billy acknowledged by clicking twice. That doggoned Ace! Did he pack a coffee pot all the way up here? Billy angled through the timber toward the meeting place. He couldn't wait to tell Ace about his call to Alden.

"Sometimes this works, and sometimes it don't," Ace said as Billy came around the shoulder of the outcrop on which stood the "contraption" as Ace called it. He had a flat, thin sliver of stone over a fire of small sticks. There were two tin cups of water just starting to steam. Ace pulled a packet of instant coffee from his vest and dumped a little in each cup.

"It'll never boil this way but it keeps the cups from getting black," Ace said. "But you better get your cup off that rock before it decides to explode. Big rocks do that more often than little ones for some reason. Must be some moisture trapped inside or something."

There was an open can of Vienna sausages at the edge of the stone, and they each took one out, split it, and put it between two crackers. Dozer watched patiently while Ace pretended not to notice.

"Look who thinks he's gonna get one," Ace told Billy while Dozer's eyebrows shot up. "See, he knows when you're talkin' about him even when I don't say words like *dog, moocher, mutt, and Dozer!*" The dog shifted visibly and both men laughed.

Ace pulled a bagel out of his vest, twisted it open and carefully poured the juice from the can on the open side of both halves. He placed them on a nearby stone and told Dozer, "These are yours old buddy."

Rather than leap up, the dog rose leisurely, walked to the stone, daintily picked one up, and carefully chewed it, and then did the other.

"Great table manners!" Billy observed.

The pair gazed at the forest and talked about the lack of logging these days. The conversation moved to the early days on the mountain.

"You ever learn much about the tie hackers?" Ace asked.

"Our school didn't teach us too much about local history. They were too busy trying to make us forget *our* history," Billy said. "but yeah, I heard they were some pretty tough guys."

"People used to work a lot harder, but they also didn't last as long as folks do now. Burned out real fast. Those guys who cut railroad ties by hand were expected to whack out sixty on a good day, and I heard they burned about six thousand calories doin' it. I don't know if you ever saw one of the broad axes they used, but they were huge. They'd saw or whack down a tree, flatten two sides with that ax, saw it into railroad-tie lengths, drag it to a pile, and stack 'em up to wait until they could be floated down to Clayton. Thing was, they stayed up here all year. I just have a hard time imagining how hard it must have been to pack a shovel, an ax, a saw, and a huge lunch and do it day after day," Ace mused.

The pair leaned back against the rock and talked about how things used to be as compared to how they are today. The afternoon was still pretty comfortable at about 45 degrees, and Ace thought about taking a nap when all hell broke loose, literally!

Chapter Seven
Continuum

BILLY'S SHARP EYES caught the movement and almost before he could point to it, the object streaked from sight into the cloud cover leaving a trail of white smoke that appeared to come from the Black Mountain Creek drainage.

Ace was just saying, "Holy . . . !" when a concussion sounded somewhere above the clouds.

Three smaller bright streaks of light shot upward, one each from the Big and Little Swampy and Gloomy Creek drainages. The deep roar of large jet engines and the sounds of smaller ones drifted down from a battlefield in the sky as three more silvery dots of light shot into the same area of the clouds, followed closely by two more. More concussions sounded from the sky.

As Ace and Billy watched, a fighter jet swooped out of the cloud cover trailing smoke, as another fighter appeared burning fiercely in a death spiral. Something broke off the first fighter causing it to pitch sharply and veer to the northwest. Two seconds later the canopy blew off, and the pilot ejected while the fighter went on to smash itself into a smudge of metal on the side of a massive stone face known as Queen Mary Point.

The second fighter appeared to go down somewhere on the mountain face above the little town of Clayton. The parachute from the fighter jet was drifting toward the ridge between Big and Little Swampy Creeks, when the well-known profile of Air Force One broke through the cloud layer. It too trailed smoke and flames as it made a labored turn taking the huge plane first north then west in a wide arc.

Ace and Billy were speechless not believing what they were seeing. Ace could see that the starboard engines, which seemed to be still functioning fully, were gradually pushing the plane around in a great turn. From his experience with aircraft, Ace could imagine the pilot was trying to balance the power to keep the plane aloft while sacrificing a certain amount of directional control. The enormous plane lumbered around to center itself over the Big Swampy drainage. Just after it passed the watchers on the ridge, something popped out of the belly of the plane and immediately deployed three parachutes. It was an escape pod.

Ace was quick to recover from his astonishment. "Billy! Mark where that pilot lands and head for it as soon as you can. I'll watch the pod."

The 747 had cleared The Arm ridge by no more than eight hundred feet and disappeared from sight. Thirty seconds later Billy and Ace saw a bloom of fire puff up over the horizon followed by a hollow boom that echoed off the mountainsides.

Only minutes before this, Air Force One had spiraled up out of Jackson Hole joined by two escort fighters. There wasn't much for the first family to see except the tops of the clouds. The pilot, Jeff Ferguson, apologized over the plane's PA system for the lack of scenery and informed them that in only a few minutes they would be over a secondary mountain range followed by a look at the northern Great Plains, which had scattered cloud cover. "You might even see a few coal mines before we get to the Black Hills," Ferguson said wryly.

President Bahktar made a mental note to have the insolent pilot fired when they got back to Washington.

Irena Bahktar watched their extremely bored daughter Kasha starting to doze off still wearing her MP3 player earbuds.

Their peaceful pampered world suddenly, if not literally, turned upside down. Alarms went off and the huge plane tilted abruptly into a fast, wide-powered turn that glued everyone down to their seats. No sooner had they straightened up, than the plane turned the opposite way, while special bodyguard Mason struggled to get near the people he was sworn to protect. The voice in his earpiece told him they were under missile attack. There was a loud bang, then another, the plane shuddered, the lights flickered, and the sound of the engines changed drastically.

"Sir! We're under attack!" Mason shouted over the din that was beginning to grow as the people around them began shouting. Some of the women were screaming.

"What?" Omar Bahktar was frozen in place at the impossibility that they could be attacked in his country. His country!

"We've got to get you out," Mason insisted. "You know the drill. This way! All of you!" Mason shouted to the wide-eyed Irena and Kasha.

Ferguson's voice, oddly calm, came over the PA, "I'll hold course as steady as I can while the first family is taken to the pod. I can position the plane over a small valley so the chutes can fully deploy before the pod hits the ground. You have less than one minute."

Mason scooped up Kasha and pushed the Bahktars along the corridor as fast as they could stumble. An attendant stood by the pod holding the hatch open. He exchanged a look with Mason that said a hundred different things in the blink of an eye. They were about to close the hatch when the chief of staff rushed up. "I've been told you're to go with them. I know the pod wasn't designed for more than three but you can hold Kasha on your lap." Mason opened his mouth to protest but the chief of staff stopped him. "Quickly! You'll be dropped in some mountainous terrain and they'll need your help. Get in man!"

Agent Mason had barely gotten his straps secured grasping the twelve-year-old Kasha tightly on his lap when the hatch slammed shut. The jolt and free fall sensation told the occupants that they were no longer on Air Force One.

X X X X X

There was no cheering or wild celebration at the Box Canyon Campground on Black Mountain Creek. The four Jihadists looked at the smoking forlorn remains of their tent and the twisted remains of the launch and communications gear, then back at Mustapha for some sort of guidance.

"Now what?" asked Zakir.

Mustapha had an almost peaceful look on his face in spite of his ruined eye. His voice was nearly inaudible. "We are done here in this world. We will meet the infidels and destroy as many as we can, for we are Allah's sacred warriors. We have destroyed the leader of the Devils, the greatest Satan of them all. Allah-hu-Akbar."

Jameel unhooked the trailer, the men checked their odd assortment of weapons, they climbed into the beat-up muddy Suburban with Zakir at the wheel, and headed north on the Black Mountain Road.

X X X X X

Calls began pouring into the sheriff's office about explosions in the mountains above Clayton and a plane that looked like a fighter jet crashing on the face of the mountain above the town.

Sheriff Harper had been told that the news would be suppressed about the president's plane being shot down until official confirmation could be obtained. In the meantime, he was to privately fuel the rumor mill and see to it that the Jihadists on Black Mountain Creek would never see another sunrise. Sheriff Harper picked up his cell phone and dialed Deputy Fulton. "Here's where you earn your pay you worthless pile of shit," he told himself.

Deputy Del Fulton was already fending off questions from an excited public in the village of Clayton. The news on the local radio station was sketchy, but it was rumored that Air Force One had gone down in the Big Horns for unknown reasons, and it was feared that everyone on board had been killed.

The Cafe was especially noisy now that loud-mouthed Bobby Joe Bentley and some of his militia friends had gathered to speculate about recent events.

"I can't say as I'm brokenhearted about losin' that worthless son-of-a-bitch," Bobby Joe proclaimed. "If he'd a lived any longer we'd all be speakin' Spanish, or Russian, or worse yet, Ay-Rab!"

The deputy's cell phone rang. People nearest stopped talking, then the need to eavesdrop spread and the place became quiet while Del responded to Sheriff Harper.

Giving the devil his due, Sheriff Harper was impressed at how his deputy played his end of the game.

"A missile? . . . Your kidding! . . . No, I didn't know that! . . . The same guys that escaped from Wesley? . . . I thought the Feds said they were headed for Canada. . . . How'd they get a missile big enough to . . . ? Yeh, sounds like the same guys I told you about on Black Mountain Creek. . . . Yeh, mud boggers saw 'em. So did Ned Sturmer. They ran him off. Um, not official yet? . . . Okay. Gotcha. I'll stand by, yeah. Bye."

Bobby Joe Bentley pushed his way to the deputy who now wore a smug self-important smirk on his pudgy face.

"What's all this about a missile, Del? And why didn't the sheriff call you on the radio?" Bobby Joe wanted to know.

"Sheriff said he didn't want it broadcast around that the unofficial word is that those ragheads that escaped from Wesley had outside help. Got 'em a ground-to-air missile and set it up by Black Mountain to shoot down Air Force One on its way back from Jackson." Then he looked around the room at the wide-eyed startled faces as he heard feet start to shuffle on the floor. "Now look here you guys. Sheriff said to keep this under your hat 'til the word gets out official on the radio." By the time Fulton got the sentence out, he was looking at the backside of everyone in the room all heading for the doors.

Fifteen minutes later a caravan of at least thirty vehicles, mostly big-tired pickups bristling with men and their guns, were headed up the mountain.

X X X X X

While Zakir gunned the Suburban as fast he dared go through the rutted Black Mountain Road, Karl was hurrying back to his camp on Big Swampy. He had to dispose of the rocket tubes and get the spy-copter into the air. He had seen one parachute from his launch point that looked like it came from the escort fighter. Although he knew the big plane went down, it had stayed aloft long enough so that it could have dropped the escape pod. He had to be sure.

Omega would be furious if this plan failed.

X X X X X

Pilot Jeff Ferguson had marveled at how the big plane had withstood the assault of so many missiles. The escort fighter manned by the Israeli pilot, who had just recently become a US citizen, had valiantly taken a missile meant for Air Force One. He hadn't seen what became of the other fighter flown by one of the few women pilots to see such duty.

Pilot Ferguson and his copilot Bob Latimore were doing everything to hold as much altitude as they could and still not stall.

Jeff's heart leaped. Latimore pointed to an hourglass-shaped flat area almost like a sloping mesa top lying right in the middle of a sea of shark-toothed peaks. They pointed the nose of the great airship toward it.

On the west coast, Monica Farizzi heard the news that the president's plane was down in mountainous terrain. "One down, two to go," she thought. Still the phone in her pocket did not ring.

The phone in Sheriff Harper's pocket did not ring either.

Air Force One pilot Jeff Ferguson knew all of the people on his plane were counting on a miracle. Jeff was praying for one too. At first it appeared there might be a chance. Their glide path dictated that there was nowhere else to go but the inviting flat-appearing plateau that was only fifteen seconds ahead. He allowed himself only a glance at Latimore's face. There was nothing left to say except, "Bob, it's been good to know you." The "plateau" was covered with boulders, some as big as houses.

It seemed that the skidding, grinding, crunching, screeching, and sliding and jarring impacts would never stop. Like a giant cheese shredder, the mountaintop ground pieces of the great plane off, while what was left of the cockpit and part of the nose teetered to a stop about a hundred yards from a sheer drop. Before he blacked out, Pilot Ferguson looked out of the left window and wondered, "What would a big old Pratt and Whitney radial engine be doing lying clear up here?"

X X X X X

The four people in the escape pod were able to enjoy the gentle swaying for about twenty seconds before they were violently jarred from the bottom, then they felt a rough scraping and bumping as the pod jerked several more times and stopped all downward movement. As soon as Agent Mason moved, so did the pod. The occupants could feel a rather "spongy" motion and more hard bumping and scraping sounds from the outside. Mason had a bad feeling about this. The pod was equipped to float and stay upright if it fell into water. It had its own batteries, locator beacon, a limited water supply but little in the way of any other amenities. In the dim glow of the emergency lights, Mason found and unlocked the watertight hatch. He slowly and cautiously pushed it open and was appalled to see a solid rock wall on one side and nothing for five hundred feet on the other. The agent craned his head around the hatch to look up. The parachutes were caught in some scraggly trees at the top of a sheer rock face.

Omar and Irena both unsnapped their safety belts and started to get up.

"Please sit down!" Mason said rather harshly when the pod rocked a little more.

"Agent. What is . . . ?" the president started to say.

Mason took a breath, blew it out and said, "Sir, my name is Richard

Mason and we're hanging off a cliff because the parachutes are caught in some trees."

The Bahktars both stared and sat speechless in stunned silence while Kasha began to cry. Mason picked her up and hugged her. "Shush, sweetheart. My job is to protect you. You know that don't you?" Kasha nodded and snuffled a little.

"Now, first of all young lady, there is a locator beacon that will let people come help us, and those trees look pretty strong up there. After all, they haven't fallen off the cliff yet, and I'll bet they've been there a long time." Mason wished he felt as confident as he sounded.

The pod shifted and dropped about six inches. Everybody screamed at once except Mason. When the pod dropped, Mason thought he heard something snap outside. He leaned out as far as he dared and saw the transmitter antenna sticking out of a crack in the rock where it had jammed, then broken off. "Oh, goody." he thought.

Mason studied the cliff, turned to the first family and said, "I don't want to alarm you but the antenna for the locator has been broken off. I'm thinking that I'm a big guy and if I get out, it will lighten the load considerably." There was no argument there and it was obvious that what was left unsaid was, "The spindly trees holding the pod in place would do a better job if this 230-pound guy would step outside."

"There is a little ledge about ten feet below us. If I hang off the bottom of the door opening, that puts my feet only about four or five feet from it. I know I can drop that far and grab hold of that outcrop to stay on the ledge. From there maybe I can find some help before . . . um, before it gets dark, okay?"

"I guess I'm in no position to make an executive decision on this," Omar Bahktar said, trying hard to lighten the mood somewhat. "Mr. Mason, you do what you think is best."

Richard Mason eased out of the hatch, gripped the sides, let his grip slip down until his fingers curled over the edge of the doorsill and looked down at his landing zone. "Shit!" he thought. "Here goes nothing."

There was an audible crack followed by a stifled scream. President Bahktar peered over the doorsill fearing the worst. Agent Mason was holding his left leg. His foot was twisted at an extreme and unnatural angle. The ledge, which looked almost as smooth as a sidewalk from above, was merely an optical illusion of sharp wrinkles, one of which reacted badly with Mason's street shoes.

As Mason was painfully inching his way along the ledge toward the place where the cliff melted into the mountainside, they were aware of a tremendous amount of gunfire that went on for probably fifteen or twenty minutes. It seemed to be coming from beyond a ridge they could see in the distance. They knew they were not alone when they heard another sound like the whine of a model airplane.

X X X X X

"Why those sons-a-bitches!" Tommy Thompson swore when his pickup burst out of the trees two hundred yards from the bog hole in the Black Mountain Road. He saw the twinkle of muzzle flashes and saw the dirt kick up in small eruptions in the road in front while a couple of slugs clanked off his vehicle before he slewed it off the road into the protection of the trees.

The Suburban was stuck in the bog again, and even at this distance, Tommy could make out the man who had been driving it the day before. Zakir was standing in the road beside Mustapha while Jameel and Shadid took refuge behind the suburban.

Bobby Joe Bentley wasn't quite as lucky. He had been on Tommy's tail and was the next vehicle to burst out of the trees. A slug went right through the windshield and out the back window taking the man leaning over the cab right below the belt buckle. Bobby Joe bailed out leaving his pickup blocking the road while the caravan of pickups piled up behind him. Zakir and Mustapha were peppering Bobby Joe's truck with little effect while militiamen were fanning out through the trees. Someone brought up a .50-caliber Barrett and set it up. There was a heavy boom and Zakir disappeared in a red mist. Mustapha was not fazed in the least. He kept up a constant fire from his AK-47. A second resounding boom and Mustapha's legs stood alone for a second then toppled over.

Shadid and Jameel began a panicked and ineffective fire from behind the stalled Suburban. A second, then a third Barrett opened up on the hapless Suburban setting it on fire. Bullets of all sizes began pouring into the Suburban from a semicircle of shooters now. The two remaining Jihadists made a run for the woods but were cut to ribbons by two or perhaps three hundred rounds of everything from .22s to long-range Magnum, big-game calibers.

When it was finally over, Bobby Joe Bentley came out from behind the tree where he had stayed until the firing stopped and loudly proclaimed, "That'll teach those lousy goat fuckers to shoot down my president's airplane!"

It did not take long for word to reach civilization by CB radio and cell phone that the people who shot down Air Force One had been annihilated by the Wyoming militia suffering only one killed in the process.

Sheriff Harper was more than happy to tell federal authorities where to go to pick up the remains and the evidence they would need to show the world who and what it was that shot down the President of the United States. In the meantime, mountain rescue teams with little hope of finding any survivors were organizing efforts to access the same peak where a B-17 bomber crashed seventy years ago.

X X X X X

Karl was maneuvering the spy-copter up the drainage of Big Swampy with the camera on wide-angle scan when he spotted the pod's parachutes. His scan showed the open hatch and a fair-sized blonde-haired man in a suit sprawled on a ledge below the pod. Karl was studying the man more closely to verify whether he was injured or not when he detected movement at the periphery of has scan. The camera had just begun to focus on the movement in the trees to the side of the cliff, when Karl almost dropped the controller.

One of the men looking at the screen over Karl's shoulder cursed, "It's that fuckin' mountain man again!"

Both men watched as Ace's 12 gauge came to bear directly at them, and both men flinched at the muzzle flash just before the screen went blank. Karl threw the controller down in disgust swearing all the way to the tent where he picked up the satellite phone.

Omega answered immediately and listened while Karl relayed events from his perspective.

"At least as far as the rest of the world is concerned," Omega said in an ominously soft voice, "the president's plane was brought down by Islamic extremists who were summarily dispatched by every redneck yahoo in the county. Our sheriff is keeping suspicion diverted for the time being. I trust you will locate and deliver Bahktar's body so it can be delivered to the crash site to be *discovered* later along with his family and bodyguard? Fortunately, the wreck is badly scattered and difficult to reach. Plus, weather reports predict a massive snowstorm in two days."

"Then there is the problem with the surviving escort pilot. You say you definitely saw the pilot eject?"

Chapter Eight
Concealment

KARL KNEW BETTER than to whine about his task but he complained, "We don't have enough men to search the whole fuckin' mountain, and now it looks like that mountain man is gonna help . . ."

Omega cut Karl off. "Ah yes the *mountain man,* the throwback that seems to be able to thwart your best efforts. Actually, I must admit that I am grudgingly impressed. Maybe I should have hired him."

"He's just lucky," Karl said defensively. "When I catch him I'll . . ."

"When you catch him," Omega interrupted again, "you shall have some help which should be arriving by private jet at the Grant City airport as we speak. Our good sheriff shall see that you will have two locators brought to your camp by late this evening. My sources inform me that the pod's locator beacon ceased to function shortly after it came to earth, which is very fortunate for us since it will not give away our quarry's present location to *other* interested parties. The escorts have been given a backseat to rescue or recovery efforts in favor of Air Force One, and since there has been no radio contact with either escort it is assumed they are both deceased."

"But how . . . ?" Karl began to ask.

"The president's personal briefcase has a short-range locator beacon. We have obtained its signal frequency and our *friends* have made a detector available to us. We also have one for standard military beacons that should allow you to locate the pilot *after* you have secured our quarry. I strongly suggest you make haste as soon as you have your locators. Goodbye and good hunting."

When Omega finished talking to Karl, he used another phone to make a call to Grant City, Wyoming. Sheriff Glenn Harper practically jumped out of his skin when the special phone in his pocket vibrated. He excused himself from a press conference, ducked quickly into a private office, and took the call.

"A man will be stepping off a private jet at your airport, sheriff. See that your *trusted* deputy is as discreet as possible in helping the man with his suitcases. Once they leave the airport, my man will give your deputy one case before he is dropped off at your Holiday Inn."

"My deputy has been on the go for sixteen hours. He just got back to town from Clayton." Harper sounded slightly irritated.

"If your deputy knows what is good for him, he will continue for another sixteen hours if necessary," Omega warned. "My man will stay there in Grant City to make sure there are no loose ends. We also have two backup teams headed that way. They will check in with you when they arrive by automobile. Please see that the suitcase is delivered to Karl at the Big Swampy Campground as soon as possible."

"We'll use our unmarked Bronco as usual," the sheriff said, hoping this would impress Omega with the fact that they were trying to keep as low a profile as possible.

"You do that Sheriff Harper, and if you successfully complete your end of our bargain, you will be appropriately rewarded." Omega's voice over the phone almost sounded like a cat's purr. "Good-bye and good luck."

Sheriff Glenn Harper shook off an involuntary chill and dialed the frazzled Deputy Del Fulton with his new instructions. He was not looking forward to listening to him whine about being overworked.

X X X X X

While Karl was waiting for his package, Billy Black Stone was closing in on the area where the fighter pilot's chute had touched down, and Ace was having difficulty trying to convince agent Richard Mason to put his pistol away.

"Young man, you just had someone shoot you out of the sky and it sure wasn't me. Now if you put your pistol back in your holster, me and Dozer will try to get you out of your fix," Ace said to the highly confused bodyguard.

"Who is that, agent Mason? What's going on out there? Was that a shot?" Omar Bahktar was peeking around the edge of the hatch opening.

"I don't know, sir," Mason replied. "He says he wants to help."

Ace held on to a tree trunk and leaned out so he could see the face in the hatch, which he recognized immediately. "Mr. President," the voice boomed, "nice of you to drop in on us. You plan to hang around for a while?" Ace showed a wide grin full of teeth.

"Can you get us down?" Omar Bahktar shouted.

"Oh, I guess I probably can if your man there will stop pointing his gun at me." Ace grinned again.

Agent Richard Mason reluctantly holstered his pistol.

"Here's what we'll do young fella, Mason is it?" Ace asked.

"Richard," the agent answered.

"Okay Richard, you can call me Ace. You stay right there and we'll see if we can get you secured so you don't fall off the edge. You're gonna have to catch these folks when I lower 'em outta that thing-a-ma-bob up there. Can you handle that?"

Mason nodded his head while Ace got busy getting things out of his vest. The first item was the wire saw that Ace used to cut a live sapling. Then he cut it into two one-foot lengths and sharpened one end of each.

Out on the ledge, Ace encouraged Mason to scoot backwards on his butt until he was under the pod. Ace took a loose stone and hammered two of the stakes into the cracks, then he took some nylon parachute cord and rigged an anchor harness to hold Mason in place on the ledge. Ace next fastened one end of a coil of yellow poly rope to another two-foot section of the sapling.

"Okay, listen up folks," Ace hollered at the pod. "I'm gonna throw this rope around that tree up yonder and let this stick down where you can grab it. Now watch me. I'm gonna put the rope between my legs and the stick under my butt cheeks like this. This is gonna be your swing. I can hold you back because friction on that tree will act like a brake. Then I'll lower you down to Richard there and when you're ready you can make your way over here. If you're scared you can keep hold of the rope until you get off the ledge, okay?"

The president leaned out of the hatch a little ways and said, "I don't think we should do this. They'll be sending rescue any moment now. I think we should wait."

Ace saw the exasperated look on Mason's face.

"Somebody's gonna come get you alright sir, but it ain't who you think. Did you see that little spy-copter I shot down? It's the same people who shot down your airplane! We gotta get you out now!"

Ace did not wait for a reply but swung the stick around to get the rope over the tree trunk. It took several tries and he had to shake the line to encourage the "seat" to pull the rope down to the level of the hatch. The rope was too far out for anyone to reach from the pod so Ace had to go back onto the ledge and toss up a thin stick to use as a grapple. It worked. Ace put on his gloves and got ready while Omar tried to figure out how to sit in the swing.

"Not you!" Ace bellowed. "Help your daughter get on. Sit on the swing sweetheart and get hold of the rope up over your head. That's the way. Now stick your feet straight out and your daddy will hang onto your feet and let you swing out slowly. No, don't look down. Look at your daddy. That's it." Ace let the rope slide as slowly and easily as he could. Kasha settled into Richard's arms and he held her for a moment.

"Okay, now crawl to me. Watch where you put your hands and knees but keep looking at me. That's the way, you're doin' great."

Kasha made it safely off the ledge with tears rolling down her cheeks.

Ace held her for a moment, then said, "You see that big old ugly dog? His name is Dozer and he loves little girls. You go up there and sit down and hug him real tight 'cause that's his favorite thing in the whole world, okay?"

Ace stood up. "Next!" he called as he pulled the swing back up opposite the hatch. Omar hooked the swing and pulled it in. "Remember the Titanic?" Ace asked no one in particular, but the meaning was clear.

Mason said loud enough for everyone to hear, "Yeah. Women and children first."

Irena straddled the rope and backed toward the hatch. Mason saw Ace's eyes widen a little and he grinned in spite of his pain. He mouthed the words, "Good luck."

Ace took up the slack and the poly rope stretched as the first lady put all of her weight onto the swing. Her butt was now below the doorsill and her heels were still inside before the rope quit settling. Omar picked up her feet and let her swing free. Ace was really glad there was only ten feet to go before agent Mason took over. Irena took longer than her daughter to traverse to safety. She seemed genuinely happy to crawl up the slope and settle down on the other side of the big dog. But she did give Ace a quiet "Thank you" as he took the rope from her.

Before Ace pulled the swing back up, he inspected the area that had borne most of the weight over the tree trunk. It looked good as new so he hauled it up for Omar to snag his ride to freedom. The extraction went quite smoothly in spite of the fact that the president insisted on bringing his briefcase. Mason crawled off the ledge and up the slope while Ace rolled up ropes and put things back in his vest. He noticed that Kasha was the only one who was intently watching everything he did.

Ace moved quickly, and as he did he spoke, "I don't know how much those people saw with that spy-copter before I shot it down. I'm sure they did not see the president or his family but they did see the precarious position of the escape dingus there. Whatd'ya think, Richard? If I whack a few of those lines and let that contraption tumble down the cliff, will that throw them off for a while?"

"It might work. We sure have to do something and I can't outrun anybody this way," Mason said looking at his ankle.

Ace took stock. "You folks rest a bit. I'll be right back." He climbed the slope to access the top of the cliff to begin cutting the parachute lines. In only a few minutes the pod lurched, tore loose, and dragged two of the chutes with it into the canyon below. Ace returned with the wadded-up third chute and some of the cord. He also carried a crude crutch.

"We'll get you fixed up to travel a little ways my friend," Ace said as he wrapped and wound strips of parachute around Richard's leg, then he bound around and around with cord to make a tight package.

"Time's a wastin'. Lets go," Ace prompted as they all rose to go. They had to travel slowly partially because of the injured agent and partially because the ladies' street shoes were doing very poorly on the mountainside.

"Any of you ever hear of the Sheep Eater Indians?" Ace called back over his shoulder. "Didn't think so," Ace continued. "Prehistoric people. Hunted mainly mountain sheep. Mostly they lived in little wickiups but sometimes they built rock shelters under an outcrop. I found one in pretty good shape up here just a little ways. You ladies'll never make it to my camp before dark, and Mr. Mason is eventually gonna slip with that crutch and we'll have to carry him, right Mr. President?"

"I . . . uh . . . I'm not prepared to harbor an opinion in this situation," Omar said lamely.

"That's okay. We'll make the best of a bad situation here. About fifteen more minutes at the rate we're goin' and you all can check in to the Sheep Eater hotel."

Ace's radio clicked once, then twice more. The little caravan stopped.

"Billy?" Ace said.

"Ace! I found her. She's alive and she's not hurt." Billy's voice carried to everyone in the little group.

"Uh, Billy, I'm thinkin' some folks might be listenin' in, so I'm goin' to assume that it's who you were sent to look for."

"That's right, Uncle. You find yours?" Billy asked.

"Yep," Ace answered. "But we had some difficulty, so some of our guests are gonna visit the Sheep Eaters tonight, okay?"

"Uh, oh, yeah, I got it. See you at camp?" Billy asked.

"Yep. See you at camp. Out," Ace said.

The radio clicked twice in response.

It wasn't long before Ace led his party around the edge of an outcrop, pushed some bushes away, and sidled along the wall until he came to a rough walled-up portion that resembled a southwestern cliff dwelling.

"Home, sweet home," Ace beamed as he motioned to a doorway. Everyone needed to crouch to get in, nor could they stand upright once inside. "You folks sit and I'll gather some sticks." Ace and his dog disappeared leaving the Bahktar family and their bodyguard to study the interior of their shelter.

Ace came back, broke a few small sticks into a little tepee, shoved a wad of dried moss under it, then pulled what looked like a rod attached to a piece of deer antler from his pocket. He unsheathed a folding knife and scraped the backside of the blade along the rod to create white-hot sparks that quickly set the moss on fire. He did this as quickly and easily as most people would flip a light switch.

"Use mostly small pieces of dry wood. There's plenty close by outside so you shouldn't have to get out of sight of the house here. After me and Omar leave, you gals can stock up on wood. I don't want Richard hobblin' around makin' things worse."

"You can't . . . !" the president began.

Ace interrupted, "Yes I can and I will. It's you these people are after. I need you to be by me and I need more help to keep things together.

This is our best option as I see it. First, we have to get better foot gear for the women. They can't go anywhere with those." Ace pointed at the ladies' feet with obvious contempt. "And if the game warden's horse is still at the campground, we can borrow her to get Mr. Mason down out of here.

Now Mr. President, we'll cut you a couple of walking sticks because I don't want you to break a leg too. Those shoes of yours are gonna act like skis on these pine needles and we need to make some time, and we've got to make a little side trip on the way."

Omar started through the door with the briefcase. "Leave that damn thing here!" Ace demanded. The look in his eye and tone of his voice squelched any argument. The president handed the briefcase to agent Mason.

Ace squatted by the door and called Dozer over. "Okay, big buddy," he looked his companion in the eye. "I need you to stay with these people. Go over there and keep that little girl warm. She's cold and scared. We'll be back in the morning so it's up to you to guard these folks tonight, okay?"

Both partners looked unhappy but both had a job to do. Dozer went in and sat next to Kasha while Ace and Omar started off along the slope back the way they had come.

X X X X X

While Ace was leading the president up a well-worn game trail, Billy Black Stone was leading a slightly disheveled lady pilot through the trees back to Ace's camp.

The pilot, Melanie Yasulevicz, expressed concern about why there were no search planes out looking for them.

Billy explained, "I checked with my Grandfather while I still had cell service up there," Billy pointed back over his shoulder to the high ridge west of them. "He said the news broadcasts say they think everyone was killed and all efforts are being spent on getting up to Bomber Peak."

"Bomber Peak?" Melanie asked.

"Yeah," Billy answered. "A B-17 bomber crashed up there during World War Two on a flight from the west coast to Nebraska. They looked in all the wrong places for it because those guys were way off course. It's pretty remote, but I heard that a sheep herder or a cowboy discovered the wreck years afterward. Now Air Force One is up there too."

"Jesus!" was Melanie's only comment.

"You say your ejection seat has a beacon in it. How long does the battery last?" Billy asked.

"They say it will last for weeks but how will they find me if I'm not there?" Melanie replied. Obviously, the pilot needed to be brought up to speed.

"I'll tell you this much Miss Yasu . . . uh, I'm sorry, how do you say your name again?" Billy was clearly embarrassed by both his clumsiness around the ladies and the pilot's dazzling smile and sky-blue eyes which didn't help matters any.

"Yah-soo-lo-vitch," Melanie pronounced phonetically. "But you can call me Yaz. Everybody else does." Her laugh was like sliver bells to Billy.

"Okay, Yaz," Billy continued. "When we get back to camp Ace will fill you in more, but I think you're safer with us because the people who shot you down are still up here. I don't think they plan to let you ever leave alive." Billy told her about his kidnapping and watching the missiles being launched from four separate locations. He expressed his doubts that anyone outside of the conspirators, except he and Ace, knew that the Jihadists got full blame for the attack while the real villains were still at large. Then he dropped his bombshell. "Ace said he rescued the president and is bringing him to camp."

"You're kidding!" Melanie's wide eyes widened even more.

"He couldn't tell me any details on the radio because everybody up here uses them you know. But it sounds like he had to stash some other people in an old Indian rock shelter, so I imagine that might be the president's wife and daughter."

"Yes, they were on the plane," Melanie said.

"I'm glad you're dressed pretty, um, what's the word . . . , ruggedly, I guess," Billy said, embarrassed again. "With all these people showing up at camp we'll run out of boots and clothes. Not to mention food. Unless you don't mind eating a lot of elk meat," Billy ventured.

Yaz laughed, "Don't worry about me, Billy. I was raised on a ranch but I always wanted to fly. That's why I'm riding a jet instead of a horse. And no, I'm not one of those vegetarians. Elk will be just fine."

Billy was liking this young woman more and more. His radio clicked once, then twice more.

"Ace?" Billy said.

Ace's voice crackled on the radio, "We'll be late for supper. We took a little side tour to show our guest what a 12 gauge will do to a *contraption*," Ace informed Billy. "I believe this will leave our *friends* a little speechless, if you get my drift."

"Well, we're not a Motel 6, but we'll leave the light on for you. Out," Billy said. The radio clicked twice in acknowledgment.

At Camp Two Karl had just taken delivery of a suitcase from Deputy Fulton, who was more than anxious to get back down the mountain.

Karl keyed his radio. "Camp three? . . . Sergei? . . . Come in, camp three," Karl shouted into the transmitter as if that would make it work better.

"Shit!" Karl shouted at the sky.

X X X X X

"Ever shoot a gun, Mr. President?" Ace asked.

"No," Omar answered. "My mother hated them. She would never allow one to be in our house."

"Why?" Ace asked.

"I asked her when I was young but she always said the same thing, so I quit asking and just accepted her opinion," Omar said.

"Which was?" Ace was not giving up

"She said they were dangerous and only good for killing people." Omar didn't sound all that convinced that his mother was entirely correct.

They had stopped walking and stood below the rock that held the metal-legged relay tower.

"If it will ease your mind, sir, your mother was right but only half right." Ace saw the interest now in the president's eyes. He continued, "Let me ask you which is more dangerous and to whom, a criminal with a gun or you with a gun?"

"I concede your point, Mr. Ace," Omar said, "but what about killing people? That's all guns are good for!"

"Ah, but you are wrong! A gun can be a tool and we're about to have a little show and tell," Ace warmed to his subject. "Follow me sir!"

The two men climbed the rock and stood beside the relay tower.

Ace unslung the 12 gauge, pumped the action, and a live shell flew out. "Now you do it 'til it's empty," Ace said as he handed the gun to the president. The slide wouldn't move. Ace showed Omar where the release button was, and after emptying the gun, showed him how to load and recharge several more times.

"Now, y'see this contraption here, Mr. President?" Ace indicated the relay. "This is what allows the guys who shot down your plane to communicate across this rugged terrain and fly the sky-spy thing around because it has line-of-sight coverage through most of the country out there." Omar nodded his head. Ace asked, "What should we do about that, do you suppose? Keepin' in mind we don't have any wrenches and screwdrivers and not a lot of time to boot."

"Shoot it?" Omar asked already knowing the answer.

"Bingo!" The word echoed several times before it died away. "And I'm givin' you the privilege of puttin' those nasty bastards out o' the phone business. Have at 'er yer honor!"

"Oh, I don't think I could . . . ." Omar began. "Beggin' your pardon Mr. President, sir. You better learn how to shoot this son–of-a–bitch because your life AND mine might depend on it, so fire away." Ace handed his shotgun to the President of the United States.

Chapter Nine
Castigation

It was less than an hour until sundown, but down in the creek bottoms the gloom was accented by overcast skies. The pine trees looked almost black and a chill air moved down the creek bottom to raise a light mist off the water.

Karl's mood was even blacker than normal. He had suddenly lost contact with the other camps. He and Rolf, the man who wore the Cabela's cap, had to drive the Yukon to camp three to pick up their ATV and game cart. Rolf, who had the privilege of riding the ATV, was shivering when they got back to camp two because he had neglected to wear a coat.

"It's bound to be a hell of a lot cooler in the morning when we take this thing up to the end of the road," Karl told his men. "Get some sleep. We have some serious hunting to do."

X X X X X

Up the creek behind their screen of trees Billy Black Stone and Melanie got the camp ready for Ace's arrival.

It was almost full dark when they heard a soft "Hello the tent," and in a few seconds Omar Bahktar and Ace slipped through the tent flap into the comfortable warmth.

"Where's Dozer?" Billy asked.

"Left him with the girls and the bodyguard. His name is Richard Mason. Nice guy. You'd both like him. He misjudged the condition of his landing zone when he dropped outta the escape pod and broke his ankle. Them street shoes didn't help any. I made him a crutch and wrapped his ankle up good," Ace explained, then addressed Billy, "Do you suppose I can get you to trot on down to the campground first thing at daylight and see if Pat's horse is still there?" Billy allowed he could easily be there in a half hour on foot if he traveled at a trot.

"Sorry folks. My manners are slippin' tryin' to keep track of everything we need to do here. I suppose you're the fighter pilot?" Ace said appraising the slender red-haired young woman in a flight suit.

They made introductions all around and while Ace tended to fixing some supper, Billy showed their guests how to find the *outhouse* and took down the trip line to forego any false alarms.

After a supper of elk steak, dough gods, canned tomatoes and coffee, Ace carried on with plans for the morning.

"Your family will be pretty comfortable in the rock shelter," Ace told the president. "That fire will heat up those stones and even if it goes out, they will generate some heat back inside. If they all huddle under the space blanket I left 'em they'll be good and warm. My water bottle won't go far between three people but there's enough to wash down those granola bars."

"I'll go rummage through the trailer tonight for some foot gear that might work for the women and for Omar here. I'm sure we can figure out some clothes that's better than what they have when we get 'em down here." Ace went on with his plans, "Billy, those guys down below us won't know who you are, but just the same I think you might want to hang that pistol belt over your right shoulder and leave the holster hang down under your left arm, then cover it with a bulky jacket. That way you'll probably just look like a regular guy out for a morning run." Billy nodded his agreement. "Besides, did you ever try running with a sidearm hangin' on your hip? It'll beat your leg to death!"

Billy agreed it would be better than running while packing the M-16.

"Yeah, that would tend to attract attention, but if they see you ride out on the warden's horse, they might get suspicious so you be damned careful!"

Ace addressed the pilot, "Ma'am . . . " he began.

"It's Yaz," Melanie smiled.

"Okay Yaz," Ace continued, feeling just a little uncomfortable using a name he thought was too personal for someone he didn't really know yet. "We're all gonna have to assume we may have to put up some sort of firefight before all this gets resolved. I figure that Uncle Sam showed you how to use that M-16?"

"Well, Mr. Gronsky . . ."

"Ace!" he interrupted Yaz this time.

"Yes sir, Ace!" Yaz snapped a salute while she melted his heart with a huge smile. The good-humored exchange got a chuckle out of the other two occupants of the tent.

Yaz continued, "I told Billy I was ranch raised and not only am I a darned good shot, but I am very familiar with the M-16."

"That makes me feel a lot better," Ace said with some relief. "We are a little short of fire power compared to our *friends,* but I have some ideas on how to even things up. In fact, I already evened it up some." And Ace told them about destroying eight of their handguns, confiscating one AR-15 for evidence, and *eliminating* the assassin Mitch.

Ace and Billy told their accounts of the Jihadist kidnappers and their destruction by the Wyoming militia as related through Billy's calls to his grandfather Alden Spotted Horse.

Billy joked, "This is how we Indians keep our ear to the ground these days. We listen to the White Man's radio." Then he added, "Grandfather says look out for a big snowstorm soon." Billy and Ace couldn't believe Omar took the bait.

"How does he know that?" the president asked.

"Grandfather says all of the White Men are stacking up big piles of firewood." Everyone laughed except Omar who genuinely seemed puzzled.

"They've got four 9-mm semi-auto pistols if the guys over on Little Swampy are equipped from the same place the other two groups got theirs," Ace said figuring out loud. "We've got my .357 Magnum revolver that Billy has which has its advantage in more power but less capacity and rate of fire compared to their Glocks. I've got my little .38 special here," Ace said as he opened his vest to show the grip just barely visible above his belt. "And down in the trailer there is a .22-caliber Ruger Mark II target pistol with a ten-inch barrel. It's got a two-power scope and is an excellent varmint getter."

Omar Bahktar was looking a little uncomfortable during this inventory so Ace elected to turn up the heat just a little.

"I hear that my .22 is the tool of choice for mob hit men because it can be up close and personal or effective at up to a hundred yards. Plus it's easy to silence." Then Ace added with a wicked grin, "Of course, my arrows don't hardly make any noise at all."

Yaz surprised everyone with her contribution to the discussion. "How are we fixed for long guns? I know we have the 12 gauge and the M-16. Do we have anything else?"

"Down in the trailer I have a single-shot aught six," Ace said. "It's a good long-range gun because it has a 26-inch bull barrel and a six-power scope. Plus I have a good variety of ammo for it."

"Pat told me that Karl said he had a .308 but I have no idea what kind," Ace said. "And we're pretty sure they've all got their AR-15s. So under the circumstances our best defense is staying out of sight which is a real pain in the ass since we have to use the game trails in the trees. Uh, 'scuse my French, Yaz."

Billy and Melanie yawned, which prompted Ace to declare bedtime. It was decided Omar should get the bottom bunk while Billy insisted Ace get the cot. Ace said since he knew where everything was he would go down to the trailer for an extra sleeping pad and bedroll for Billy. Billy insisted on going along to help.

As they dug through the trailer for the clothes and extra boots and socks, Billy whistled a soft sound and said, "Doggone, Uncle. She's really cute!"

"I hadn't noticed," Ace faked indifference.

"I'll bet you didn't, you old billy goat!" Billy poked Ace in the butt as he leaned further into the trailer.

"If I come outta here with that extra camp ax, you better have those fancy runnin' shoes on," Ace gruffed.

By ten o'clock, everybody was settled in. The simmering sound of the coffee pot died down as the stove cooled, and the shadows on the canvas told Ace that the skies had cleared and the moon was out. Sunrise was going to be colder than a witch's teat in a rainstorm.

At the sound of the ATV and a flash of lights through the treetops, Ace and Billy quickly extinguished the gas lanterns. As the sound grew closer, slightly filtered by the screen of trees, the occupants of Ace's tent could hear the hollow thumping of what probably was a game cart. There were a few curses that floated back to the camp at Elephant Rock, while the people on the ATV and cart struggled to get them past the boulder pile at the end of the road. From there the road was strictly a trail suitable for only the hardiest of ATVs or horses.

"Hunters goin' up to pick up an elk maybe?" Ace asked Billy.

"Sounded like it," Billy replied as he re-lit the lantern. "But you never know. Especially now."

"Well, it's nearly light enough now for us to keep from bumpin' into trees so we might as well hit it," Ace said. Ace led the way south followed by Omar with Yaz bringing up the rear. Billy took off north through the trees like a ghost. He would find a good spot to come out onto the Big Swampy Road where he could make better time to the campground.

After crossing Big Swampy Creek, Ace and his party paralleled the creek south planning to cut away on an old skid trail that angled up to a spot below the Sheep Eater's rock shelter. They weren't making as good a time as Ace would have liked, but he realized that even though the president was in pretty good shape, the high altitude kept him gasping and wheezing a lot.

About thirty minutes into their hike, Ace's radio clicked once, then twice more.

"Billy?" Ace asked in a low voice.

"Ace, I hate to tell you this, but the Game and Fish came and took Pat's trailer and his horse." Billy's voice sounded out of breath.

"Okay, Billy. We'll make do somehow. Make a travois or something," Ace answered, already thinking of options.

Billy's voice came back full of chilling news. "That isn't all Uncle. Camp two is empty. Nobody's there and the fire pit's just warm. And worst of all, from the tracks, I'd say that was them that went by this morning."

Ace got a sick feeling in the pit of his stomach. "Billy, I hate to run you all over the mountain, but I need you to head back up this way. We're goin' to get up to the rock shelter as fast as we can. Maybe you can catch up to us before we get there. We're on that old skid trail on the west side of the creek. And be careful!"

"Gotcha!" Billy said. Ace clicked the radio twice and turned to his companions trying to put on a cheerful face. "Saddle up troops!"

That's when they heard the shots.

X X X X X

Pain was keeping Agent Richard Mason awake most of the night so he kept the fire going against the rock wall. The women huddled under the silver space blanket while Dozer rose numerous times to stand in the door lifting his nose to test the air and to look about with those liquid-brown sad eyes for his human buddy.

Richard noted how cleverly the shelter was constructed. The fire against one end allowed the smoke to flow up and out through a natural chimney while the heat reflected back inside. He also noticed the moonlight as the skies cleared and felt the chill deepen prompting him to scoot further from the door.

Nonetheless, the bodyguard kept his pistol in his lap as he alternated between dozing and shivering.

As soon as the sun cleared the horizon, the first rays fell through the rough outline of the rock shelter's door and almost immediately began to chase the night's chill from the room.

Agent Mason hobbled outside to relieve himself and when he came back, the women followed suit.

Ace had told them to stay out of sight so Irena and Kasha settled onto the space blanket against the back wall, nibbling on one of the last granola bars. Richard posted himself just inside the door where he could look down the steep slope.

Pine squirrels scolded Dozer every time he got up to make a short foray away from his post near the girl. The occupants were actually lulled into a sense of peaceful drowsiness by the soughing of the wind in the pines and the tiny animal sounds outside their open door.

Almost at the same time that Dozer stiffened and began a grumbling growl, Richard Mason noticed that the forest had stopped making all of its little sounds. The quiet was deafening.

Agent Mason turned briefly to motion with his left hand, "Stay! Stay back!" he whispered. When he turned back to the door, he saw the head and shoulders of a man laboring up the slope looking at something he must have been holding in his hand. Mason waited and clicked off the safety on his pistol and winced at the sound which he was sure could be heard by the man coming up the slope.

The man was breathing hard and watching a device that looked like a TV remote. Even at twenty feet now, Richard could hear the beeping increasing in frequency as it melded into a steady whine.

Mason stood up outside the door as the man looked up from his locator, threw it on the ground, and reached to bring his rifle around on its sling to bear on the agent. The man was working the slide back to chamber a round as Agent Richard Mason crouched in a two-handed combat hold and centered the sights of his pistol on the man's chest.

Things happened faster than it takes to tell about it.

Mason's three quick shots took the man off his feet causing him to slide down the slope on his back until he crumpled up against a log.

Even while his comrade was falling Karl leveled his rifle at the agent and viciously emptied his magazine into Richard Mason's body, even after he fell across the doorway of the rock shelter.

A third man named Jorge charged past Karl who was fumbling to insert another magazine in his rifle. Jorge had one foot in the air to step over the prone agent when Dozer hit him in the chest and rode him down the slope knocking Karl off his feet. Karl lost his magazine but not his rifle. Jorge was screaming for help when he and Dozer stopped up against the man Mason had shot. Karl got there in three giant steps, held his rifle by the barrel and used it like a club on the dog. The fiberglass stock broke against Dozer's head and he collapsed on top of Jorge. Karl pushed the dog's body off of Jorge just as Rolf came puffing up to join them. Karl threw the useless rifle away. "Let's go get 'em. Hurry!" and the trio climbed to the rock shelter.

At the doorway, Rolf scooped up agent Mason's pistol and stuck it in his empty holster while Jorge and Karl roughly tossed Mason's body down the slope.

Karl stuck his head through the door, "Good morning, ladies. Where's your old man?"

"If you mean my daddy, he's with Ace and you'll never get him," Kasha scolded Karl through her tears.

Irena was speechless. All she could do was say, "Shush! Shush!"

"Good idea, twerp. Keep your mouth shut and life will be a lot more pleasant for you," Karl growled.

Karl picked up the president's briefcase. "I can't believe he left this behind. Omega will be *very* interested in the contents.

The three men led Kasha and Irena callously past the bodies causing both women to sob at the sight.

"Shut up, both of you." Karl yelled. "If we didn't need you as bait we'd add you to the pile!"

Irena was stumbling because of her fashionable but worthless street shoes.

"Stop!" Karl ordered. "Get his boots, Jorge." Karl pointed to their dead companion. Jorge unlaced the dead man's boots and removed them and the socks.

"Sit down and put these on," Karl ordered as he tossed the boots at Irena. "We gotta get out of here and I sure as hell ain't packin' *you* down this mountain," Karl warned. Irena got his meaning and hastily donned the boots.

As they started to move, Dozer moaned and began to stir.

"Dozer's alive!" Kasha exclaimed.

"No he ain't," Karl said as he pulled Mason's pistol out of Rolf's holster and shot the dog in the belly.

Kasha screamed at the senseless, ruthless act. Karl handed the pistol back to Rolf, picked up the sobbing Kasha, threw her roughly over his shoulder, scooped up the briefcase, and the group began making their way down the mountainside.

Sounds in the mountains, especially gunfire, sometimes seem to be coming from nowhere and everywhere, making it difficult to pinpoint the source or direction. In this case, however, Ace could tell that it came from the direction of their destination. He translated what he heard for Yaz and Omar. "Three shots from a big bore pistol . . . about twelve to fifteen from an AK or similar weapon. Do you concur, Yaz?"

"Yes, that's what it sounded like to me, too," Yaz agreed.

"Damn it, damn it, damn it! How could they find them so fast?" Ace asked no one in particular.

"Find who?" Omar asked. "Are you talking about my family?"

"Yes, I am sir," Ace said as he started off. "Keep up best you can. I'm gettin' up there fast as I can." Ace called over his shoulder, "Yaz, you keep an eye on Omar. If you guys get into trouble he knows how to operate that 12 gauge now. Just follow this skid trail south, then turn uphill where it comes up against a big rockslide. There's a long outcrop near the top of the ridge and that rock shelter is under that. Can you handle it?"

"You get going Ace, we'll be just fine," Yaz assured him.

Ace reached the north end of the outcrop and crept along it hugging the wall until the stonework of the shelter showed around a bend in the formation. He picked up a small stone and bounced it off the wall near the door. The rock clicked and clattered, then relative silence settled in again. Ace eased up to the door and tossed another rock inside. It made a thud, then a rustle, as the stone rolled onto the crinkly surface of the space blanket.

Empty! Agent Mason's blood had soaked into the loose sandy soil by the door and the foot traffic in and out of the door had almost obliterated it, but as Ace looked around, he saw the splatters on the stones.

A light breeze moved up the slope swaying the treetops. The locator that had escaped notice where it had been tossed into the shade was now alternately exposed to sunlight. The flash caught Ace's attention so he slid down the slope a little ways to retrieve the device.

"That goddamned briefcase!" The realization suddenly dawned on Ace that he was holding a locator that had guided Karl and his cohorts to this place. His eyes followed the skid marks down the slope. He did not see Dozer at first but he did see Richard Mason and another man lying still as death near a large log. As he started to move down the slope, his radio clicked once then twice.

"Billy?" Ace spoke into the microphone.

"Ace!" Billy sounded excited. "That scooter just went by. I heard 'em comin' so I hid. That mean-lookin' guy I figured must be Karl from the description you gave was sittin' on the back facing the trailer."

"I figured as much," Ace responded. "Did they have passengers in the trailer?

"Yeah, a black woman and a girl. Looked like her daughter maybe," Billy said.

"That's the president's wife and daughter. Just two men you say?" Ace asked.

"Yeah, just two guys and the two women. Say! How did they find them so quick? They don't look like they could track an elephant through a cornfield," Billy said.

"Locator. Those sons-a-bitches got their hands on one somehow and I'll bet the president's briefcase has a beacon in it . . . Oh, oh," Ace said thinking out loud. "I'll bet you anything they have a locator for the ejection seat too. Did you bother to hide your tracks to camp after you found Yaz?"

"Ace, I'm really sorry. I didn't think it was really necessary. What do you want me to do?" Billy asked.

Ace was really worried now and he hated to put the young man in any more danger, but they had to keep their camp from being discovered. "I'm sure the third man was dropped off the trail near where Yaz came down and he's probably halfway to the landing site now. Can you intercept the path you took to camp and try to waylay him if he's following it down?"

"No problem, Uncle. And don't worry about me. Okay?" Billy sounded more confident than Ace felt. Just then a moan drifted up the slope on a breeze that also carried the scent of death.

Chapter Ten
Collation

"Billy, I gotta go," Ace said as he started down the slope digging in his heels to keep from sliding. "You be damn careful. Out"

The radio clicked twice as he slipped it into a vest pocket. On the way down the slope Ace made note of the broken AR-15, the discarded magazines, and the scuff marks of many feet. But his main focus was on what he feared to find most near the log that lay crosswise on the mountainside.

Dozer's black form was in the shadow just beyond the bodies of the two dead men. If Ace had been looking harder he might have noticed sooner, but now he leaped over the bodies and skidded down beside the prone form of his faithful friend.

"Dozer, buddy!" Ace croaked as he slid down to lie beside the great dog.

Dozer lifted his head weakly. Blood trickled from his mouth and nose and his breath rattled with each shallow exhalation. Ace slid his arm under the dog's head and stroked the area beyond the torn scalp. The blood from the stomach wound had soaked immediately into the pine needles.

"Good boy, good boy," Ace crooned over and over. "You're a hero, buddy. You did a good job. I'm proud of you. You're a good, good boy."

Thus reassured by the human to whom he gave unconditional love, Dozer heaved one last sigh and went limp. Ace was gazing into the brown eyes as the light went out of them. Great sobs shook the shoulders of the old man as he lay down beside his friend for the last time. He wasn't sure of how long he had stayed that way until he suddenly became aware of voices calling his name.

"Here. Down here," Ace called.

Yaz and Omar came sliding down the slope dislodging stones and small avalanches of pine needles.

Yaz spotted the blood on Ace's arm. "Did you get . . . ?" She was interrupted by Ace shaking his head while he pointed at the inert form of Dozer. He couldn't trust his voice yet to give an answer.

"Oh, Ace, I'm so sorry," Yaz said as she gave him a clumsy hug.

The sight of the two dead men had taken the starch from Omar's knees and he weakly sat down trying not to look at the bodies.

"Where is my family?" Omar asked no one in particular as he gazed dazedly down the slope.

Ace finally found his voice as his mind came back to tackle matters at hand. "Bait!" he said through gritted teeth.

"What?" Omar had the blank look of someone in shock who was not really comprehending what was going on around him.

"Bait!" Ace repeated. "Your family would already be dead if they didn't need them for bait to get their hands on you."

Omar stood up mechanically, dropped the 12 gauge on the ground and said, "Then I'll just go give myself up. We can negotiate. I am very good at it."

Yaz stared in disbelief at what she was hearing and in two giant strides, Ace was blocking Omar's path. He grabbed the man by the shirtfront, and for a moment Yaz thought Ace was going to bitch slap the man.

"You . . . ," Ace sputtered, searching for some epithet to fit the occasion but was at a loss for words. In spite of his dark skin, Omar's face turned ashen when he beheld the raw fury he saw in Ace's eyes.

Ace took a deep breath, let Omar go to stumble back a step or two, then found his voice. "Look around you, sir. There is no negotiating anything with these people. If they get their hands on you, your family is finished. They'll figure out a way to make it look like a terrible accident. Remember, your escape pod is wrecked in the bottom of Big Swampy Canyon. Right now we have some work to do here and it will give me a chance to figure out our next move. I sure hope Billy is going to be all right. Does somebody want to help me get this asshole's coat off?" Ace asked as he dragged the body away from the log.

As an indication that he was thinking clearly now, Omar asked, "Why is this man barefoot?"

"I'm guessing your wife is wearing his boots. She would have slowed 'em down considerable without 'em. That bein' the case, she's probably damn lucky Mason shot this asshole here, or they'd have shot her too and just took your daughter." Ace noticed the shocked look Omar gave him so he said, "I'm just sayin' probably . . . You know . . ." He trailed off, realizing that it was just too much information for Omar's state of mind.

"We've got some chores to do here so we can get on down to business," Ace said, trying to sound a little more cheerful. "Omar why don't you work your way back up the slope to the shelter and pick up everything you can find. I noticed a broken rifle, a couple of magazines, and the locator thing for starters. And then fold up that space blanket and clean up any trash. You know, paper and stuff, and put it in your pockets. Okay?"

Omar nodded eagerly apparently eager to get away from the grisly business by the log.

"And take your shotgun!" Ace called after him.

Ace spread the dead man's coat out and gently rolled Dozer over into it.

"Those rotten sons-a-bitches." He cursed as he saw the chewed up earth where the bullet had exited the dog's body. Yaz bent closer to look as Ace pointed it out. "They shot him while he was down and out."

"Poor dog," was all Yaz could say.

"Yeah, and Mason. They didn't have to pump him so full of lead like that," Ace said bitterly. "Their day is comin'." and the tone of Ace's voice made Yaz shiver slightly.

Yaz helped Ace carry Dozer along the slope to the rockslide area. Ace scrambled around on the acre-sized boulder field until he found what he was looking for. They struggled to get the dog to a space between the rocks that resembled a natural crypt.

It was harder to get Agent Mason's body to the pit. Ace had used the other dead man's shirt to cover Richard's face. It slipped off a couple of times and Ace unconsciously said "sorry."

Yaz and Ace laid the two heroes side by side, then they went to get Omar to help with the last phase of the burial. Ace found a section of tree trunk that was not rotten and the three of them used it to pry a boulder loose near the top on the slide. The boulder began to roll in slow motion but picked up speed and fellow travelers as it tumbled and bounced down the decline. The avalanche filled the burial crypt leaving one elongated boulder standing upright marking the spot.

As the rumble died away, Ace walked out on an overlooking rock and stood for a moment posing with his spear. He slowly lifted the spear, tucked the butt cap into his armpit and pointed the tip at the far horizon. Ace drew a deep breath and issued the strangest bellow of rage, frustration, anger, sorrow, and challenge all mixed together.

Omar visibly recoiled and Yaz felt a shiver run up and down her spine.

X X X X X

The sound echoing off the rock walls on the east side of Big Swampy Creek made the man inspecting the ejection seat look up to wonder what sort of animal made a sound like that. He hoped he would never meet it in the dark. Rolf had been picked by Karl to use the second locator to find the ejection seat because he believed Rolf to be the best tracker in the group.

The trampled area around the seat and evidence that the pilot had been there long enough to relieve herself behind some bushes led Rolf to believe she had been there for several hours before someone came to lead her away. He found an embossed tag that had the name, Melanie Yasulevicz, on it that probably had been attached to a kit bag or something. He stuck that in his pocket, then found the battery lead to the locator beacon and yanked that out.

Rolf made a circle and found the distinctive tread marks from the pilot's boots leading north on a game trail through the woods. "This is too easy," he thought. The pilot's tracks were considerably smaller than the other boot prints, which bore a distinctive but dissimilar pattern.

Billy trotted up the trail stopping now and then to look and listen. His tactics were sound, jogging through one clear stretch to stop near a large tree or boulder for concealment and to watch and listen before completing another segment.

Rolf was halfway across a grassy park when he looked up to see a tall young man watching him from the far side of the park. He was standing beside a large rock shaped like a loaf of bread.

"Busted," Rolf thought, but to stop now would look suspicious.

"You huntin' elk?" Billy asked as the man drew near.

Rolf wished that he had not opted to carry his AR-15 slung across his back. The young man appeared to be unarmed, probably a nature freak or something.

"Uh, yeah," Rolf replied as he passed Billy.

"Where's your bow?" Billy called, after the man passed by a few steps.

Rolf stopped as if he'd run into a wall. "Shit!" he thought.

Billy had opened his coat but stood turned a little sideways. "It's bow season you know and I hear the wardens are out checkin'."

Billy saw Rolf look down and almost do a double take. He realized Rolf recognized his boot tracks in the dust. He saw Rolf's right elbow move back and up as he reached for the pistol he had taken from Richard Mason.

Rolf whirled and fired at the spot where Billy had been standing. Three of the shots were wasted into the dirt since he started shooting before he had fully turned around. Three more screamed off the rock sending stone chips flying. And two more, uselessly wasted into thin air, emptied the magazine.

Billy heard Rolf's feet thud on the trail as the man ran to the end of the rock nearest the trail.

Rolf unslung the AR-15 as he ran, charged the chamber with a live round, and leaped past the end of the boulder to find no one on the other side. Rolf was halfway along the south side of the boulder when he heard the "click-ka-latch" sound of a hammer being cocked directly behind him.

Rather than put his hands up Rolf opted to turn.

The 158-grain, hollow-point, .357-Magnum slug punched a cigar-sized hole just behind Rolf's left ear. It immediately began to expand, bulging out the left eye as it carried away about a fourth of his brain and pushed it out through the right eye socket leaving a coffee cup-size hole on that side of his skull.

The sound of the heavy revolver's report was still echoing back off the canyon walls after Rolf's body crumpled to the ground, quivered a couple of times, then lay still.

Up on the west side of Big Swampy Creek, Ace paused while putting Richard Mason's personal effects into the sack with the boots and things they had planned for Irena and Kasha to use. He held his breath as the flat staccato of rapid pistol fire rattled off the rock walls. About twenty seconds went by followed by a single healthy boom.

The radio clicked once then twice more. "Billy?" Ace almost shouted.

"Hey uncle, you'll never guess what I found." Billy's voice over the little radio caused a wave of relief to wash over the trio below the rock shelter.

Ace keyed the radio, temporarily feeling his old self. "You Indians are always *finding* things. So what did you *find* this time?"

Billy was feeling pretty cocky now. "Oh, let's see. There's a nice AR-15, a 9-mm auto that's out of bullets, a real nice pair of boots, a real nice new jacket with a couple of stains on it, the cap ain't worth a shit, nice knife, holster, belt, no ID, no money. Can I keep the scalp, pretty please?"

The look on Omar's face was priceless so Ace played along. He pulled out a Lapp Puukko that hung under his shirt from a cord around his neck. "I'll bet my scalp will look better than yours!"

"You get one too?" Billy asked.

"No. Agent Mason got one of them before they cut him down with a full magazine. That means there's only two of 'em left at camp two now unless they send for reinforcements," Ace said.

"Damn! I'm sorry to hear about the bodyguard. Okay, now what?" Billy asked.

"Take that locator and that guy's stuff back to camp. It might be a good idea to brush out your trail in case they get another tracker too. I hear we'll get some snow soon. Then it won't matter, but better safe than sorry. Can I get you to go on back down to their camp and spy a little? See if the women are okay and scope things out?"

"You betcha," Billy answered.

"Oh, to be young and indestructible again," Ace thought. "We'll be down in about an hour and a half and we'll all get something to eat when you get back from your scout. And you be damned careful." Ace got two clicks back on the radio.

Ace still had the puukko in his hand as he pulled the trousers off the stiffening corpse. He then grabbed the body by the feet and dragged it over the top of the log where it tried to slide down the slope.

"You folks might want to turn away," Ace said.

"Are you really going to scalp that man?" Omar was probably pretty close to breaking down now.

"Here's a reality for you Mr. President. I didn't tell Billy about Dozer because I didn't want him doin' anything crazy. That's why I kept it light. Understand?" Omar nodded while Yaz looked with new respect at this man she barely knew.

"Here's another for you. I don't want the damned bears tryin' to dig out my dog and your bodyguard, so as distasteful as it may seem, I'm fixin' to rig up some distraction that'll last, hopefully, 'til things freeze up. So once again I'm warnin' you to turn away!"

The puukko was a product of Finnish craftsmanship and the tool of choice for Lapp herdsmen from Siberia to the North Atlantic coast. The elegant knife was a gift from a Finnish exchange student twenty years ago. Every time Ace used it he thought of Mikko, but this time he wondered what Mikko would think of how it was used today.

Ace straddled the body, split the corpse open from crotch to sternum and kicked it down the slope where it spilled and trailed entrails as it went. He wiped the knife first on the log, then in the pine needles, and finally on the dead man's undershirt that he wadded up and pushed under a large flat stone.

Ace picked up his spear. He took the 12 gauge from Omar and carried it in the crook of his elbow as he headed down the mountain toward the road.

Yaz and Omar looked at each other, picked up their burdens, and silently followed. When they reached the bottom, Ace stepped out onto the openness of the trail.

"You two stay well behind me. This is one time I don't feel like sneakin' through the trees."

Ace was mad. He was leaving his buddy behind. Tears were flowing freely now. It would be so easy to just walk on past his camp and tear into those sons-a-bitches, but after a half mile he slowed his pace and let Yaz and Omar catch up. It was a somber trio that marched into the camp at Elephant Rock early that afternoon.

In the tent Ace tried to avoid looking at the old saddle pad that had been Dozer's bed since he was a pup. The large metal can of dog food stood as a mute reminder that made his eyes tear up again.

Yaz noticed this and quietly picked up the container. She carried it outside and set it behind the propane bottle that stood against the tent wall.

When she came back in Ace held out the saddle pad. "Horse trailer?" Yaz asked.

"Yeh," Ace said, and quickly turned away.

Omar, lost in his own thoughts, was not so engrossed that he did not fail to notice. He focused on the man with the white beard stubble getting the coffee ready and rummaging through the dry locker for the ingredients of a meal for four. Omar recalled how Ace had treated his daughter so considerately and the emotion he displayed over the death of his dog, and minutes later disemboweled a human corpse to treat it like a piece of disgusting garbage. Mentally he shrugged his shoulders, "Well, the nameless dead man *was* a piece of garbage." He was just beginning to wonder what these circumstances and this place was doing to him when the radio in Ace's vest clicked for attention.

"Ace!" Billy's voice sounded excited. "There's three more guys at camp two and another Yukon. I think they are the guys from camp three 'cause there's a huge guy with a long square jaw, a little weasel lookin' guy, and another that looks like he might be a Mexican or something."

"That sounds like the crew from camp three alright. How about the women?" Ace asked, and he noticed Omar move closer to listen.

"I saw them come out of the tent and the guy you call Karl walked 'em to the public restroom. Do you want me to stay here and watch?" Billy asked.

Ace thought about it, then told Billy, "No, you better get back here now. At least we sort of know what to expect and I imagine you're getting hungry."

"You got that right," Billy agreed. "It looks to me like these guys are settin' things up to spend the night in their vehicles, but I'll bet they post guards all night too."

"They'd be stupid not to," Ace said. "You better get back here before someone sees you. We'll figure out what to do when you get here."

The radio clicked twice.

Yaz heard the last part of the conversation as she entered the tent.

"I'm glad he's alright and he's coming back," she said, showing considerable relief.

Ace's eyebrow shot up just a little higher than its normal position on his forehead. "Me thinks the girl likes the boy," he thought to himself.

"Yaz, have you wondered why there haven't been any military rescue choppers looking for you?" Ace asked.

"Well, my plane *did* crash and people saw it from the highway. We know that from the news on the radio. You'd think somebody would have figured out I wasn't in it by now unless, like they say, all efforts have been on the Air Force One site," Yaz speculated further, "and the news said Ari was found in his plane, but it was easy to find since it went down on that ranch in the foothills." It was Melanie's turn for tears. "Ari turned right into that missile headed for Omar's plane. They seemed to be coming from everywhere all at once. I just couldn't keep track of them all."

Ace hugged the young woman tight and said, "There's someone else worried about you and it ain't that young, hungry, warrior." Yaz looked puzzled for a moment while she pawed at the tears on her cheeks.

"I can't imagine a youngster like you would not have a cell phone," Ace said. "I think it's past time to tell your folks that you're okay."

"I tried it and there's no signal in this canyon," Yaz said.

"That's why we don't turn 'em on down here. They use up their battery power too fast searching for a tower. After Billy gets here and we get something to eat, I'll have him take you up behind Elephant Rock. There is one place that looks out through a notch toward a tower in the valley and I think you can get out from there," Ace told the young pilot. "But here's what I think you should do. Can your folks get text messages?" Ace asked.

Yaz nodded her head. "They can but they sure don't like to use them."

"Good," Ace said. "I suggest you send a short text that says elk hunters found you and will bring you out in a few days. Tell 'em you don't have much battery left but to tell everybody you're just fine and you'll call . . . , and cut it off like your phone died."

"Shouldn't I just tell them where I am and what's going on?" Yaz asked.

Omar, who had been listening, jumped up. "I think she's right! We could have my people up here all over the place. They'd send in special forces . . ."

Ace held up his hand. "Stop!"

Chapter Eleven
Convergence

As if explaining why it rains to children, Ace began, "Think about everything that's happened so far. If I had a chalkboard I'd write it all out. First, somebody arranged for those Jihadists to escape *and* furnished them with a good-sized missile. From Billy's description I'd say that was a pretty complicated thing that took a lot of arranging with the complicity of the local law. So we know that whoever is behind this at the top can reach pretty far down the ladder. Second," Ace continued, "there's the flight path of Air Force One. Who knew which route you would be taking? Third, there's these *teams* up here equipped with multiple missiles and probably charged with any mopping up which they are trying to do now. Fourth, they got their hands on locators that sure as hell didn't come from Radio Shack." Ace was on a roll. "Then there's why? Correct me if I get this wrong, but according to the polls, doesn't about half the country hate your guts? Who stands to gain by having you gone? The oil companies? The coal companies? The Israelis? The Russians? The vice president?"

With that last suggestion, the president snorted, "He isn't smart enough to . . ."

Ace cut him off. "So that's why you hired him on?"

"Look. This isn't getting us anywhere." Ever the adroit sidestepper, Omar was whining now, and Ace almost felt sorry for the man.

"Okay, let's start over," Ace suggested. "Whoever is behind all of this has way too much influence and power. So let's ask ourselves, what did you do to piss 'em off and what do they gain by killing you?"

"Well, there were a lot of people who expected a lot from me and were highly disappointed when things didn't go their way," Omar said.

"That's an understatement if I ever heard one. What you're sayin' is the road looks a hell of a lot different from the driver's seat than it did from the back of the bus, which is where you claim to have come from," Ace ventured.

"Yeah," Omar admitted, "after I took office, there was a tremendous amount of information I had to absorb, and I had to renege on a lot of promises that just couldn't be kept because of the conflicts it caused. And because of their nature, I could never explain why. But there are still a lot of those promises I plan to keep and things left undone. It will be a struggle, and if I get re-elected, it's doubtful that there will still be time to accomplish all of my stated goals, but I will still try."

Ace listened while the coffee brewed and an elk stew bubbled on the stove. Omar rattled on about glorious plans for the transformation of America and it was too bad that so many people just didn't "get it."

When Omar finally wound down, Ace cleared his throat, took a sip of scalding coffee and said, "So . . . , what happens if these people are successful in creating a martyr? What if your party can't field a viable candidate except the vice president? What if everybody moves up a notch, and even if the opposition wins the next election, how can anyone compete with a dead president who can't be here to defend himself and his policies? Who would be so heartless as to not honor your memory by instituting all the things they will claim you were fighting for? And how easy will it be to manipulate the survivors when they understand the consequences of thinking for themselves?"

The call, "Hello, the tent," halted the discussion as Billy pushed the tent flap back. "Ummm! Smells go . . . Did I interrupt something?" he asked as he beheld Ace's grim look and Omar's dropped jaw still hanging open.

"Nope, just politics. We didn't get around to religion yet," Ace grinned at the irrepressible good nature of his young friend.

"Let's get some food in us and then my young Indian scout will lead Miss Yaz up behind the rock here so she can send her folks a text message," Ace said as he began setting out bowls, spoons, a loaf of bread and coffee cups. "Oops, I need a couple more sticks of wood .You guys go right ahead. I'll be right back."

Billy was dishing up his bowl when he noticed the pattern in the dirt where Dozer's saddle pad bed had been. "Where's D . . . ?" Yaz poked him in the ribs so hard he almost dropped his bowl. She held a finger to her lips as Ace ducked through the flap with an armload of firewood.

"This'll keep the coffee hot and me warm," Ace said with a forced cheerfulness he really didn't feel.

X X X X X

While Ace and his crew at Elephant Rock were having a late lunch, the five men in camp two were grumbling about their meager rations. They had not planned to be here this long. The three men in camp three had been waiting for instructions when Jorge drove up in the Yukon from camp two. They were at a disadvantage now since their radio system had been literally shot down. To a man, they would all have been flabbergasted to know that it was their quarry who had blasted their communications relay to smithereens. Jorge helped them load their food, bedding and other gear into their Yukon, abandoning their tent and trailer to whoever decided to take them.

Karl was sure that by tomorrow they would all be headed down the mountain where Omega said another crew would be waiting for their *cargo*. Although Omar was still at large, Karl was confident he would be showing up either this evening or in the morning.

Given time to think about it, Omega was certain the *bait* at camp two would be too hard to resist. Omega was also sure that as arrogant and sure of his own importance as he felt the president to be, he would probably march in demanding his family's release, and be prepared to make a deal with their captors.

X X X X X

Far to the south, just over the Grant County line, the sheriff of Absaroka County was in his second day of trying to straighten out the mess at the wilderness boundary.

The Wyoming Alpine Association along with a half dozen other groups, including Earth First!, had mobilized hundreds of supporters to block any recovery on Bomber Mountain with anything but backpackers or packhorse outfits. Of course, nearly all of the horse packers were dispersed throughout the mountains at hunting camps, and rescue teams were frustrated at not being allowed to at least use ATV's and helicopters to access the peak.

Monica Farizzi was at the forefront throwing her support behind the environmentalists because, after all, hadn't the president just addressed the "invasion" of pristine lands by anything other than "natural" means?

A national Conservative talk show host was having a heyday with the conundrum posed by the former Speaker's alleged support for the president and his ideals, while supporting a restriction on recovering his remains, citing her desire to "Remain true to our most sacred convictions." Adding with a straight face no less, "I know he would approve," meaning she had already crossed Omar Bahktar off the list of the living.

X X X X X

When the news came on the TV over the bar at the Cave Inn, Frank Wellington sat absolutely still staring at the screen. As soon as that news segment was over and the anchorperson began speculating about the crash of Air Force One, Frank was already out the door.

The stocky old cowpuncher had given up working for other people years ago, but he hadn't given up his horses. He operated a leather shop, and in the fall he contracted packing hunters into the wilderness area that began only a couple of miles from his backdoor. His completely bald head and Teddy Roosevelt grin were very well-known trademarks all over northern Wyoming. At 80 years of age, Frank was still tough as latigo leather and hard as a frozen railroad spike. Apparently, the only thing that slowed him down was the bane of many an old cowboy, stiff joints and bad hips.

It took Frank only ten minutes to get to his house, and in another ninety minutes, he was unloading a saddle horse and two loaded-down packhorses from his trailer at the Engelmann Park Trailhead. Frank was very familiar with his destination. He remembered years ago when a sheepherder had spotted something shining on a high peak. It turned out to be sunlight reflecting from wind-scoured aluminum on the wreck of a B-17 bomber that had disappeared in 1943 on a flight from Washington State to a base in Nebraska. The Army Air Corps, busy with fighting World War Two, looked for as long as they could in all the wrong places.

Two years later in 1945, Frank, at thirteen, was working for an outfitter who hired kids because of the shortage of men. They were among some of the first people to reach the scene on a recovery detail. He would never forget finding one young man who had survived the crash sitting propped against a rock with a Bible in his lap. The young pilot's desiccated corpse stared out over the breathtaking vista from 12,840 feet. Frank never quit thinking about how sad it was that someone couldn't have seen the wreck and gone up to the site sooner. Maybe, just maybe . . . The image haunted him, and now with an urgency that drove the old cowboy to get as much speed from his horses as possible, Frank headed for Bomber Mountain again.

X X X X X

Three cell phones were operating almost simultaneously. Yaz was sending a short text message to her astonished, but joyfully relieved, parents. Billy Black Stone was getting the latest news from his grandfather, Alden Spotted Horse, and Frank Wellington was beaming down the news that pilot Jeff Ferguson and two other crew members had survived the crash of Air Force One.

In her office, Monica Farizzi threw her glass of iced tea against the wall and said, "Shit!"

In his tent, Karl was watching the two Bahktar women huddle in the corner while Omega gave ominous orders to him on the sat-phone.

"I trust that shortly after sunrise you will tell me you have not two, but three birds in hand?" Omega asked.

"I'm surprised he isn't here already." Karl sounded peevish. "If it wasn't for the damned mountain man, we'd be done with this."

"I suggest you underestimate the man and I also suggest you should be on an alert for a surprise visit. What are your men doing right now?" Omega asked.

"If we had some night vision gear we could go out tonight, but I'll post the men around the area. It's too bad we couldn't contact Shamus at camp one. He's probably wondering what happened," Karl said.

Omega sounded more agitated than usual. "I'll see that Shamus is apprised of your situation by way of our good sheriff. He will send his deputy up in a marked vehicle to lend some semblance of legitimacy so that you may leave the mountain unmolested by other law enforcement that is not under our control. Other events have complicated things. It seems that some citizen has taken it upon himself to visit the crash site of Air Force One and found the pilot alive. The escort pilot has just sent a text message to her parents saying she is alive and well and staying with an elk hunter. I believe you assured me that that had been taken care of!"

Karl was becoming very nervous now. Things were falling apart. "Look, we lost Miggs when the bodyguard shot him and that mountain man let the air out of Mitch with his spear. Then I sent Rolf after the pilot. I didn't know it was a woman pilot, but still it should have been easy to track her from the ejection seat, only . . ."

"Only he didn't come back and the pilot is still alive." Omega finished with a distinct sound of disgust in his voice.

"Look, we'll do the job and get off this fuckin' mountain, alright?" Karl was the one becoming agitated now and it came through loud and clear, for he noticed the added fear in the eyes of Irena and Kasha.

Omega's voice assumed the deadly purr that made Karl's blood run cold. It was as if his boss could read his thoughts through the phone connection.

"I must caution you that if you think of just disposing of your *problems,* then it becomes *my* problem. If you are thinking of abandoning your mission, I have other options available to me and I assure you that you will not survive any *adjustments* I may be forced to make. Is that clear?"

Karl signed off, glared at his two prisoners, and stalked out of the tent. It would be a long night.

X X X X X

At the camp at Elephant Rock, Ace was instructing Omar on camp etiquette.

Omar was learning things like: Everyone in camp helps with the chores. There was no *free meal.* Someone had to cut and split wood, someone had to peel potatoes, someone had to carry in the wood and water, someone had to dispose of the stove's ashes, someone had to heat water to wash socks since clean, dry footwear was critically important. Someone had to tighten loose tent ropes and someone had to bring up extra bedding and supplies from the horse trailer.

Omar had broken the ax handle by missing his swing at a chunk of stove wood. "You break it, you fix it," Ace said sternly as he dropped a new handle at Omar's feet.

"I haven't got the slightest idea where to start," Omar pouted.

"I was going to make some snide comment, but I've thought better of it," Ace said. "I can't blame you if you don't know how to swing an ax properly or replace the handle, just as I wouldn't have the slightest idea how to organize a community, so let's go to ax-handle school, shall we?"

Ace talked while he worked. "Lots of people used to carve their own handles but Wyoming has a shortage of hardwood unless you're down around Medicine Bow. There's a lot of good hardwood there and back in the day, the Indians came from miles around for stuff to make their bows. That is unless they could trade one of the Sheep Eaters for one of them super powerful bows they made from sheep horn. Anyway, everybody I know just buys 'em nowadays. Hickory mostly. Now see the way this splintered in long stringy splinters instead of just snappin' off? That's because I keep the handles on all my tools soaked up with linseed oil. You drill a quarter-inch hole in the end of all the handles, fill it with oil and pound a little plug in it. Oil migrates through the wood and keeps 'em from gettin' brittle."

"Now after I saw off the splinters next to the head here, I drive out the pieces and save the wedge. See that?" Ace asked. Omar nodded his head.

"Now I got a little chore for you," Ace said as he tied the new handle parallel on a short stout horizontal tree limb. "You can use my puukko like a draw knife to shave the end of this handle to fit the ax head like this, while I go start some supper." Omar tried a few strokes and after a rough start and some coaching, was doing a pretty good job of getting the new handle ready. Ace returned several times to check the progress and although the fit was crude, it was good enough. Ace showed Omar how to hold the ax head down and hammer the end of the handle with the back of a hatchet to seat the head.

They had just cut the protruding wood off with a small hacksaw and driven in the wedge to finish the fit when Yaz and Billy came through the trees.

Billy spotted the old ax handle. "Is this all you White Men have to do all day is make fire wood from perfectly good ax handles?"

Yaz noted the startled look Omar gave Billy in response to his remark, but he recovered quickly, and with the first good humor he had displayed since they had made his acquaintance, quipped, "Old Indian saying goes, 'If White Man breaks ax, then White Man has to fix ax,'" he said with mock sternness, and held his handiwork up for all to see.

Ace said, "He did a pretty good job too. You know that ax has been in our family for six generations?"

Billy already knew what was coming so he played the straight man. "Looks pretty good for an ax that old."

"Yep," Ace went on. "We have replaced the handle at least thirty times and the head four times!"

Yaz treated them all to that silver-bell laugh while Omar had to think about it for a moment, then began, "Let me guess. Is that a redn . . ." and cut himself off for fear of offending anyone. Ace finished for him. "Yep, that's a redneck joke! Welcome to the club!"

With supper over and the chores all done, Ace pulled out a toolbox from under one of the cots.

"We still have enough light to check these out," he said as he picked up the AR-15 Billy had confiscated from Rolf. He picked out something that looked like a pen with a long thin tail, selected a tip of .22-caliber size and screwed it onto the tail. "Laser sighter," Ace explained as he slipped the tail into the rifle's muzzle and pressed a small switch. A red dot appeared on the tent wall.

Ace took the rifle outside where it was still almost full daylight, settled the rifle into the sawbuck they used for cutting wood, and put the red dot on a tree trunk about fifty feet away. The dot illuminated a round spot where a small branch had been cut off.

Ace squinted through the gun's open sights. "Aha!" he proclaimed. "No wonder those guys shoot up so much ammo." Over his shoulder, Ace said to Billy, "This gun you stole couldn't hit a barn wall even if you were inside,"

"I stole? I stole?" Billy donned his indignant act. "I *found* it the same way your people *found* this country!"

Ace had removed a small screwdriver from his shirt pocket and busily adjusted the sight while he countered, "Your people weren't doing anything with it anyway, and besides *WE* bought it from France fair and square. I think there's a bill of sale somewhere but I forgot where I put it."

"Guilty!" Billy pointed a finger at Ace. "Guilty of receiving stolen property."

Ace picked up the M-16 and winked at Yaz and the wide-eyed Omar. He inserted the laser and addressed Billy. "Okay, mister high and mighty, what did your people do with the folks who built the Medicine Wheel? Weren't they here first?"

Billy gave Yaz and Omar a dramatic stabbed-in-the-heart look.

"Damn! Every time the Indian thinks he's got the upper hand, the White Man does the forked tongue thing again!"

Ace stood up and handed the M-16 to Billy. "All zeroed in for close work. They were both off something terrible. You'll have to admit, us White guys do some things right."

"Do you know Shooby White Clay?" Ace asked Billy.

"Yeah, he's always bitchin' about how the White Men are always screwin' the Indians, and he's made some pretty good points, you know," Billy said.

"I know," Ace replied. "But I about fell over when he finally admitted that he could thank the White Man for one thing."

"What would that be?" Billy asked.

"Indoor plumbing," Ace replied. Yaz, Billy, and Ace laughed uproariously, but Omar didn't quite get it.

The light was fading and the temperature was dropping dramatically. They went into the tent relishing the warmth inside.

"I've been giving this a lot of thought and it's time to get serious now. Billy knows your family is alive and they look to be okay," Ace addressed Omar.

"We have to figure out how four of us, unless you want to stay out of it," Ace looked at Yaz, "can take on five mean sons-a-bitches who know we're comin'."

"No way I'm staying here. You'll have to tie me to a tree," Yaz stated emphatically.

"Okay," Ace continued. "Here's the way I see it. They'll have someone behind the camp probably no more than a hundred yards out. If we try an ambush attack, he could get in behind us. We'll need a distraction. Omar, if you're willing, and remember these people want you alive until they have you *and* your family together, you can be the distraction. Do you want to hear the rest?" Ace asked.

Omar nodded his head. He had begun to respect this man's ability to improvise by assessing and judging, and using whatever was at hand to an advantage.

"If we head out before daylight, we can be at camp two as the sun comes up. We can move up from the southeast so the sun will be in their faces and we'll be in the shadows. Since we use these little radios for hunting, four of them have ear buds. We'll be wearing them."

"Omar will stay out on the road. He'll wear Rolf's big coat and he'll carry my .38 special in his coat pocket. Omar will wait a couple of hundred yards south of the camp two turn off until he gets the word to walk. Here's the hard part for you, sir. When you start walking toward their campground, they'll see you and be watching you. One of them will walk toward you, I can almost guarantee it. Yaz and Billy will have crept in close and will let us know when they can cover the campground. I'll take care of whoever is out back." Ace tapped his compound bow meaningfully and added, "Hopefully, I can do it quietly."

"If there are four men in sight, then that means one man is most likely back in the woods patrolling the back door. That's one-on-one for me, and three against four for you. Omar, no matter what they tell you, keep your hands in your pockets. They are fully aware of your anti-gun stance and will never expect you to be armed. When he's close enough I want you to shoot the man in front of you right in the belly without ever taking your hand out of your coat pocket." Ace watched Omar's eyes as he told him this. "Any hesitation on your part will jeopardize the rest of us and your family. Do you understand that?"

Ace saw the president's Adam's apple bob and his dark face blanch slightly. He thought to himself, "Maybe he will and maybe he won't. We'll have to play it by ear."

Omar's voice sounded dry as if he needed a drink, "I'll do what needs to be done. I . . . , I mean we need to save my family."

"Good! Billy, you need to have the AR-15 as backup, but I think you'll be more effective with this." Ace brought out the long-barreled .22 pistol. "I took the liberty of cutting a hole in Omar's pillow and helping myself to some of the sponge rubber stuffing which now fills the inside of this plastic pop bottle. I've split the neck and I popped it over the end of the barrel like so, . . . and Voila! we have zee silencer. The electrical tape will cut any glare from the plastic and the scope caps will subdue any shine from the glass."

"If you use the .22 they won't know where you are, Billy, but make sure you have good cover. I think you can knock down two of them before they can get a shot off." Ace handed the lethal and exotic looking weapon to Billy.

"Yaz, you get the M-16. Set it on the three shot burst. As soon as you fire, they will definitely know where you are, so pick a good fat tree trunk and stay behind it," Ace warned. "That's our plan, any questions or suggestions anyone?"

It was a sober crew that looked back at Ace. He had seen the same look from troopers about to jump from a perfectly good airplane. He had also seen the same look on the faces of paramedics jumping out of an ambulance at a horrific crash site.

They knew they had a job to do. Two of them had already faced trial by fire. Ace had concerns about the third.

"Let's all drink as much water as we can hold before we turn in for the night," Ace ordered.

Billy caught Omar casting a curious look toward Ace at that statement. "Indian alarm clock," Billy explained. Yaz giggled, "That's a new one on me. Does it work?"

"Yeah," Billy replied. "If it doesn't, you'll wake up in a waterbed."

No one slept very well at Elephant Rock and all were up scurrying outside in response to the *Indian alarm clock* well before sunrise.

Ace made fried egg sandwiches with bagels toasted on the stove top, and while Yaz and Billy cleaned up the *kitchen*, Ace put Omar through a dry-fire drill with the .38 revolver.

After he was confident that Omar could fire the weapon, Ace loaded it and handed it to Omar with instructions to keep it in his coat pocket. Ace emphasized the value of surprise if Karl and his men believed him to be unarmed.

There was just enough light from a waning moon to keep from tripping over the rocks in the road but it still took forty-five minutes to reach their dispersal point.

One more radio check and Ace gave his last-minute instructions. "I need to neutralize any lookout that might be behind the camp and try to get a head count. When you hear from me, I want you two," Ace nodded to Yaz and Billy, "to take up your positions. Crawl on your belly if you have to and take it slow. All you have to do is whisper 'ready.' I'll make a final assessment and give the word to move to Omar who will stay out of sight beside the road until we're ready for his walk-on performance. Clear?"

This was taking a little longer than he anticipated, but Ace was moving as a good hunter should. He walked slowly for a short distance, then squatted to scan under the tree branches. The lodgepole pines had done their duty after a long-ago fire had cleared the forest of trees. They grew thick and fast racing to the sun leaving their trunks bare up to twenty feet. The weaker ones died, fell over, rotted, and provided material for the spruce that flourished in the shade of the *cover crop*."

It was behind one of these spruce trees that Ace froze in place. Cigarette smoke drifted on a barely discernable movement of air.

Ace bent to one knee and the single shot 30-06 rifle shifted awkwardly on his back. He placed his bow down slowly and dropped further to one elbow. Fifty feet away Ace saw two booted feet at the base of a large lodgepole tree trunk.

CHAPTER TWELVE
Complications

KARL STALKED UP and down in front of the fire pit stopping now and then to warm his back. They had built up a big blaze all night that lit up the campground, but now the sun was striking the trees on the west side making the shadow on the east side seem even deeper.

He watched Sergei, Kelly, and the other man they called Paolo saunter around the perimeter looking more bored than alert. He hoped Jorge had posted himself strategically enough to warn of any surprises from the woods.

Karl was confident that Omar Bahktar would be worthless in any kind of physical confrontation. He knew the mountain man to be extremely dangerous IF indeed he was really even helping the president that much. Maybe he had just given him a place to stay. Then there was the pilot. Had she done away with Rolf? Maybe Rolf just plain had an accident. What if the mountain man and the pilot were going to try something rash? That would still be five against two. Maybe he was just being too cautious.

Karl had already decided that if things got any further out of control, he would just shoot all the hostages, hijack a car that would not be recognized, and disappear into the underworld from whence he came.

These thoughts were swirling in Karl's head when Kelly called, "Here he comes."

X X X X X

While Karl was pacing his campground, Ace never took his eyes off the booted feet.

It took a full minute and a half to slowly lower himself onto his back. Although the scoped rifle he had left slung across his back was almost unbearably uncomfortable, his discomfort was eased somewhat by the rifle being pressed into the deep pine duff of the forest floor. Ace removed three arrows from the rack on the compound bow and laid two on the ground with the tips pointed toward the boots.

The feet shifted and Ace froze. The feet rearranged alignment as the sentry moved a little, probably fishing for another cigarette.

A painful thirty seconds went by while Ace placed the arrow in the arrow shelf. He had only made a shot like this once before with the bow parallel to the ground. Lying on his back and drawing the bow to its sixty-five-pound peak draw was no time to start shaking from the strain. Ace held that pose for precious seconds until the feet shifted again. Perfect!

The arrow pierced both calves and imbedded itself into the soft pinewood. With his legs pinioned securely to the tree, Jorge pitched clumsily, face forward in a belly flop that knocked the wind out of him. Jorge's rifle flopped onto the pine duff but his left hand still had hold of the sling.

Jorge rolled onto his right side dragging the rifle with the left hand. Ace already had another arrow laying in the arrow shelf as Jorge now looked right into his eyes. Ace drew back and stopped and waited. Jorge had twisted the arrow out of the tree when he rolled partway over but his legs were still pinned together. The two men locked gaze, then Jorge made his move trying to scrabble the rifle to his shoulder. The second arrow to puncture Jorge went clear through his body cavity, not seeming to affect him much except to make his movements clumsy. The third arrow was left center of Jorge's chest and this one left the fletch sticking out. Jorge gasped, made a last effort to get a finger on his rifle's trigger and failed. He sagged face down to lay still on the forest floor while his life soaked into the spongy carpet of rotting pine needles.

Ace relaxed flat on his back for a few seconds taking huge gulps of air. Only then did he realize how long he had been holding his breath. He rolled up on his knees, using the bow to aid standing up. "Where's a spear when you need it?" he thought. He walked over to Jorge and pulled the fallen rifle away from the dead man's hand. "If it's any consolation," he told the corpse, "you *did* show a lot of spunk."

Ace spoke quietly into the radio, "The sentry back here is out of business for good. Stay put until I can get a look at the campground."

Behind the tent was a dry streambed about knee-deep that angled away from the campground. Ace crouched there and counted four men including Karl.

"Okay you two, time to creep up," Ace whispered into the radio. "When you're in place, give your radio three quick clicks, then I'll give Omar his marching orders."

Ace had taken some small bunches of long grass and poked it under his hatband to break up his head and shoulder profile. He thought he probably looked like the scarecrow from the Wizard of Oz.

Ace was about to shift his position to ease his aching knees when he got three clicks in his earbud. Thirty seconds later there were three more. "You're on, Omar." Ace was about to give the call again when he got the double-click response. Omar's slow response made Ace uneasy but he chalked it up to inexperience at such activity.

When Kelly called out, all eyes in the campground turned toward the entrance road. This allowed Ace to sprint doubled over to the area directly behind the tent. With his rifle in one hand and his puukko in the other, Ace carefully split the canvas tent wall. "Shhh!" he said before the hostages could react with any sound to give away his presence. Ace finished splitting the canvas and beckoned the shaking Irena and wide-eyed Kasha to step through. As soon as she was out of the tent, Kasha threw her arms around Ace and hugged him with a power that surprised him. "Whoa, whoa! Quiet. We're not out of this yet," he whispered. "See this little old streambed? You get down on your hands and knees and crawl that way. If some shooting starts, you lay down flat and don't look up no matter what. Otherwise, you keep going 'til you come to a pipe under the road. You get in there and stay. Okay?" They both nodded, but hesitated. "He's okay," Ace said reading their minds. "Now git." He watched as they started off.

Ace eased back to a spot behind the tent just in time to see Omar approach Kelly.

Kelly was not going out to meet him so Omar kept walking. The men watched silently until Omar had reached the edge of the campground.

Ace double-checked his single-shot rifle. There was a hunting load in the chamber. He snapped the rifle shut and waited. Then Omar did the unthinkable. He pulled his hands out of his pockets and said all too clearly, "I want to see my family!"

"Oh, for . . . !" Karl spun on his heels and walked briskly toward the tent, hanging his rifle over his shoulder by its sling as he moved.

"Oh, oh." Ace breathed as he positioned himself in the streambed directly behind the tent, which put him out of sight of anyone in the campground.

Karl jerked the tent flap aside and, not seeing his prisoners, presumed they had tried to hide under the folding cots along the walls. Then he noticed the vertical slit in the back wall. "Shit, shit, shit!" Karl repeated with each footfall as he strode to the back wall.

Karl pushed through the slit removing his rifle as he did so. He had one foot outside the tent arrested in mid-step as his eyes fell on Ace who was looking at him along the barrel of his Ruger Number One. "Hi, Karl," was the last thing Karl ever heard. The 180-grain hunting load designed to bring down a grizzly bear totally devastated the man. He was dead before he hit the ground. As the dust of the tent floor puffed up from the body's impact, Ace was already snapping his rifle shut on another live round.

At the sound of the shot, Omar began a stumbling run toward the tent, shouting over and over again, "No, no, no, no!"

Sergei was not sure what had happened but was bringing his rifle up to bear on the running president, when three shots from Yaz's M-16 spun him around to fall, rolling over once before he lay still. Simultaneously, there was a faint Whap! Whap! And Paolo dropped as if an unseen hammer had hit him on top of the head.

Kelly, who was closest to the vehicles, reacted instantly. He threw his rifle away and made an adrenaline-fueled leap that carried him right over the hood of the closest Yukon. Out of sight of the still unseen shooters, Kelly was not sticking around to find out what happened. He jerked open the door of the second Yukon and jumped behind the wheel. In a shower of dust, gravel and pine needles, Kelly gunned the Yukon out from behind the other vehicle to carom off a picnic table, and disappear out of the campground with only a half dozen souvenir bullet holes in the tailgate and back window to speed him on his way.

Omar burst through the front of the tent frantically asking Karl's corpse, "Where are they? What did you do with them?" He finally remembered the pistol and fumbled it out of his coat pocket pushing it ahead of him like a flashlight as he looked under the folding cots.

Ace stepped through the slit in the back wall still wearing the camouflage on his hat. Omar spun around wide-eyed bringing the pistol to bear when Ace smacked his forearm smartly with his rifle barrel causing the distraught man to drop the revolver from numbed fingers. "Calm down, man, calm down. They're okay!"

Ace herded Omar out of the tent as Yaz and Billy emerged from the trees. Ace was stuffing his .38 into his concealed-carry holster and Omar was holding his arm.

"Did he get shot?" Billy asked.

"Naw," Ace affected a laconic manner he didn't feel. "He was just a little too agitated and I had to remind him not to shoot his friends."

"Where is my family?" Omar wanted to know.

"Hold your horses, your worship," Ace told the clearly distraught man. "Yaz, do you remember that culvert under the road back that way?" Ace asked as he pointed south toward Elephant Rock.

"Yes, I think so," the pilot answered.

"There's a dry creek bed behind the camp here, and when I busted them out the backdoor I had 'em follow it to the road. I told 'em to hide in the pipe, so if you'll go fetch 'em back, us heroes will get to work here," Ace said.

Yaz took off at a trot and Ace gave rapid instructions to Billy and Omar. "I hate to leave you guys with all this work, but I gotta get over the knob here and take care of some other very urgent business," Ace said as he patted his rifle. The meaning was clear.

While Ace started off east through the trees, Billy and Omar dragged the dead men behind the big log at the edge of the campground. They had removed all of the men's boots and gathered two sleeping bags out of the tent that they placed in the ATV trailer. Billy looked up.

"Ace better hurry. Here comes the snow." A few flakes drifted down. Not only did Billy remember the forecast he got from his Grandfather, but he also had been in these mountains long enough to know that this was just the beginning.

While searching through the camp's equipment, Billy discovered the plastic tube in the Yukon from camp three. He pulled the cap and called Omar over. "Here's one of those rockets they used to shoot down your plane, sir. I think we should take this for evidence. Besides, I don't like the idea of them maybe getting their hands on it. We'll take it along."

Billy and Omar had just about gotten everything Ace had told them to gather, when Yaz showed up with the shivering Irena and Kasha. Billy got them dressed in coats he found that didn't have blood on them and sent Yaz, Omar, Irena, and Kasha on their way to the Elephant Rock Camp while he finished the chores Ace had assigned him to do.

First, Billy lowered the air pressure in the Yukon's tires to the point that they still appeared to be fully inflated. Next, he worked on the .223 ammunition. Using his leather belt as a pad, Billy used pliers to pull the bullets from a half dozen shells, dumped out the powder, replaced the lead into the cartridge case, and fired each of the AR-15s he was instructed to leave behind. The explosion of the primer drove the bullets about halfway up each barrel. Next, he pulled the top two cartridges from the extra magazines, pushed in a powder-less round, then put two live ones back on top. He left two rifles in the Yukon and three in the tent.

Ace had said that if there was time, he would like to have Billy hook the cargo trailer to the Yukon and back the trailer up near the north end of the campground. Billy worked frantically to complete a task that, "May or may not have some value," Ace had said. So Billy loaded close to a thousand pounds of granite rocks into the rear portion of the trailer and covered them with a tarp. He left the trailer attached to the Yukon and beat the latch down with the backside of a single-bit ax so that it would be extremely difficult to disconnect.

Billy wanted dearly to follow Ace across the ridge to camp one, but it was imperative that he help Yaz get the Bahktars settled and then get the contents of the horse trailer transferred to the campsite. When that was completed, he needed to get the ATV and trailer as far up the trail past the camp as possible where he would find a place to conceal it and the little game trailer.

Billy looked around camp two for anything else that he felt he should take. He took one last look inside the tent at the jumble of cooking gear, plastic sacks, and general disorder of the place, and left to finish his chores. Amid the stuff on the table in the tent, the message waiting light softly pulsed on the sat-phone.

Kelly's flight from the ambush at camp two took him out to the Boulder River Road where he turned right to follow the long looping route. The apex of the loop bent around the end of the ridge separating the drainages of Big and Little Swampy Creeks where it squeezed itself between a sheer rock wall and the aptly named Boulder River. From there the road continued in an easterly direction before it evolved into a series of squiggles that descended into the Little Swampy Creek

Canyon. In his haste, Kelly flew past the turnoff to the Little Swampy Campground and camp one. He lost more time looking for a place in the narrow road to turn around.

X X X X X

By the time Kelly skidded into camp one, Ace was making his way through a pass in the spine of rock that formed a virtual wall between camp one and camp two.

Age was making itself felt as Ace shed first his coat and then a hooded sweater, and still he was puffing and sweating from the climb. The temptation to stash his extra clothes and the survival vest was great, but long experience taught Ace that it was better to have it and not need it than to need it and not have it.

As scattered flakes drifted down, Ace stopped to blow and take a sip from his water bottle. "Downhill from here should go a lot faster," he said to himself.

In slightly less than thirty minutes of fast walking Ace had reached the last shelf that overlooked the Little Swampy Campground. He allowed himself a solid ten minutes to cool down and to observe the scene below. Ace was not particularly surprised to see the Grant County Sheriff's SUV and Deputy Del Fulton's pear-shaped form standing close to a large blaze in the fire pit. Ace recognized Kelly and assumed that a person wearing a brown beret might be the Shamus fellow that he'd heard Karl mention the night he had listened outside Karl's tent. Shamus seemed to be the one in charge. As he cooled down, Ace donned first the sweater, then the coat, then the survival vest.

Ace had cut the sleeve from Karl's bloody coat, and now he pulled it out of a coat pocket. He scooped loose dirt into the sleeve, folded one end over and shook the dirt down, scooped in more, then folded the other end over and placed the improvised "sandbag" on the natural rock parapet behind which he had taken a position. This made an excellent solid rest and good cover from any return fire.

Ace noted with satisfaction that the camp had remained pretty much like he had first seen it on one of his excursions. He also noted that only one man carried his rifle while the rest wore pistols. That meant the long guns were probably either in the tent or in the Yukon, a companion to the one Kelly had just parked nearby.

At three hundred yards, he could easily shoot one or possibly two men before they all took cover, but his sense of decency and natural aversion to killing anyone or anything that was not an immediate threat cancelled out that option. He also had to make the absolute most from every shot, so Ace chose the large propane bottle standing beside the tent as a primary target. There were nine 180-grain hunting loads in the cheek pouch on the rifle stock. In his pocket were six Full-metal-jacket military *ball-ammunition* rounds. Ace had left his M-1 Garand at home, but his ammo box always held a variety of ammunition types. It was not by sheer luck that the Ruger single-shot rifle was the same caliber as the M-1. Ace laid all six full-metal-jacket rounds on his glove beside the *sandbag*.

X X X X X

Kelly had related his version of what happened at camp two and why he had shown up at camp one weaponless and in a panic.

Shamus could not believe that they had been attacked by an overwhelming force of some sort of *mountain-man militia*. He had read the note that the deputy had brought that instructed him not to even consider capture as an option. He was instructed to get rid of everyone who could dispute the "new plan" in which the president and his family had escaped the shoot down of Air Force One, but had been found and killed by right-wing extremists running loose in the mountains. Omega said he would see to it that the media would push that story until it was accepted as the truth.

In the meantime, Shamus was assured that Omega's influence had been used to manipulate reports so that search efforts would be concentrated south of the actual resting place of the escape pod. When the mistake was eventually acknowledged, the excuse offered would be that combined "faulty information" and failure of the tracking beacon had led to the confusion.

Shamus was now discussing the need to post watchers to make sure their quarry did not escape down the mountain. He doubted they would try to use Karl's Yukon. He was about to tell the deputy sheriff to post himself down on the Boulder River Road in case they tried to make a run for it when the propane bottle exploded with such force that everyone in the campground was knocked off their feet. The tent and everything in it was obliterated in a sheet of flame.

As happens during such an event, the six men in the campground were temporarily deafened, so they were unaware of the "Thunk," as a steel-jacketed bullet punched through the Yukon's hull amidships where it angled through one layer of the steel frame and tore a hole in the gas tank located between the frame and the driveline.

In his scope, Ace could see the gasoline dripping on the ground. He lined up on the second Yukon and fired but the angle was too high, so he adjusted his third shot, which left a second hole three inches below the first. He waited only a few seconds to be rewarded by the sight of gasoline dripping under the second vehicle. By now some of the men could hear well enough to determine the general direction from which came the assault, and they began firing their pistols up the hill from behind overturned picnic tables and tree trunks. That is when both Yukon's exploded knocking everyone down again. The windows of the sheriff's SUV were blown out on one side and the paint blistered badly, but it survived.

Because none of the pistol fire ever manifested itself anywhere close to his position, Ace was assured that they had no idea where he was.

"Two left," Ace said to himself as he picked up the last two rounds that he had laid out. "And they quit shooting already. Come on boys, waste some more," he said as he inserted a round into the Ruger. Ace had seen the underside of a Yukon before. He remembered where the gas tank was located but was unsure of where to hit the sheriff's SUV, so he picked the middle of the "O" in the word County and fired. The response was another fusillade of ineffective 9mm pistol fire. As it started to taper off he put the last round in the "G" of the word Grant. More pistol fire, which stopped abruptly in response to an angry command from Shamus that contained the words idiots, assholes, dumb shits and stupid fuckers.

Ace grinned and slid back away from his parapet, and with the rock outcrop and trees to protect his back, he retraced his steps back to camp two, leaving an easy trail to follow in the new snow.

X X X X X

As Ace was working his way back to camp two, the men in camp one surveyed the damage. Their food, shelter, and transportation were gone. The deputy was edging toward his SUV when Shamus stepped over to block his exit. "Going somewhere?" he asked menacingly.

"I was, uh, just . . . , going to see if, you know, my outfit would run."

"Tell you what, deputy. I'll furnish a chauffer for you. Kelly, you go with the Law here out to the main road, or wherever it takes, to call his boss. You tell him to relay the recent news here to someone who is definitely *not* going to be happy. Then when you get any new orders, get on back to camp two, and if we're not there, sit tight and wait."

"What should I be tellin' our good boss ye'll be doin'?" asked Kelly.

"Tell him we'll be trailing the son-of-a-bitch that shot up our camp. Maybe he'll lead us to his lair. If we don't hurry and this snow gets heavier, we won't be able to track him at all. Let's go boys."

Shamu's crew spread out up the mountainside west of camp one, and before too long one of them stumbled across Ace's quickly disappearing tracks.

Kelly and deputy Del found a spot for cell service, passed their information, and waited for a reply, parking the SUV so that the good windows faced the increasing wind and snow.

By the time Ace made it to camp two, Shamus and his crew were through the pass at the top of the ridge. They were having trouble in the open spaces because the wind was erasing Ace's boot prints, but still they kept doggedly on.

Ace looked quickly through the stuff at camp two and found what he needed, two new sections of three-inch stovepipe and a five-foot walking stick someone had cut from a sapling. He tucked those under his arm and made clear distinct tracks in the snow out to the Big Swampy Road. Some hunters who had been spooked by the snow were already moving out and had left ATV tracks in the road. Ace turned right and walked beside the tracks for a way, stepping in and out but leaving a very clear trail of boot prints until he reached the main campground. There was a crisscross of tire and boot prints all over the place. Ace bent and spread the stovepipe sections and let them snap closed onto his ankles. He reached down and bent the front edges up. "Clumsy, but serviceable," Ace thought. Placing one foot in front of the other, Ace used the walking stick to push himself along on one of the sets of tire tracks on the Big Swampy Road.

Looking back down his back trail, Ace decided that by the time a little more snow blew into these tracks it would take a crackerjack tracker to follow his trail.

Had Shamus or any of his men gone straight out to the road and looked left, they might have seen Ace melting into the gloom of falling snow. But Ace's tracks had led them right past Jorge, which caused them some pause.

"Arrows!" Shamus cursed for not having even considered that they would be up against a skilled hunter. He had badly underestimated Karl's nemesis.

At the camp, they spent a few more precious minutes locating Karl and the two other men, then while Shamus and one other man followed Ace's tracks to the main campground, the other two were trying to duct tape the tent back together and get the stove going.

Shamus and his companion, a man they called Sharky, were just about to start back to camp two when they heard the sound of an approaching vehicle. It was Del and Kelly so they got in with them to ride on in to camp two. Had they walked back to camp two, it's possible they may have noted the anomaly of one vehicle track being slightly different than its companion.

Kelly said there was a checkpoint at the bottom of the mountain and the people manning it had not seen any of the people they were interested in. The checkpoint's cover was that they were from the government monitoring traffic due to the existing circumstances and no one seemed interested in checking their credentials. That was the official word through the sheriff from Omega.

X X X X X

While Shamus was getting camp two straightened out, making sleeping arrangements for six men, and figuring out how to feed them with the food they had on hand, Billy was busy directing the erection of the cowboy tepee as a sleeping quarters for the men at Elephant Rock Camp.

They had cleaned the snow off a section of the pine-duff forest floor and pegged down four corners of the tepee. They tied the top center rope to two crossed sticks and scissored them up to pull the simple steep-sided tent up in one motion. "That is really slick," Omar said, impressed with the simplicity. "Why don't you just tie it to a tree branch?" he wanted to know.

"Trees move with the wind," Billy explained. "You want to keep those walls as still as possible and you don't want the stakes pulling out in the middle of . . ."

"Well done, well done!" boomed Ace's voice from the snowy gloom. "But we're not finished yet, Billy me lad. Where's the big plastic tarp?"

Under the circumstances of wind and blowing snow, it took Ace,

Billy, Yaz and Omar to pull the huge plastic tarp over the top of the wall tent and secure it. The hardest part was keeping the plastic tarp away from the stovepipe until the opening to accommodate the pipe corresponded with the place where the chimney stuck through the tent roof.

Stretched taught, the tarp extended three feet past the tent walls on each side and ten feet past the front to form a portico of sorts. "A fine home, sweet home," Ace declared.

Chapter Thirteen
Confinement

The setup crew at Elephant Rock retired to the warmth of the tent where they shed wet outer clothing to be hung from a pole, which was hung six inches below and parallel to the tent's ridge pole. "Highest and driest place might not be the best for headroom here, but it sure does the job nicely," Ace explained.

As they all sat on bunks, cots, and folding chairs, Ace decided to steer the conversation away from more serious matters by explaining some of the rules of camp etiquette.

"First of all, whoever is closest to the stove not only gets to pour the coffee for everyone else but also gets to make a new pot when it gets empty." He grinned.

Kasha looked ar ound while the other five inhabitants held out their cups, waiting. She blushed, but dutifully began to reach for the big pot from her chair next to the stove. Ace gently trapped her slender arm in his big paw of a hand. "Here," he said as he offered her an old padded leather glove that lay on the small chopping block next to the stove.

"Nothing here has an insulated handle, so always use the glove," Ace smiled.

"Mister . . . , uh." Irena stopped when she saw the eyebrow over Ace's right eye shoot up and then relaxed when she corrected herself. "Ace, I'm sorry, I just wanted to say that . . . ," The eyebrow shot up again as Ace detoured the direction of the road he felt she was beginning to take by finishing for her. "You are wondering why we covered the tent?" Before anyone could answer, Ace continued, "Snow; if enough piles up on the tent, it will collapse. That's not a maybe. Up here it's a certainty. If you try to brush it off, the canvas will leak We'll keep the stove going while we're here, but in a hunting situation, a tent like this will be unoccupied for long periods. When the snow piles up good and deep, the canvas hardly ever gets a chance to dry out. That's especially true for the end farthest away from the stove."

"The *rainfly*, which is what they used to call this arrangement in the old days, keeps the strain off the tent itself, and now with these new plastic tarps, the snow just slides right off. When we use the larger tarp, it adds extra eaves on each side. It keeps the snow from piling up against the walls, which is great when it comes time to strike the tent. At least the sidewalls don't get froze to the ground."

"The covered area along the sides allows us to store firewood and equipment out of the weather, and the extra piece out in front gives us a place to stomp off the snow so we don't track so much inside. Anymore questions?" Ace asked, feeling that he had adroitly sidetracked the thanks he suspected Irena was about to express. Ace was unsure why he thought he would be uncomfortable with that, but he felt this was not the time or the place.

Omar held up his hand as if he were in school. "That little tent, a tepee you called it? It seems awfully small for three people, and won't it be very cold?"

"We'll go through the drill on how to get in and out without getting the inside all full of snow," Ace explained. "The tepee has several advantages that aren't obvious until you have had some experience with tent camping. First and foremost, you can actually stand up while you get dressed in one of these, and that's something you'll really appreciate if you ever had to try to get dressed on your hands and knees in one of those little plastic bubbles."

"We can heat that small space with a double-mantel Coleman lantern, and if it gets really cold, we'll use two lanterns. And don't worry; ten by ten is more than enough room for three people. But if you're cold blooded, Mr. President, we'll put you in the middle. But," Ace said and looked around at the group and winked with an exaggerated squint, "you have to promise to keep your hands to yourself!"

Everyone laughed at the thought of Omar jammed into a tepee between a rough old mountain man and a young Crow Indian.

"You guys take it easy while Billy and I put on our oilskins and whack up some firewood," Ace said.

"Yaz stood up. "I want to help."

"I won't turn you down, missy. Can you run a chain saw?" Ace asked.

"Hey, you old grizzly!" Yaz replied gaily. "Remember, I said I was raised on a ranch? But shouldn't we be concerned about the noise?"

"That's why we need to cut now. The wind is from the north and sounds don't travel when the snow is comin' down like it is now. Also, it's damn good and cold so we can just knock the snow off the dry stuff we drag in and pile the chunks against the tent. It's early in the season, and if we wait until it stops snowin', it'll melt and get our firewood wet."

"Well then," Yaz said as she pulled on a pair of gloves, "you know what they say?"

"What's that?" Ace asked.

"Let's git'er done!" Yaz imitated Larry the Cable Guy as she pushed through the tent flap.

Billy was the last one out and he turned with a dramatic shrug of his shoulders as he grinned at the Bahktar family. "Some bunch of lumber jacks we got, huh?"

After the firewood crew left, Kasha assumed an air of extreme importance. "And I'm in charge of the stove and the coffee. Want some?"

Irena and Omar looked at each other and smiled for the first time in days. Their daughter was actually enjoying herself.

X X X X X

While the Elephant Rock Camp was preparing to get snowed in, the men at camp two were grumbling about the lack of firewood and the breeze coming through both ends of the tent. Now the floor was getting muddy from all the snow they were tracking in.

Since the place they picked seemed ideal at first - dry, bare, earth - they began to realize a ground cloth or a spot on the pine duff may have been a better choice.

Experienced campers faced the tent flap east. Karl had pitched the tent facing west and now the wind from the northwest blew right into the entrance.

Shamus cursed the snow, the men around him, Karl for having been such a screw up, and the whole situation in general.

Deputy Del Fulton was probably the unhappiest of all. He tried, with limited success, to duct tape some cardboard into the spaces on his sheriff's department SUV where the windows had been He knew he couldn't spend the night in the vehicle running the heater because Shamus had confiscated the keys. By the looks of the groceries he saw in the tent, he would be missing a lot of meals. On top of everything else, these guys scared the crap out of him so he tried to be as inconspicuous as possible. The only time there was a positive note was when Shamus discovered the satellite phone amongst the clutter on the table in the tent.

"You may not think so right now, but this snow storm has given us time to consolidate our resources now that all search and rescue efforts have been suspended," Omega told Shamus. "That was a serious mistake on the part of your mountain man to leave your camp intact and to overlook the satellite phone. It appears all we have to do is wait, since no one is going anywhere under these conditions."

"Yeah, we're making the best of the situation. I'm just thankful we found a case of MREs in all this junk that Karl left," Shamus said with a definite tone of dissatisfaction.

"I'm sure you'll be fine," Omega reassured. "Make sure you keep the deputy there. Park his vehicle near the main road and be sure he monitors any vehicles that might be coming in after the storm is over. He can use the excuse that he is working under the direction of the FBI or Homeland Security to keep curiosity seekers from interfering with the recovery teams."

Shamus had seen how resourceful his unknown adversary had been and expressed his concerns about them slipping out of the mountains by traveling overland.

Omega reassured Shamus that the president and his family could not make such a trip, especially now during a snowstorm. "I've looked at the terrain on Google Earth and I am certain they will find transportation and make a run for freedom. If they do get past you, it will be your job to pursue them into the waiting arms of people we have waiting at the bottom of the mountain," Omega said more confidently than he felt.

"You know there's more than one way off this mountain, don't you?" Shamus reminded his boss.

"We are very well aware of that. That's why we sent extra people into the area and have reminded our contacts in law enforcement that they are expected to cooperate in every way. As far as they know we are pursuing right-wing extremists who are trying to finish the job the Jihadists failed to do."

Shamus signed off by saying, "Okay, you're the boss." He looked around their camp at the sorry mess they were in, then out toward the road which was now totally lost to sight in the blowing snow. Shamus shook his head as he tried to tie the tent flap shut against the wind. "How the hell are we supposed to watch for anything in this shit when we can't even see fifty feet?"

Kelly seemed to be in better humor than anyone. "Well, if we're supposed to chase 'em if we see 'em, and we can't see 'em, then I guess we won't have to chase 'em, I'm thinkin'"

Shamus looked at the small Irishman with more than a little suspicion. "You got some whiskey hid out I don't know about?

"Well, I used to, but gone it 'tis I'm afraid!" Kelly said gaily.

"Shit!" was the only word anyone heard out of Shamus for the rest of the day.

Deputy Del had heard the weather report on his vehicle's AM radio. "A three-day snowstorm?" he thought to himself. "This was really going to be a long three days."

Since this was an established campground, the loose firewood had been scavenged from the immediate surrounding area. The men at camp two were very unhappy indeed at the prospect of locating suitable fuel for their stove. They had moved the gas bottle inside for cooking but were extremely nervous about it, remembering the explosion at camp one.

X X X X X

Darkness came early due to the falling snow. The chores at Elephant Rock were pretty much done for the evening and everyone seemed to be lost in their own thoughts.

While Ace set a three-gallon metal pail on the stove to heat, he quizzed Billy about his last conversation with Alden Spotted Horse.

"Grandfather says the newspapers are full of conflicting reports about the fate of our honored guests," he said, with a nod at the Bahktar family sitting on the bottom bunk at the west end of the tent. "Some are saying that they didn't survive the crash, some say they did. The government won't say anything except that they haven't been able to pick up signals from any transmitters indicating their location."

Omar looked at his briefcase that they had recovered at camp two. "At least they didn't get to keep it and it doesn't look like they were able to open it."

Ace nodded agreement. "And I'm glad my eagle-eyed scout here found that locator, or they'd be tracking us down even in a blinding snowstorm. It's darn funny that the signal isn't any stronger."

"It used to be, but we had to trim it back," Omar explained. "It's just like the restrictions on cell phones and stuff like that on airplanes. They tell me it's very short range. It also messed up other detection devices whenever I took it to . . ."

"Cell phones!" Ace interrupted. Everyone looked startled. "Billy! Did you think about that satellite phone Karl had?"

Billy smacked his forehead with the palm of his hand. "I'm sorry. I forgot all about that. It means they can call anytime and we're still stuck with finding a high spot to call out."

"That's okay, my friend, nobody's going anywhere until . . ." Ace was interrupted by a swoosh and a dull *flump* that shook the tent startling Omar, Irena, and Kasha. Snow had slid off the plastic tarp in a small avalanche. Ace chuckled and jerked his thumb toward the sound and continued, "Until it quits doing that."

"Did your grandfather get hold of Jason?" Ace directed the question at Billy who was trying to disguise the fact that he was stealing glances at Yaz.

"Wha? . . . Oh, yeah," Billy stammered, embarrassed. "Jason said he'd bring Brutus up as soon as the storm was over. Grandfather filled him in on what was happening up here so he knows to be careful. He said Jason said to talk over what we wanted to do and let him know any details."

"I've got some ideas we'll bounce around, but right now I think we need to think about the ladies," Ace said as he walked over to the stove and checked the water temperature. "Here's how it's done, ladies. We set this forty-gallon trash can that normally contains the tent right here next to the center support. Next, we thread this small rope through the pulley up there and attach one end to the shower bag. Now if someone will be so kind as to fill the bag about half full of hot water and the rest of the way with cold until it's about right for a shower, we'll get started. Guys?"

Omar held the bag while Billy dipped hot water with a pitcher. Once the bag was filled, Ace hoisted it aloft to dangle from the ridgepole. The shower bag was one of those that could heat itself if left in the sun. It had a short piece of tubing attached to the bottom with a small push-off pull-on nozzle at the end.

"Now it seems to me that I sense some trepidation on the part of the shower-ees," Ace joked. "Us men will leave while you ladies help each other to stand in the trash can to take your shower bath. I suggest that you use the water sparingly or us guys will be forced to come back in to fill the bag."

Ace lit the spare double-mantle lantern and the men left the tent to stand outside under the overhanging rain fly. It wasn't long before they were rewarded with giggles and shrieks coming from the tent as the women took their turns in the shower.

Billy finally broke the quietness outside the tent. "Do you suppose someone should tell them to put the lantern on *this* side?" Omar and Ace turned to look at the enlarged and distorted silhouettes dancing on the tent's end wall when Omar cracked them both up by remarking, "So this is what the pioneers did before they invented television."

The men were surprised when Yaz stuck her head through the space between the door flap ties. "So what are the guys going to do, jump in the creek?"

Ace punched Billy on the shoulder. "No. Tomorrow our representative from the Crow Tribe is going to set up an official sweat lodge. Right, Billy?"

"Yeah, just like the old days. Us warriors will be doing the sweat lodge ceremony while you women are down at the creek beating our laundry clean on the rocks," Billy grinned. Yaz stuck her tongue out and pulled her head back inside the tent.

Ace picked up the scoop shovel leaning against the wall tent and walked to the tepee. He cleared off a spot in front of the door, then smacked one of the support poles to send a shudder through the canvas that dislodged some of the clinging snow. He beckoned Billy who brought him the lantern, tapped the snow off one boot, and stepped partway into the tent to hang the lantern from the strap dangling from the center. Ace closed the flap, shoveled more of the snow away from the front of the tepee and went back to join Omar and Billy in front of the wall tent. "That'll take the chill off and we can put our boots on that dry locker when we turn in. That locker will make a handy table for the extra lantern and my pistol too."

It wasn't long before the women had finished cleaning up which made a tremendous difference in their mood. "Okay, you guys can come in out of the cold now," Yaz called through the canvas.

"Hot chocolate all around and then we hit the sack," Ace proclaimed.

But before we do, I believe we have within our presence an official stove tender. I believe also she is called by the name of Kasha, the Princess of fire and warmth." And Ace placed a wreath of pine needles on her head.

Irena and Yaz clapped their hands, then Omar and Billy joined in. Kasha beamed with pride.

"Do you know what happens when the Fire Princess goes to bed?" Ace asked. Kasha shook her head.

"Well, I do believe the fire goes out," Ace said with a very serious look on his face. "Tell you what," Ace said. "You just stay in bed in the morning. I'll come over and we will have a little lesson on how to get a tent warm, okay?"

Kasha agreed that would be fine, and everyone at Elephant Rock Camp prepared to go to bed.

Early morning was still pitch black outside and the sounds in the tepee seemed oddly muffled as Ace zipped open the heavy canvas cover of his sleeping bag. He reached out to fumble for the butane lighter lying on the large plastic cargo box he called a dry locker. Soon, the hiss of the Coleman lantern told the other two men that the lantern was attempting to chase away the chill in the little tent. Billy and Omar had both covered their heads completely during the night, and now peeked out blinking against the sterile glare of the gas lantern.

Ace rose from his sleeping bag and lit the second lantern hanging from the peak, then quickly slipped back into his bed. "Damn! That was refreshing. This place will be nice and toasty in no time."

Billy started to stir as if to get up. "Better stay put until I get out of the way. It's way easier for one guy at a time to get dressed in this thing or somebody's gonna get an elbow to the eye socket," Ace said as he stood to pull on his pants that he had kept between his sleeping bag and it's cover. After he was fully dressed, Ace cautiously untied the top flap tie and looked out. "Whooee! It's bettern' knee deep to a tall Indian out there and puttin' down more!" Ace undid the middle tie and stuck first one leg out, then the other as he backed through the opening, then stuck his head back inside.

"I suggest you two climb out the same way or you'll be lettin' a bunch of snow fall inside. We'll clean out around the tepee later when this starts to let up," Ace said as he headed for the main tent. He stomped most of the snow from his boots, finished with the broom that was kept just inside the door, and prepared to give Kasha a lesson on fire building.

As he lit the lantern in the wall tent, Ace looked at the top bunk where Kasha peeked sleepy-eyed from out of the depths of her sleeping bag. "Hey, Fire Princess, do you know what the hardest part of starting the morning fire is?"

Kasha shook her head.

"It's getting out of your nice warm bed to start the fire," Ace laughed.

"Come on kiddo, rise and shine and do your chores. I want to get out of bed in a *warm* room," Yaz teased from her cot.

Kasha leaned over the edge of her bed. "Mom?"

Irena pushed the sleeping bag's flannel liner off of her face. "It looks like you got yourself a job, honey, you better hop to it. You can use that big coat for a house robe."

Kasha reached out and pulled the coat from the bedpost, stuck her arms through the sleeves, and clambered down out of the bunk bed.

Ace explained the procedures as he worked. "First thing is, you have to clean out yesterday's ashes. Here's the little shovel, and use this bucket."

Kasha struggled with the stove's door latch until Ace told her to pick up a piece of stove wood to tap the latch loose. "You can use a stick of wood for lots of things, you will soon see," Ace said.

Kasha took one shovelful of ashes and dumped them into the bucket. A cloud of dust flew up into her face and made her sneeze.

"Here, watch me," Ace said as he took the shovel. He scooped a load onto the shovel, tipped the bucket slightly, and put the shovel clear down in the bottom. As the ashes slid off, he pulled the shovel slowly out. Kasha copied the procedure while Ace explained that some stoves of this type would have a layer of dirt in the bottom that must be left there to keep from burning the bottom of the stove out. "There is no clay in the mountains, so I brought my own, mixed up the mud in a bucket, and coated the bottom of the firebox. The first fire baked the clay into a brick that we'll throw away when we're done. Did you know that we can fold this stove up flat and pack it away in that canvas bag over there?" Ace asked. He noticed from the corner of his eye that Irena was taking this all in, as was Yaz.

"Okay, the firebox is clean so I need you to loosely wad up as many of those old newspapers as you can and stuff the firebox clear full and light 'em," Ace instructed.

As the fire roared and the stovepipe crackled, Ace explained that tar and residue build up in the pipe, and a quick roaring blaze would burn up most of a day's accumulation.

"Now we're ready for the real fire. If we haven't gone out the day before and gathered a bunch of little sticks, we have to make our own, and here's how we do that. Since you are pretty new at using an ax, I'll show you how to do this safely, okay?" Ace asked.

Ace guided Kasha through standing a piece of cut wood on the chopping block, setting the ax blade where she wanted to make the split, then hit the back of the ax with another stick of wood. He was very pleased to see that she had a natural feel for using her dexterity, and by the time there were enough splinters for starting the fire, she was quite good at the task.

"Now, lay all your splinters in the firebox and mess 'em up so's they're not all layin' the same way. Yup, just like that. Now put some bigger ones on top and sort of lay 'em side by side. That's my Fire Princess!"

"Lots of times we'd take some treated sawdust like we have in that can there and sprinkle it on that pile and light it, but today I think everyone is anxious to head for the outhouse so we'll use an old Indian trick I learned from Lewis and Clark that'll have this thing going in no time. I'll let you practice this later, but here goes."

Ace produced an aerosol can of WD-40, sprayed some on the kindling, then held a match under the spray as it came from the nozzle to make a blowtorch. The stove roared to life for real and the chill immediately began to leave the tent.

Ace clapped Kasha on the shoulder. "We've done our job. Now all we have to do is roust out the cooks."

"You ladies can slip your feet into those five-buckle overshoes there in the corner. They'll get you to the outhouse. Take the broom. Go in pairs 'cause somebody will have to hold the lantern. It's not getting light very fast is it?"

The women had put on long-tailed men's shirts as nightgowns and now giggled at the sight they made wearing coats and huge overshoes.

The *outhouse* was a five-gallon bucket with the bottom cut out sitting over a hole in the ground. Its saving grace was that it had a toilet seat and lid fastened to the top. The toilet paper was kept in a gallon coffee can. The users were warned to put the lid back on the can and the lid down on the seat to keep rodents from getting at the paper.

By the time the women had made their visits to the *bathroom* there was plenty of light to see by. Ace swept the snow away from the tepee and was pleased to see that not too much snow had spilled onto the floor inside the door. He would bet that this snowstorm would probably last through the day and quit sometime tonight, since his experience and the last weather report seemed to jibe pretty closely. The temperature was actually not bad considering the time of year. The snow was pretty wet now and would be settling. They would just have to sit tight.

Omar and Billy were passing firewood into the tent when Yaz called that breakfast was served. The pilot had found the bacon and the pancake mix. She had discovered that the eggs in the cooler had not frozen, so she added those to the menu. Everyone ate just like people usually do at hunting camp - like they were starving and hadn't eaten for days.

"Before the snow gets any deeper or harder to walk in, Billy, do you think I could get you and Yaz to make one last trip up top here and give Alden and Jason a call?"

Billy was all up for some action, especially if it involved going somewhere with Yaz. Ace tossed Billy a pint can. "You guys smear this on your boots. Open up where the tongue is and work it in there, too. This stuff works good to keep your boots dry, but you have to put it on every day when you walk in snow. It'll wear off pretty quick, especially if the snow gets a crust on it.

While Yaz and Billy waterproofed their boots, Ace told Billy to tell Jason to load that piece of plate steel that he had planned to use on the horse trailer floor onto Brutus. "Tell him to blow a half-inch hole in each corner, then strap it down good on the flatbed. Oh, and tell him to make sure he's got the two-inch ball on the hitch. His excuse for coming up will be to get his horse trailer. If someone asks where the horses are, tell him to say the hunters rode 'em out to the main road. That'll give 'em something to think about. Something else I've been thinkin' about, and see if you agree, since you Indians have this *sixth sense* you always show in the movies . . ."

"The movies are full of it," Billy interrupted.

"Just checkin' to see if you're listenin'," Ace grinned and winked at Yaz. "I'm confident we can leave these guys down the creek here in the dust. But I know for sure now that the sheriff is in cahoots with 'em, or that stupid deputy wouldn't be hangin' out with 'em. That means we can't head for town, and I wouldn't be surprised if there ain't more of these sons-a-bitches, sorry ma'am, waitin' at the bottom of the hill. Are you thinkin' what I'm thinkin?" Ace asked.

"Head for the res?" Billy asked back.

"Yup," Ace answered. "I think our best bet is to let Alden know we'll be headed his way and he can start calling the right people to meet us somewhere public. We have to wait until the last minute, otherwise, the word might get to the wrong folks. I want all of those kind behind us, not in front. What do you think of that Mr. President?"

Omar shook his head. "I don't know what to think anymore. This whole thing is beyond anything I was ever prepared to deal with."

Ace noticed that Irena kept silent while she looked at the floor, and Kasha looked at her father, then back to him with an expression that was difficult to decipher.

CHAPTER FOURTEEN
Counterpoise

"KASHA, HOW WOULD you like to wrap a set of gaiters on your legs and accompany Billy and Yaz up on top of Elephant Rock?" Ace asked. When she hesitated, he added, "That is if her majesty, the Fire Princess, will turn over tending the stove to the old shoemaker."

Ace selected the smallest pair of boots they had from their collection, greased them, and made them fit with an extra pair of socks. "Those gaiters will keep your legs dry and the long sleeves on that big old coat will be your mittens. You youngsters have a nice walk, and be careful!"

After the trio left, Ace turned to Omar and Irena. "Irena, can I get you to do the breakfast dishes and tidy up while Omar and I go look up Kasha's new shoes?"

Irena approached the *kitchen* hesitantly. As Ace and Omar stepped through the tent flap, Ace called back into the tent, "Hot water's in the spare coffee pot and just holler if you need more. We'll be over at the meat pole."

At the meat pole, Ace lowered the front quarters down to shoulder level and went to work with the puukko. He made a circular cut in the hide around the rib cage from the neck back around to the armpit area. The quarters were hanging leg down, so he began loosening the hide near the top while peeling it down towards the leg which had been cut off at the knee.

"I'll need your help here, Omar. You grab hold and keep pulling down with all your weight." With the help of the skillfully handled puukko, the hide began to peel off over the leg, turning itself inside out. They repeated the process with the other quarter, then raised the meat back up out of reach of any interested parties.

Omar was clearly uncomfortable with the blood and gore on his hands.

"It'll wash off, and we have a fine pair of boots here," Ace said cheerfully as he dangled the bloody hide up high, and as if displaying a trophy scalp, he did a little war dance in the snow. Ace noted with grim satisfaction that the gesture clearly upset the president. "Good!" he thought.

Ace gathered the things he needed, then sat on the floor with the tubular hide stretched over a length of firewood and began scraping off the flesh with the ubiquitous puukko. As he worked, Ace began to talk: "Now that the kids have left, there are a few things we need to clear up. Do you have any idea who is behind all of this? I need to know who to look out for, and it seems to me, so do you, Mr. President."

"I have many enemies. Some I can think of used to be friends, or I thought they were, but no one I know of would go this far. Chances are we will never know for sure. They seem to have almost unlimited resources and are obviously deeply influential within my Administration," Omar admitted.

"So basically we can't trust anyone you know, which leaves us with my connections, right?" Ace asked. Omar nodded his head.

"Who . . . ? Uh, who is Jason and who is Brutus?" Irena wanted to know.

"Sorry. I didn't make that clear. Jason is my son and Brutus is our one-ton dualie four-by-four crew cab." Irena and Omar gave Ace a blank look. "Down here in fly-over country where we *cling to our religion and our guns,* I guess we speak a foreign language," Ace said sarcastically as he watched the crimson creep into Omar's face. "A one-ton dualie is a small dual-wheeled truck. Everybody knows four-by-four is four-wheel drive, and a crew cab is a truck cab that will seat six people.

"Okay, sir, you got me started now, so we might as well get this all out before the kids get back," Ace said. "Let's just pretend that you and your asshole attorney general and the rest of the antigun people were successful in grabbing everyone's guns, where do you think you would be now? You know it isn't just having a gun; it's knowing how and when to use it. By now you should realize that responsible people could just save your sorry ass some day."

"Well, I still don't think . . . !" Omar began.

"That's your problem, you don't think!" Ace's voice was beginning to rise.

"Omar Hakim Bahktar!" Irena shouted as she stood and faced her husband. "How utterly stupid can you be? We're miles from any place, isolated in a snowstorm, and you're arguing with a man holding a bloody knife!" Tears of frustration were running down her cheeks.

Omar hung his head and stared at the floor clearly embarrassed. Ace got up quietly, laid the knife aside, and walked over to put his arms around the first lady who began to sob convulsively. "You lasted longer than I thought you would," he said. "Your show of bravery, I'm sure, is what kept Kasha from losing it. That was a lot of trauma for you guys, hangin' over the cliff, having agent Mason shot in front of you . . ."

"And your poor dog. That man, Karl, just shot him out of pure meanness," Irena quavered. Irena sat back down on the bunk bed and patted Omar's knee. "Sorry," she said through her tears.

"If you two never saw evil before, I'm sure you'll agree you've seen plenty of it now," Ace said softly.

"I'm sorry. Really sorry," Omar said, with an air of sincere humility Ace had not heard before. "I guess I've been wrong about a lot of things. Being here, seeing how *you folks* handle things, shows me a side of this country I never saw before . . ."

"It's been here all along, sir," Ace interrupted. "You just didn't see it. It was there when those firefighters ran into the Trade Towers, it was there when Richard Mason gave his life trying to save your family. It was there when neighbors aided tornado victims before FEMA ever arrived. What's telling is, that it was *not* there with those people in New Orleans waiting with their hands out and doing nothing to help themselves after Katrina hit. *But,* it is still there in those youngsters who *volunteer* to go into the military. I've heard people in your administration denigrate our service men and women by implying they're somehow substandard. I'm sorry for my outburst a few minutes ago, but it's frustrating to me that the man sitting in the president's chair doesn't seem to have the balls to chastise the people under him who talk that way."

Ace had the skins scraped and was scrubbing them with a stiff-bristled brush and lye soap.

"I've made up my mind. Things are going to change . . ." Omar stopped when Ace gave him a sharp look, then he continued, "No, not *Hope and Change*, I mean a different attitude and approach. A new understanding. I was disillusioned and now I see how things have twisted out of control. The momentum of what is already in place will be hard to stop, but this episode, I believe, will be a new awakening for this country."

"If we make it out alive," Irena added.

Ace had washed off the soap and was brushing in some neat's-foot oil to keep the hide from stiffening. "Don't look much like boots yet do they?"

"I can't even imagine how you're going to make anything out of that," Irena said.

"We'll have a good start on 'em by the time the kids get back," Ace said, "but let's talk about other stuff while I have your ear, okay?"

Ace talked about the forest and why many of the environmental concerns were not using sound scientific knowledge to guide management of healthy forests. He pointed out that the small country of Finland had reached a good sensible balance on forest management that he had seen first hand. As an example, Ace used the beetle infestation, the resultant tree kill, and the inability of anyone to make use of the wasted wood due to unrealistic and nonsensical laws.

They talked about the wolves, declining elk population, and the grizzly bear problems.

They discussed game management, cattle grazing, mining, oil production, housing, and wasteful government programs. Ace described how one-size-fits-all decisions in Washington often failed, or were inferior to letting states, counties, and local governments make their own rules according to local circumstances. As an example, Ace talked about the Homestead Act. Lawmakers in the east with no concept of the reality of the arid west, decided people could make a living from 160 acres, when 1,600 acres would have been a minimum in many places.

The talk eventually turned to self-sufficiency and dependence on government for everything.

Ace said, "Our Founding Fathers did not sign the Declaration of Dependence, did they? This country was founded on *Capitalism*! Let's take a look at a small example of cause and effect, and the consequences of responsibility on a local level shall we?"

Ace had Omar and Irena's full attention now as he dug out his leather awl and Kasha's street shoes for a foot-size pattern, but continued his lecture.

"It turned out okay in the end, Omar, but your actions yesterday could have got your family killed. It wasn't in the original plan for me to help Irena and Kasha escape through the back of the tent, but I *read* you pretty accurately didn't I?" Ace said, and Omar nodded sheepishly.

"If Karl had found your family in the tent and brought them out into the mix of people in the campground, do you realize how difficult it would have been for Billy, Yaz, and me to put those guys down without you and your family getting in the way?" Ace asked. Then, noticing how Irena looked at her husband, Ace continued, "Don't beat yourself up over it. Most people are not mentally prepared or have the experience to deal with situations like that. I should not have asked you to shoot another human being. My bad, sir."

"Now Kasha is learning a little something about responsibility; it's a small lesson, but one that may stick with her, and it goes like this: If you want to be warm, or cook your food, you have to build a fire. If you want to build a fire, you have to gather the wood, and so on. Every kid in America should be raised on a farm, and if not, at least spend some time camping." Ace looked at Omar and added, "Old habits are hard to break aren't they?"

"I don't get your meaning." Omar responded.

"Correct me if I'm wrong, but running through your head right now is the thought that, hey, yes, the government could set up youth camps and make it mandatory for every kid in America to spend a couple of summers in one, right?" Ace said, looking Omar straight in the eye.

"Busted!" Omar said, embarrassed again.

"Okay. I'm waiting. Spit it out!" Ace grinned.

"Um, tax breaks or incentive programs for church groups, Boy Scouts, Girl Scouts, and youth clubs with maybe more access to federal lands for outdoor activities?" Omar ventured. "Maybe encourage employers to allow parents *extra* vacation time if they include their children, and extend tax breaks to make it more attractive to do so."

"BINGO!" Ace yelled.

"Who won?" came the question from outside of the tent. The tent flap shook as the hikers undid the ties. Kasha was the first one in,

"Mom, Dad! We saw some deer, a moose, and a *porkypine*!" said the girl breathlessly.

Yaz and Billy spent more time kicking snow off their boots than Kasha did, but no one noticed. They stepped inside and Billy asked, "What's for lunch?"

Yaz looked at Ace's project and asked, "What's that?"

"Those are *supposed* to be Kasha's new boots. Leave it up to an old White Man to try to make something from a piece of road kill," Billy grinned.

"At least I don't stick a few feathers in my hair and ride naked through the middle of the Seventh Cavalry! Oh, I forgot," Ace feigned embarrassment. "Somebody already did that."

Everyone laughed.

Irena and Yaz started lunch while Billy and Omar brought in more wood and some groceries from the lockers still hanging from the trees. Kasha settled down to watch Ace sew the hide together for her boots.

"These are patterned after the footwear of the Sami people who live in Lapland. This hollow piece came from the elk's front leg. Now, I pull it down on itself like this, and we have a boot top with hair inside and out. This piece that's still attached is the heel, the sole, and the sides. We fold them all up like this, trim off what we don't need, turn up the toe, and sew it all together and pretty soon we have a boot. This will be a special snow boot because the hair on the bottom slopes back. In other words when you slide your foot forward, the hair lies down. When you push back to take a step, the hair stands up to give you traction. It's another one of those old Indian tricks."

Ace took a break for lunch. Then while everyone else sat back with a second cup of coffee, he finished one boot and handed it to Kasha to try on.

"Hmmm, that feels nice," she said with a big smile. "This looks just like the shoes elves wear."

"You'll eventually wear the hair off the bottom, but the softness of the sole will let you feel the ground better. That way you can walk quieter and sneak up on people. An Australian Aborigine Shaman will wear hair shoes on special missions, so the idea is not unique," Ace said.

It didn't take long to finish the second boot and Kasha gave Ace a hug for his efforts.

"Okay, Fire Princess, you can tell your friends at school about your boots and how the hunters don't just eat the game they kill, they can use just about all of it for something. You know, the leg bones can be pulverized and boiled to make the oil I used on the leather. It doesn't get stiff when it gets cold," Ace told her, and he continued to explain about other animal parts and what they were used for.

Ace and Kasha were startled by a snort and turned to see that Omar, Irena, Yaz, and Billy were all sleeping. The warmth of the stove had made everyone drowsy. Ace encouraged Kasha to climb up on her bunk while he retired to the tepee, lit the lantern for some warmth, and stretched out for a nap. He knew that in roughly an hour the stove would have digested its last feeding of wood and the rapidly cooling tent would automatically wake everyone up.

X X X X X

While everyone at Elephant Rock was taking an afternoon nap, Jason, *Jay Gee*, Gronsky had his eye on the weather and an ear to the radio. It had rained over most of the valley earlier during the storm, then turned to a sloppy snow. Before the clouds lowered and the precipitation began in earnest, there had been a parade of hunters vacating the mountain.

The local news related complaints of the "check stations" at the foot of the mountains stopping and inspecting everyone and everything. The people in the black SUVs were purported to be from Homeland Security and Sheriff Harper's comments to the news media were terse and noncommittal.

Jay Gee had gone to school with Under Sheriff Riley Mossberg and had seen him at the adjacent gas pump in downtown Grant City. Jay Gee was waiting for the big saddle tank on Brutus to fill, so he sauntered over to say "Hi." The two men could have almost been twins. They were both a stocky six foot two and two hundred and thirty pounds. They both sported military buzz cuts, had been on the same high school wrestling team, and attended each other's wedding. Jay Gee wore a light brown beard while Reilly adopted the latest craze, the Fu Manchu style in red hair.

"Keepin' busy?" Jay Gee asked.

"Ha!" Reilly snorted.

Jay Gee knew that nearly the whole sheriff's department, and everyone else in the county for that matter, detested the *California Cowboy* which is what most folks called Sheriff Glenn Harper. It was an epithet in this part of the west that carried no terms of endearment, to say the least.

Looking around to make sure he wasn't overheard, Reilly said, "We're sittin' around down here twiddlin' our thumbs while all sorts of strange people are rollin' into town, flyin' in to the airport, flyin' out of the airport, settin' up road blocks and who knows what, and Harper has us out lookin' for lost dogs and breakin' up family fights."

"Hey! Pay's the same fightin' or marchin' ain't it?" Jay Gee grinned and slapped his old friend on the shoulder.

"I'd feel a whole lot better drawing my wages workin' on the road crew than doin' this shit," Reilly said bitterly.

"Hang in there, buddy," Jay Gee said. "Your boss ain't no Sam Elliott, he's just a poor excuse for a wannabe, and dollars to donuts he won't be around after the next election." The gas pump thumped as it shut off indicating the saddle tank had filled.

"Gotta go up and *rescue* my dad in the morning if it clears off like they say it will. He probably won't come down, but I'd better pull that trailer out before we have to leave it there 'til spring," Jay Gee said.

"Yeah. Used to be you could leave something like that up there and it would still be there in one piece in the spring, but not anymore," Reilly said. "Different kind of people are moving in. They come here and go crazy for a while thinking it's all wild and free and they can do anything they want just because somebody isn't lookin' over their shoulder twenty-four/seven."

Jay Gee laughed, "Here we stand talkin' like a couple of old fur trappers pissin' and moanin' 'cause the pilgrims are movin' in on us."

Reilly opened the door to his patrol pickup. "Look, you be careful up there, Jay Gee, there's been an awful lot of craziness what with the president's plane going down and those terrorists with their rockets and all."

"Hey, we'll be just fine. Don't we have the Wyoming militia to *protect and serve* us?" Jay Gee grinned.

Reilly threw his vehicle in gear, shook his head, gave Jay Gee a friendly one-finger salute, and peeled out causing the other customers to look after the departing sheriff's department pickup.

After topping off the gas tanks, Jay Gee went back out to the ranch and wrestled the piece of plate steel onto the flatbed truck. Pushing the plate first over one side, then the other, he used the ranch's cutting torch to blow a hole in each corner. He then centered the plate on the bed, laid a six-by-six timber on top, and lashed the whole works down with three ratchet straps. He next tossed in some bottled water, a couple of bags of cookies, and some jerky. It would not look good to have a lot of supplies on board if his purpose was going to be retrieving the horse trailer.

The final item was his dad's M-1 Garand .30-caliber rifle which he placed in a gun pocket that hung on the back of the front seat. Jay Gee would be up at first light and if the snow had stopped, he would be on his way up the mountain.

In a phone call from Alden Spotted Horse, Jay Gee learned that Alden suspected the best destination for them, once they got off the mountain, would be to come directly to the reservation on the old two-lane highway. His reasoning being that there would be no one of any concern using that route to meet them from the north on the old highway, and if they did, they would be immediately noticeable. The parallel route, the interstate highway, would be a bad choice.

Alden said he would make some calls to people he could trust telling them to stand by. Since they had no trust in the federal government for fear that any plans might be leaked to the wrong people, they would have to keep their plans secret for as long as possible.

X X X X X

The men at camp two had finally gotten their tent to hold in some heat from their struggling stove, and those who were not sleeping in shifts were taking turns monitoring the Swampy Creek Road which remained unmarred by any tracks save for a moose that wandered aimlessly looking for some browse.

Deputy Del Fulton had made up his mind that he was going to bail out of this mess at the very first opportunity. Shamus and Kelly must have sensed the deputy's intention for they never let him out of their sight, and they certainly didn't trust him with the keys to his mid-sized SUV. Del knew his vehicle's capabilities and knew that unless some larger vehicle broke the road open, he would never make it out on his own anyway.

They all knew something had to happen soon because the storm appeared to be tapering off. A small, battery AM radio told them that tomorrow should be sunny and warmer. That meant the early season snow would settle quickly to become heavy and wet.

X X X X X

At his home in Grant City, Sheriff Glenn Harper furtively packed a suitcase and slid it under the bed where he doubted Gloria would find it. The call from Omega told him to stand by for further instructions and make plans to meet the private jet at the airport at a moments notice. That notice should come tomorrow, Omega hinted.

X X X X X

In her office on the west coast, Monica Farizzi was also making plans. Somehow Eric had replaced her old butler. Although to all of her visitors he appeared to be a servant, she knew she could not make a single move without him finding out about it. "That damned Santorini isn't going to let me out of his sight," she thought to herself. She felt trapped while things were spinning out of control. Control was the focus of her entire career, and now it seemed she was only a fly caught in a web that had no end.

What irked Ms. Farizzi more than anything was that suck-up Vice President Sheldon Parker had arranged to have Air Force One pilot Jeff Ferguson flown to a hospital in Washington where he denied access to the man by anyone but himself and his private staff. So far, the vice president hadn't made any moves to permanently take over the president's office, but told the press he would handle all urgent presidential business in a manner consistent with President Bahktar's policies.

"What does he know that he's not telling?" Monica asked herself out loud, then remembered that Eric had "debugged" her office, or had he? The knot in her stomach made her reach for her third antacid in an hour.

X X X X X

While all of the other players in this game figuratively held their breath, anxious or fearful of what tomorrow would bring, the people in the camp at Elephant Rock had just finished a hearty elk steak supper and now sat around in the wall tent discussing plans for tomorrow.

"It'll be too time consuming to run up in the morning to call Jason 'cause I know he'll be right behind the snowplows. We'll have to assume that he'll be making his way up the Boulder River Road by an hour after daylight," Ace speculated. "I don't think he'll have to chain up 'cause Brutus has plenty of ground clearance, but still, he will more than likely be the first outfit to break a trail up the main road. This snow will slow him down so I imagine it would be another hour before he gets here."

"Can we make a run for it?" asked Yaz.

"No, that damned deputy will probably be right down there at the campground to check Jason in and out. Even if we didn't stop, they can hear us coming, and I don't want to risk that sort of firefight, which I'm sure it will be with a cab full of people. They'd have the advantage of being in front or to the side of us. What we have to do is make them think we're still up here," Ace said.

Lending an air of lightheartedness to a serious situation, Billy quipped, "So do we use devious White Man tactics or sneaky Indian tricks on these guys?"

"Remember what happened to Fetterman?" Ace asked.

"You mean decoys and ambush?" Billy asked.

"Well, sort of," Ace replied. "We'll take out of here on foot at first light and just march right down the road. Jason will see our tracks where we leave the road, and I'll tie a plastic bag to a tree branch where he can see it. It will have one of our radios in it and a note. He'll go on up and hook on to the trailer, while we circle the campground. When he comes out, the cab will still be empty. We can keep in touch on the radios and come out of the timber when we're safely past the camp. I'm sure there will be more of these people further on down, but I think we can get by them before they know what's going on."

"What if they shoot at us?" Irena wanted to know.

"Well for one thing if they are behind us, we'll have the horse trailer back there and when we meet Jason, we'll real quick-like prop up that sheet of plate steel for extra protection. I'll have Jason throw in the *evidence* onto the floor behind the seat and cover it with a blanket just in case we need some *help* getting through the *check* station."

"What evidence is that?" Omar asked.

"Remember that piece of pipe that said US GEOLOGICAL SURVEY?" Billy said, catching onto the plan.

"We still have one of their rockets," Yaz said, clapping her hands in delight, and then added, "and I know how they work!"

CHAPTER FIFTEEN
Checkmate

"FRONTIER SOLDIERS USED to travel on this stuff," Ace said as he prepared the side pork and dough gods. "I know you guys don't feel much like breakfast, but choke down all you can. We got about a half hour 'til there's enough light to travel on. On your way to the outhouse, you might want to look up. Those stars are sparklin' cold as ice up there. I don't think you'll see anything like that back in Washington."

A half hour later, Ace lead the way north through the timber until they were past the dog-hair stand of young trees. "No point in gettin' covered with snow pushin' our way through that stuff," he explained. "Stay in my tracks as much as you can." Ace made good use of the spear knocking snow off the lower branches so it would not fall on the travelers.

When they left the tent, Ace handed Omar the shotgun. "I'm gonna trust you with this. Don't let us down now, okay?"

Omar nodded and looked sternly into Ace's eyes. "I know you won't let us down and I'll do my best to do the same. Lead on."

They soon angled out to the Swampy Creek Road making better time there than they had in the timber. Ace stopped, selected a branch that hung out into the road, and tied an orange hardware store bag to it. "Jay Gee can't miss it here," he said.

"How will he know it's for him?" Irena asked, apparently worried that the plan could go wrong.

"This is where we leave the road and get back in the timber. He'll know when he sees the tracks. And from here on there will be no talking," Ace said as he led the way into the forest once more.

They made quite a parade. Ace in front with spear and single shot rifle, Billy with the old revolver and AR-15, Omar with the shotgun, Irena with a couple of water bottles and Omar's briefcase, Kasha carried a bag with two extra radios, and Yaz brought up the rear carrying the M-16.

As they trudged through the area where Ace had pinned Jorge to the tree trunk with his first arrow, they heard a deep rumble from the south getting closer and closer. Ace stopped his little caravan and listened. The rumble stopped for close to a minute, then started again and began to fade to the south.

X X X X X

While Ace and his party waited in the trees only a hundred yards east of camp two, Deputy Fulton held up his hand in a signal to stop the big four-wheel-drive truck.

The driver grinned at the deputy, "Anything wrong?"

Del stepped up on the running board and peered into the cab. "No, we're just tryin' to control the sightseers and curiosity seekers. What's your business in here?"

"Just come to get my horse trailer before it gets bogged down for the winter," Jay Gee said.

"Where's your horses?" Del wanted to know.

"Hunters rode 'em out to the main road before all this white shit came down." Jay Gee pointed his chin, Indian fashion, toward the rat-faced man behind the deputy, "Who's your friend? Or is he family?" Jay Gee was enjoying making the deputy uncomfortable.

The question flustered Del. "He's uh, Ho . . . Homeland Security. You b-b-better go get your trailer."

Jay Gee couldn't resist. He said loud enough for the second man to hear, "Homeland Security. Huh? Boy, I know I'll sleep a whole lot better tonight!" He fired up the truck, spun the wheels, and wallowed on up the road.

At the orange sack, Jay Gee reached out the window and snagged it off the branch as he went by. "Good old pop," he said to himself. "Always thinkin'"

Ace's radio clicked. "Jay Gee?"

"Got the sack dad, anything else?" Jay Gee said.

Ace told Jay Gee to get the trailer hooked up ASAP and be sure to toss the PVC pipe onto the back seat floor and cover it with something. They would keep going through the trees until they heard the truck and meet him on the road.

X X X X X

Almost a half hour later Shamus heard the big truck approaching from the south. He quickly stationed his men on either side of the road.

Deputy Fulton again stopped the truck, and the thought crossed his mind to try to jump in and tell the driver to step on it, but that little weasel Kelly was never far from his side. Del stepped up, looked in the cab, and shook his head while Shamus jerked open the horse trailer door. Empty!

"See anyone up there?" Del asked, indicating the direction back toward Elephant Rock.

"Nobody but us chickens, boss!" Jay Gee grinned.

"Okay, get out of here, then," Del said as he stepped off the running board.

Shamus watched the truck and trailer disappear slowly down the road. "I don't like it! Kelly, you and the deputy follow him out to the highway. I have a feeling about this."

Jay Gee looked in the mirror and picked up the radio. "I got a tail. He can't keep up very well but he's still comin'. It's that dip-shit deputy and his bodyguard."

Ace's voice came back, "Kick Brutus in the ass 'til you get to the top of that first steep hill, then unhook the trailer. We'll meet you on the other side."

"Come on folks let's hustle. We got a bus to catch!" Ace said as he picked up the pace.

Jay Gee easily pulled ahead of the struggling SUV. He made the trailer fish tail a few times to make steering more difficult for Del, then slammed on the brakes at the top of the hill. Jay Gee jumped out, swung the dolly wheel down and jacked the trailer tongue off the hitch. As a last gesture he pulled the keeper pin from the jack pivot and stuck it in his pocket. The spot was perfect. There was no room between the trees to allow a vehicle to get past and if they tried to move the trailer, the dolly wheel would collapse dropping the tongue down to the ground. Down the hill and around a bend, Jay Gee stopped. He let the truck idle so it could be heard, and began loosening the straps holding the steel plate in place.

Ace and company could hear the truck so they headed toward the sound. Just as they broke out of the trees not far from Jay Gee and the truck, they heard the siren on the deputy's SUV begin to wail. Deputy Del was apparently signaling the men in camp two that he needed help.

Omar and his family cast anxious glances back down the road.

"Don't worry. It's going to take them some time to get that trailer out of the way," Jay Gee said as he and Ace struggled to get the steel plate leaned up against the headache rack behind the cab. They tied the plate in place with bailing wire while everyone else was loading up. They laid Ace's spear across the bed behind the headache rack, lashed it down with more bailing wire, and then they were gone.

Shamu's head came up when he heard the siren. "I knew it! They're up to something. Antonio! Grab the rifles and ammo. Dan! Get that trailer unhooked!" Shamus yelled as he and Sharky ran toward the Yukon. The vehicle started immediately, which was no surprise. When they arrived at camp two, Shamus was surprised to see Karl's Yukon had not been destroyed like the other two. It was still hooked up to Karl's cargo trailer as if they had been planning to leave at a moment's notice. Still suspicious, Shamus started it, checked the fuel level, and everything seemed to be okay. He gunned the engine impatiently. "What's takin' so long back there with that trailer?"

Dan called back, "Somebody's buggered this hitch up so bad I can't get it unhooked without using some tools,"

"Forget it then. Get in!"

As soon as Dan slammed the door, Shamus jammed the Yukon into gear and four-wheel drive and left the campground throwing rooster tails of snow from all four wheels. Shamus noted the trailer was causing him to continually countersteer but chalked it off to the deep snow. The rocks Billy had loaded into the back end of the trailer were doing exactly what Ace had figured they would.

Kelly and the deputy were standing helplessly beside Del's SUV. Shamus jumped out and made a quick survey. "Get that little piece of shit off to the side so I can get by!" Shamus yelled at Del. Del complied immediately, backing his SUV out of the road.

It took the encumbered Yukon and the men pushing, a full ten minutes to move the horse trailer far enough to get by. Shamus was in a red rage as he revved the Yukon's engine unmercifully and screamed at the men.

As Dan, Sharky, and Antonio piled in, Shamus yelled at Kelly to make sure the deputy followed them as close as possible. It was fortunate that there was no traffic on the Boulder River Road, and very few vehicles on the recently cleared highway. They could see the looping curves of the highway below them and Antonio, in the passenger's seat, suddenly pointed, "There they are!"

Shamus had been driving like a wild man in spite of having the cargo trailer still attached. He smiled wickedly, "We're catching them!"

X X X X X

Less than a mile ahead, Omar was leaning forward to look in the side-view mirror. He caught a glimpse of the black Yukon pulling the small cargo trailer and the sheriff's SUV close behind with the emergency lights flashing.

Although the sun was quickly turning the snow to water, the highway was noticeably clearer as they lost elevation. They now were on a stretch of road that clung to a long southern exposure that offered them a lot of dry pavement.

"Shouldn't we be going faster?" Omar asked, clearly worried.

No sooner had Omar voiced his concern, than Jay Gee said calmly, "They're right behind us."

Ace leaned a little forward so he could watch in the mirror. "Yeah, that's just about right. Keep 'em there for a little bit." Jay Gee skillfully kept the Yukon from passing. As he drove, he kept a watch in the side-view mirror.

"One of 'em's leaning out the passenger side with a rifle, wanna watch?"

"No, we shouldn't obstruct your view," Ace said.

"Wow!" Jay Gee exclaimed. "That's the first time I ever got to see a rifle blow up!"

Pieces of the exploding AR-15 inflicted serious injuries to Antonio's face and minor cuts to Shamus. The shattered rifle dropped to the road where it was run over by the trailer and Del's SUV.

Kelly looked at his rifle. He was clever enough to put two and two together. His suspicion was borne out when he and Del saw Dan pitch two more rifles out the window of the Yukon.

Kelly opened his rifle's action, turned the weapon around, and looked up the bore. The little Irishman shrugged his shoulders, punched the cardboard out of his window, dropped the magazine in his lap, and tossed his rifle away. Del gave Kelly a puzzled look. "Clever bastards they are. They spiked our guns! I reckon Antonio's lost an eye if not worse. Well, we still got our pistols." Then he smirked and added, "And yours!" Kelly reached behind the seat and pulled Del's M-16 out. "At least here's one they didn't get to."

Shamus was having a really bad day and it was getting worse because the truck they were pursuing was now pulling away. They passed a sign that said *Fallen City*, but Shamus could care less. He was focused on getting closer and getting some revenge. Forty-five, now fifty miles per hour. The trailer was causing a great deal of trouble, and the Yukon's steering seemed awful mushy.

The truck had just disappeared around a sharp corner, but Shamus did not see it appear going around the next. The Yukon's speedometer said only sixty-three miles per hour when the truck appeared nearly stopped in the middle of the road. Instinctively, Shamus stomped on the brakes to be rewarded with the sickening feeling of the trailer pulling the rear end of the big SUV around. Shamus let off the brake and hit the accelerator in an attempt to straighten out. The truck he had been chasing squatted down as it squirted up the road out of his way.

Shamus had the whole road to himself now but it was no use. The more he tried to straighten out, the worse things got until they were completely out of control.

Kelly and Del watched transfixed as the Yukon and its madly swaying trailer headed first toward the sheer rock wall on the north side of the road, then toward the guardrail on the south, then toward the wall again. Finally the Yukon and it's trailer rocketed through the rail to disappear leaving a cloud of dust, rocks, metal, and glass debris raining down over the gap in the guardrail.

It seemed longer, but it was only six seconds before anyone on the highway above heard a muffled boom and saw a puff of black smoke that made a perfect mushroom cloud in the brilliant blue sky.

Del had stopped his SUV in the middle of the highway and sat totally speechless. Kelly didn't say anything for a few seconds while he watched the smoke dissipate .Then he sighed, shifted in his seat, and told Del, "Well then, my friend, it's just you and me, but I think we'll follow at a discreet distance, don't you think?"

Del's dry throat wouldn't let him reply so he nodded his head and put his battered vehicle in gear. As they rolled past the gap in the guardrail, Kelly said, "Del, would you be a dear and turn off that friggin' light? I don't think we want to attract any more attention than need be, eh?"

Jay Gee brought the truck down to normal traffic speed now that the deputy's vehicle seemed content to follow at a respectful distance. After the highway made a major change of direction from east to north, they could see the valley of Boulder River spread out below. Ace pulled binoculars from the glove box and scanned the highway past the foothills. "Looks like a road block down on that straight stretch just out of Clayton. Yaz, do you have any idea if we can use that rocket without one of those launch frames?"

"If it's the right kind, it has a manual override. You have to break a seal and there's a small access door that covers a twist timer. I think twenty seconds is the most you can set it for," Yaz said.

"I have an idea for dealing with the roadblock. Here's what we'll do," Ace said, and he laid out his plan for approval.

At the end of the mountain portion of the highway was a pullout for people putting on or removing tire chains. They pulled in but parked in the borrow pit to give the passengers extra protection. Everybody had a job to do. Irena and Kasha kept an eye on the people at the roadblock more than a mile ahead. Omar and Billy ran back and flopped down at the highway's shoulder to fire at the deputy's SUV as it rounded the corner behind them. Del almost turned his vehicle over swerving into the borrow pit on the south side of the highway to get out of the line of fire. Kelly had fired only two shots from Del's M-16 when the third shot only produced a sickening snap. Kelly was about to chamber another round, thought better of it, and checked the rifle's bore. He laughed bitterly and threw the rifle out on the road toward Billy and Omar. In answer to Del's questioning look, Kelly replied, "Those clever bastards buggered the ammo too! Well, it's too far for pistols, so we'll just sit right here, shall we?"

The two lone shots from Del's M-16 screamed off the steel plate leaning against the headache rack on Brutus. Everyone flinched and ducked but went back to work when Billy signaled on the radio, "All clear, Ace. They used one of the magazines of doctored ammo."

Ace and Yaz held the PVC pipe tight against the edge of the flatbed while Jay Gee used the ratchet straps to hold it in place. Ace sighted through the pipe to ascertain that the forward end had a clear path unobstructed by any protuberances on the truck, while Yaz and Jay Gee worked on the missile. When everything was ready, Ace called Billy and Omar back. They sent a couple of parting shots toward Del and Kelly to remind them to keep their heads down, then sprinted toward the truck. Everyone got in and Yaz took the seat by the right-hand rear door.

Jay Gee pulled up out of the borrow pit and started down the road toward the roadblock. At about a half mile from the two black vehicles positioned nose-to-nose on the highway, they stopped again.

Yaz jumped out and while she was knocking the caps off the plastic pipe, she could see men scrambling behind the big black SUVs down the road. She pulled the rocket back far enough to expose the access door, flipped it open, twisted the timer, and yelled, "Twenty seconds!"

She pushed the rocket back into the tube and jammed the cap onto the back to make sure the missile didn't slide out backwards.

The truck began to roll as Yaz swung in and slammed the door.

This is gonna be sooooo cool!" Yaz grinned.

Jay Gee gunned the truck and headed straight toward the blockade. The black SUVs were lost to view momentarily in the rocket's exhaust plume, but as the smoke thinned, Ace and Jay Gee could see the men by the vehicles sprinting away to either side. Even as he spoke, one of the SUVs disappeared in a ball of flame. The other was knocked backwards into the ditch, but was still on its wheels. "Windows down and everybody fire at anything that moves. Make 'em keep their heads down 'til we get by," said Ace.

The men bowled over by the explosion were too busy trying to recover to even think about shooting as Brutus flew past the wreckage on the highway.

More than a mile southwest of what was left of the roadblock, Kelly looked at Del as the deputy pulled his vehicle onto the highway. "That had to be the slickest play of guerilla tactics I've seen in a long, long while."

Del had to admire the move, "Yeah, they did good, didn't they?"

Kelly directed the deputy to head toward the smoldering roadblock. "We should offer to help pick up the pieces. Since your sheriff hasn't come up with any further instructions and Shamus took the satellite phone with him to the bottom of the canyon, we'll have to rely on these chaps for further guidance, eh?"

As the deputy's SUV rolled to a stop, Del and Kelly could see Brutus disappearing around the curve leading into the town of Clayton.

One of the survivors of the roadblock approached Del's SUV. He was a heavy-set man with a wide forehead, ice blue eyes, and a wisp of blond hair. Kelly took the man to be of Swedish extraction so he flippantly addressed him. "Well Sven, looks like we just missed the party. Are we havin' fun yet?"

The blonde man was not amused. "My name is Brynulf. Remember that." Brynulf looked back up the highway. "Where is the rest of your crew?"

"You're lookin' at it, me lad," Kelly said, clearly not liking this person.

Brynulf was stunned. "There were supposed to be three crews. Twelve men and three vehicles . . . !"

"All dead and gone except me, bucko!" Kelly said cheerfully.

"Shit!" Brynulf stamped a size twelve boot and thumped the top of Del's SUV with a huge fist, denting the roof. "We need to get going here before more locals show up asking too many questions," Brynulf said as they all noted several vehicles approaching from both directions. "Evald and I will ride with you, the other four will take the Yukon. Evald! Bring the phone and your weapon," Brynulf said as he stuffed himself in behind Kelly. As Evald slid in beside the big blond man and slammed the door, Brynulf slapped Del on the back of the head.

"Go, you idiot, go!" The deputy's SUV shot out past wide-eyed civilians gawking at the smoking mess along the highway.

"There is another road they might use rather than the main highway to Grant City?" Brynulf wanted to know.

"Yeah, there is a secondary farm-market road that connects to the old two-lane highway that eventually ends up in the reservation," Del volunteered.

Evald had been tapping buttons on the satellite phone and handed it to Brynulf.

"Speaking!" he said, then listened. After a while he said, "Good, we will catch them easily. They are driving an old truck that can't possibly outrun our vehicles. Yes, yes, okay."

X X X X X

Omega pressed the off button and laid the satellite phone on the big gleaming desk in his yacht. The sun would soon be gone from the coast of Spain. Perhaps it would be wise now to put Operation Disconnect into action.

His contact in Cheyenne Mountain had accessed the satellite surveillance system once too often, or had he? His last transmission showed the truck carrying the fugitive president headed north on a secondary two-lane highway into Montana. Omega feared that perhaps he had exceeded the bounds of influence with a request to launch a predator drone strike.

Almost immediately he had been informed of the arrest of a young, idealistic airman inside the super secret Spy in the Sky facility. The man had been very useful in diverting search and rescue efforts at and near the crash site of Air Force One. Other sources suggested that Vice President Sheldon Parker had launched his own investigation based on personal interviews with Air Force One pilot Jeff Ferguson.

Ferguson was showing uncharacteristic behavior that belied his public image of a stumblebum buffoon. Perhaps they had misjudged the man.

Omega alerted his network to stand by to be ready to put Operation Disconnect into motion in ninety minutes; that done, Omega ordered the captain of his yacht to set sail for the Mediterranean. Although his benefactor had not survived the Arab Spring, the billions he had dedicated were still working to destroy what he considered *The World's Greatest Enemy* by any means possible.

That influence, like the ivy vines that worked their way between stones and through brick walls, had worked its tentacles into the ideology of the Left and the halls of learning in the US. Recruitment to the cause had not even been an issue and now *useful idiots* existed like a cancer spread throughout the body of the US.

Ninety minutes; just enough time to enjoy the sixteen-year-old cheerleader who was lured aboard a private jet so she could wave to her friends from the air. He imagined the parents were now plastering the neighborhood with missing posters. He sighed; in a couple of weeks they could look for her on the bottom of the Mediterranean.

While Omega's yacht weighed anchor, Monica Farizzi and Sheriff Glenn Harper had both received a call to stand by for a second call in an hour and a half. The same call went out by robot to hundreds of other people who, like Farizzi and Harper, were busy packing.

X X X X X

Cell phone service was spotty around the border between Wyoming and Montana, but Billy Black Stone was able to reach his grandfather Alden Spotted Horse.

"I been talkin' to Larry Ring Shield about this," Alden said. "He said Crazy Horse liked to make traps. Maybe we could make one that would keep innocent people out of the way, while we surprise these guys from behind."

"I'm listening, Grandfather," Billy replied. Alden had just started to lay out the plan when they passed out of a coverage area. Billy looked at the cell phone in dismay. "Leave it up to a White Man's invention to let the Indians down."

Billy laid out as much as he could find out before the phone went dead.

"Who is Larry Ring Shield?" Kasha wanted to know.

"He's a Rosebud Sioux. Pretty smart guy and a good singer," Billy said. Before he could continue, Ace interrupted, "A Crow giving a compliment to a Sioux? What's this world coming to?"

"At least *our* treaty is doing waaaaay better than *your* treaty," Billy said as he poked Ace in the ribs.

"My treaty?" Ace pretended to be deeply wounded by the affront. "I didn't sign the damn thing!"

"Hey, you two, knock it off! Those guys are still back there, and now there's another vehicle with them; looks like they got some reinforcements," Jay Gee said as he checked the road behind them in the mirror. "What did Alden say about where we should go next?"

"Grandfather said to go through the battlefield monument and take the one-lane road south that goes to Reno Hill. We can stop at a spot on high ground right near the end of the road where it follows along the spine of a ridge. I know the place. It's a good spot. We can hold them off and they can't get around. They'll have to stay on the road. There's no cover for them except sagebrush, and the civilians will be safe on the south side of the hill, out of the line of fire. That's when the phone went dead."

"Ah!" said Ace. "And the reservation cops and their *deputies* can come swarming up from behind. Brilliant!"

"What if the plan doesn't work?" Irena wanted to know.

"We do a *Wagon Box* thing and fort up," Ace said.

Jay Gee said over his shoulder, "This all sounds great as long as this rescue party isn't operating on *Crow time*."

"Hey! Did you ever hear of Indians being late for a massacre?" Billy shot back.

As they turned into the Little Bighorn Battlefield National Monument, they watched a trio of vehicles turn off the secondary highway behind them and head up the hill. Apparently, Alden had cleared the way because the gatekeeper, a pretty Indian girl, waved them through the entrance.

They roared through the parking lot and were approaching the Last Stand Hill monolith when Jay Gee steered violently to the right. A huge motor home swerving the other direction was doing a slow-motion roll on its side blocking the entire road. The motor home laid over behind Brutus while the front of the truck was stuck up against the big concrete monument inscribed with the names of troopers from the Seventh Cavalry.

"Wagon box time!" Ace shouted. "Everybody out!"

The little party of refugees had just found places to hunker down when the three pursuing vehicles screeched to a halt disgorging men who sought cover behind the scattered stone markers of Custer's fallen men.

CHAPTER SIXTEEN
Conclusion

THE NATIONAL PARK Service had decided that the elderly iron picket fence surrounding the small plot where Custer fell should be temporarily removed for grounds maintenance before winter set in for good. The plans for replacing the fence with something that had a little more class were still on the table, so a *Do Not Cross* ribbon fluttered in the wind to hopefully keep the visitors from trampling the area.

The ribbon meant nothing at all to Brynulf, Evald, and the other men who had followed them. The plan to charge Ace's little group dissolved quickly when two men went down to a single blast of "buck and ball" from the 12 gauge wielded by Omar. The president was now protecting his family, but he forgot Ace's instructions about holding the shotgun tight against his shoulder. Omar had followed Ace's instruction to lay flat behind the concrete curb at the monument's base as he fired at the men still bunched up as they exited the vehicles. The butt stock smacked his collarbone so hard that for a moment he thought he'd been shot!

Ace, Billy, Yaz, and Jay Gee were firing from whatever cover they could find without exposing themselves. Their attackers found refuge behind the stone markers where they fired random blind shots in the general direction of the monument. The stones didn't offer a lot of cover and they soon learned that any portion of a body left exposed was likely to be perforated.

The firing died down to an occasional shot now and then as each side appeared reluctant to waste ammunition or risk exposure for a shot.

"Omar!" Ace hollered. "If any of those people get up to run to another position, cut loose with that 12 gauge. You have as good a chance as any of us to hit 'em!"

"Jay Gee! Where's that ammo box?" Ace asked.

"Damn it! It's still in the truck," Jay Gee said, and before there was any more discussion, he jumped for the still-open driver's door. A few poorly aimed pistol slugs clanked into the truck that were answered by return fire from the defenders at the monument.

Jay Gee gave the heavy box a fling in Ace's direction, then followed it to the relative safety of the cement monument base.

"I got an idea," Ace said as he popped open the ammo box. "Ah, here they are!" He held up two clips of M-1 ammunition. "Trade you," Ace told Jay Gee who handed Ace the Garand while he took the single-shot. "Ready?" Ace asked.

"Any time, pops!" Jay Gee replied with a grin.

Ace fired, and a coffee cup-sized divot appeared about four inches from the edge near the base on one of the markers that hid one of the attackers. The second shot put another divot in the center next to the first. "Watch him now!" Ace warned. The third shot's result was a crack clear across the marker which stood for only a second before it toppled flat on the prairie grass exposing the man behind it. The attacker tried to roll to the next marker, but two simultaneous shots from Ace and Jay Gee flattened the man in the grass.

This tactic did not go unnoticed by Brynulf who signaled his men to back away and to try to encircle the defenders.

Kelly and Deputy Del Fulton were watching the action from the deputy's SUV. Del had declined to follow Brynulf and his men, while Kelly made as if to join them, but as soon as he saw they were focused on their task, he spun on his heels and sauntered back to join the deputy.

"You know, I been thinkin', my fine chubby little friend," Kelly said. "It would be expedient for us to claim we was kidnapped by them fellas, if we get caught, that is. But you can do whatever you want. As for me, while everybody's watchin' the show, I think I'll just *mosey,* as you cow-persons are inclined to say." Kelly slid out of the passenger seat, stood, turned, and bumped into the biggest Indian he had ever seen. The little Irishman's nose only came up to officer Jefferson Iron Bird's shirt pocket. The pistol Kelly had been carrying clattered to the pavement as a huge hand lifted him by the shirt collar.

"Didn't your mother feed you when you were a baby?" asked the Indian cop.

Another Indian policeman had approached the driver's side. "Are these the guys Alden told us about?" he asked his big fellow officer.

"Looks like them, alright," said Jefferson. "Lock 'em up in the wagon. I don't want these snakes shootin' us in the back while we figure out how to deal with that mess up on the hill." Del tried to protest that he was the law, but was told succinctly, "Not up here you aren't!"

Del and Kelly had just been locked in the police van when the two cops turned their attention to the thunder of hooves thudding on the sod and clacking on the pavement behind them to the north.

Larry Ring Shield and thirty-five young Indians who had been practicing for the Indian Relay Races down at the fairgrounds, came flying by headed for the museum.

The ponies milled about several park rangers who were handing out the replica weapons used during demonstrations of Plains Indian warfare.

Marvin Rhythm Dancer, Chief Ranger, told Larry, "I'd give anything to be twenty years younger and sixty pounds lighter so I could go with you guys," as he handed Larry a mean-looking war hammer with a stone head. Seeing that they all had weapons, Larry let out a wild whoop and the cavalcade rumbled past the museum toward Last Stand Hill.

At first the attackers could not understand the meaning of the commotion behind them. Nearly all of them turned to look. A few forgot about exposure and were reminded to keep their heads down by fire from the monument.

For the second time in one hundred and thirty six years, Indian warriors swept through the ranks of invading white men. Some of the men stood up to surrender and were bowled over by a blow from a war club. Some tried to fire their weapons, but the targets were too fast and too many and they fell pinioned by lances or by arrows fired from only a few feet away.

Billy Black Stone was up as soon as he saw the riders coming. He ran to the truck and loosened Ace's spear from its bailing wire wrap. Movement from the corner of his eye revealed that Brynulf had wormed his way to the east and around the slope beyond the overturned motor home. He was running clumsily through the sagebrush and tall prairie grass.

Ace stood to watch through the sight on the M-1. Jay Gee saw what Ace was looking at, and then the whole crew noticed and turned to watch the drama.

"If that son of a bitch turns to shoot that boy, I'll nail him!" Ace muttered.

Billy ran like an antelope. Brynulf had begun his run a good seventy-five yards ahead of Billy. He figured he had plenty of time to look back at his pursuer, so he concentrated on watching the ground ahead. Brynulf didn't stand a chance. Billy was right behind him in seconds. The lithe Indian reached the seven-foot length of the spear forward to stab the fleeing man's right calf. Brynulf stumbled and cartwheeled into the dirt losing the pistol he had been carrying in his right hand.

No sooner had the big blond man rolled onto his back, than he felt the point of the eighteen-inch blade drawing a trickle of blood from his throat.

Billy shifted his grip on the shaft so he could pull a second pistol from Brynulf's belt; that done, Billy removed the blade from the man's neck, reversed the shaft, and rapped the startled man sharply on the shoulder with the butt. The Indian boy gave the Swede a look of utmost contempt, turned on his heel and stalked off, leaving Brynulf to wonder what the hell had just happened. Billy Black Stone had just counted coup.

The fight was over almost before it began. The battlefield was curiously quiet.

Ace still had Brynulf covered with the M-1 while Jay Gee walked out to escort the man back to the monument.

In the distance, everyone could hear the heavy thump of rotor blades as the Montana National Guard made its way down from Billings.

Marvin had called them as soon as he knew Ace and his party would be arriving for sure.

Not all of the attackers had been killed, but all of them except Brynulf were very much the worse for wear.

The *warriors*, almost to a man, were still jittery and excited from the adrenaline rush.

Jefferson Iron Bird used up his entire supply of plastic restraints and had to resort to some of Ace's bailing wire to the accompaniment of much grumbling from the prisoners.

Some of the young Indians helped the wide-eyed and disheveled old couple out of their motor home. They were banged up but uninjured. The old man was heard saying, "Boy are we ever going to have something to talk about when we get back to Florida!"

Ace leaned against Brutus and surveyed his crew. Kasha ran up and threw her arms around the old man. "Do we have to leave now?" she asked.

Ace nodded toward the helicopters. "I'm sure your ride home has arrived."

"I'm going to miss you," Kasha said, as her eyes welled up with tears. She looked down at her feet for a moment then asked, "Are these boots really all mine?"

"Yes, they most certainly are, young lady. When you get back to school, I imagine you will be a tough act to follow if you use them in Show and Tell," Ace grinned.

The helicopters were getting closer. Omar and Irena came close to Ace. Omar put out his hand. "You know, this is the first time I have taken your hand during all of this?" the president said. They shook hands.

Irena took Ace's hand while Omar still held it. "I don't know how we can ever repay you, Mr. Gro . . . , uh, Ace," she said, embarrassed somewhat by the blend of formality and familiarity.

"I'll see that you're well paid for your inconvenience and your loses," Omar began, but Ace cut him off.

"Don't worry about it. If you want to pay me back, I'd like to think that you took something away from this experience that teaches you something about the people who inhabit the heartland. I'll tell you now that the reason I jumped in to help you is the same reason other Americans kicked Germany and Japan's asses when the chips were down. I truly believe there are people like us all over this country, from coast to coast and border to border, who would do the same. They just do what has to be done and then go about their business."

"That's what I intend to do now," Ace continued. "The best I can hope for here is that you'll change things for real back there in Washington. Speaking of which, it looks like your ride has arrived."

The big Guard chopper landed and disgorged troops ready for action, but there was none. They fanned out professionally and it was good to see some form of organization.

A colonel strode over and saluted. "Mr. President, we're here to take you and your family and Lieutenant Yasulevicz to Billings. There is a plane waiting to take you to Washington. Please follow me sir."

The man was all business Ace noted. He called after the officer, "Excuse me! Hey!"

The Colonel stopped abruptly. "Yes? We're in a hurry. What do you want, and who do you think you are? We . . ." The officer suddenly realized he was addressing a wild-looking man wearing dirty clothes and holding a vintage automatic rifle backed by some other armed people who had now all turned to face him holding a variety of weapons.

"Uh . . . !" The man seemed out of his element in spite of his rank. Probably a pretty nice guy in civilian life, Ace thought, but before he could say anything, Omar stepped in.

"Colonel, these people saved our lives and kept us alive in spite of overwhelming odds. Whatever they want or need, I expect you to see that they get it, whatever it is, no questions asked. Is that clear?"

"Yes sir, Mr. President!" the Colonel responded, a little red faced.

Ace stepped forward. "Whoa, whoa, whoa! It just occurred to me with all of these husky soldier boys standin' around, maybe we could tip these poor folks' home back on its wheels. What do you say?"

Omar asked, "Is that all you need?"

"I don't need anything, but maybe you could get Uncle Sammy to fix up these nice folks' motor coach and have them checked out by a doctor just in case, you know," Ace said.

"But your truck! There's bullet holes . . . ," Ace interrupted the president. "Souvenirs, sir, souvenirs! Look, you guys better get going. I'm sure things are gonna get real busy real fast, and I'll also bet you dollars to donuts that when you finally round up enough people you can trust, they'll be busier than a cow's tail during fly season trying to catch all the rats jumpin' off your ship."

"I know there will be some people who want to talk to you, Ace, and Billy too. Where will you be?"

"If we're not at the ranch, we'll be at the Big Swampy Campground. I'll move my camp down there now that the first snow has come. And if it makes no never mind to anyone, I'd like to *confiscate* their ATV," Ace said, nodding his head toward the prisoners who were being herded away, "and their tent and cargo trailer they left at Gloomy Creek."

"That's the least I can do. I'll try to remember to pass the word along . . ."

"Kasha interrupted her father, "I'll remind you every day, daddy!"

"Sir . . . ," the Colonel reminded them.

"Yep! Gotta go. We will never forget what you folks did. Bye!" And the president, his family and Yaz, who had given Billy a long hug, hurried to the waiting helicopter.

The soldiers and the relay racers tipped the motor home back on its wheels, but it wouldn't start. Ace walked over to the still-shaken couple from the motor home. "Come with me, hurry."

Ace and the old couple hustled down the hill where Jefferson Iron Bird was attempting to figure out what to do with all of his prisoners. After some hurried negotiations, the Indian Police *appropriated* all the cash they could find among the prisoners, which amounted to nearly eight hundred dollars. The big policeman handed the collected cash to the couple. He said they were welcome to take either one of the Black Yukons that sat abandoned in the parking lot, drive to Billings, and get a nice room at the Holiday Inn. He handed them a card with instructions to call his office in a day or two.

Billy and Jay Gee got Brutus backed away from the Monument and headed down the hill to the parking lot which was beginning to fill up with ambulances, police and highway patrol cars and finally, some trucks from the National Guard. As Jay Gee, Billy, and Ace drove out toward the park's gate, they caught a glimpse of Kelly and Del looking very dejected behind the glass in Iron Bird's patrol car.

Billy shook his head, "I don't know about that Kelly fella. Somehow, his type always seems to come out smelling like a rose, but I sure feel sorry for Del. He's in deep, deep shit!"

"All I want to do is get back up to camp and sleep for a week," Ace said, and as Jay Gee steered Brutus back toward the Big Horns, Ace laid back and began to snore.

There were no commercial or professional TV cameras present and the only pictures the world was now getting were grainy and jerky out-of-focus video from some phone cameras.

The news was electrifying. All of the previous rumors were now forgotten as it was officially verified that the president and his family had been found alive after being lost in the mountains of Wyoming during a snowstorm. It was very difficult to keep track of what actually happened as the talking heads blathered on and on about what went right and what went wrong, who was to blame and who was to be congratulated. It would actually take years to sort it all out.

Epilogue

Bernie and Sarah Bernstein did not wait until they reached Billings, Montana, to call their children on Sarah's iPhone. She began calling as soon as they were on their way.

Bernie had slammed on the brakes and jerked the steering wheel to the right when the flatbed dualie suddenly appeared racing up the hill toward his motor home. Sarah was thrown to the floor when Bernie slammed on the brakes, and then found herself laying on the bathroom's slim door as the behemoth rolled on its side. The door handle left a big red welt on her ribs that turned a nice deep purple a few hours later.

Bernie yelled at Sarah to get in the back. He was struggling with the seat-belt buckle while he watched the twinkle of gunfire from men finding protection behind grave markers. The wide expanse of the windshield glass in front of him left him feeling very exposed.

Bernie didn't know what or who was doing the shooting; he just knew that he and Sarah needed to get as far to the rear of the motor home as they could get.

That is when Sarah burrowed beneath the mattress in the rear bedroom where she had a clear view through the rear window of Ace and his companions defending themselves. As Bernie joined Sarah, she reached for her ever-present phone, selected the camera function, and began recording the activity.

Less than an hour later, before any news organization had any graphics to accompany the wild stories that were beginning to trickle out of Montana, Sarah's pictures went viral on the internet. With the entire world watching, there was the President of the United States shooting at some people yet to be identified!

Thirty minutes after the pictures were out and verified, a famous talk-show host was the first to note: "I kid you not folks, and please pardon my pun here, but the anti-gun crowd has gone ballistic after watching their poster child for gun control actually defending himself and his family with (pregnant pause) a GUNNN!"

X X X X X

The day after the latest Battle of the Little Big Horn, Ace, Billy, and Jay Gee moved the hunting camp from its hiding place at Elephant Rock down to the public campground on Big Swampy Creek.

Even as they were setting up the tent, investigators from the Air Force and federal and state agencies were pestering them for information. In desperation, Jay Gee drove out to an area that had cell phone service and put in a call to Under Sheriff Riley Mossberg.

"I heard your boss disappeared," Jay Gee said. Riley affirmed that Sheriff Harper had indeed gone away, and no one knew where. There was an unconfirmed report that someone resembling the truant sheriff had scurried aboard a private jet at the Grant County Airport.

Jay Gee told Riley if he wanted to do them a big favor, he could come on up to Ace's camp, do an in-depth interview with Ace and Billy, and with the aid of a good topo map, he could set himself up as the "go to" guy for all those investigators.

When Riley expressed his reluctance, Jay Gee reminded the under sheriff he would garner a tremendous amount of name recognition that couldn't hurt in the next election.

Riley Mossberg finally got used to the TV cameras enough to focus on the business at hand, which was to shuttle the various requests and questions to people most qualified to handle them.

Riley made a pile of copies of his very detailed notes that he had gleaned from Ace, Billy, and Jay Gee. He even managed to pry some details out of Frank Wellington about his trip to Bomber Mountain to pack out the crash survivors, and then handed them out to whatever agency happened to be next in line clamoring for information.

The news channels could not keep up with "the latest developments" as more and more people were swept up in a growing conspiracy scandal.

X X X X X

Vice President Sheldon Parker shared the news spotlight by contributing all of the information his people had learned from the few survivors of Air Force One. It became quite obvious that there had been a concerted and deliberate effort to delay and confuse rescue and recovery operations, and the VP wanted to make it clear that he was doing everything possible to deflect any suspicion away from himself.

X X X X X

Monica Farizzi suddenly declared she had urgent "family business" to handle on her Guatemalan plantations, stepped aboard a private jet, and was never heard from again.

X X X X X

There was some vague report that the former Speaker had stepped aboard a jet belonging to Pavel Santorini, but the man, when contacted, said he was vacationing on a remote Greek Island and could not vouch for the whereabouts of one of his several airplanes.

X X X X X

Two months after the disappearance of Sheriff Glenn Harper, people photographing wild horses in the Red Desert stumbled across a pile of clothing in a small depression. Upon closer inspection, they discovered pulverized human remains. Investigators speculate the late sheriff had bailed out of an aircraft from a very high altitude without the benefit of a parachute.

X X X X X

The list of people scurrying to abandon the sinking Progressive Party grew longer by the day. Some merely wanted to disassociate themselves. Others were found to be implicated to one extent or another, while others in the Party, different bureaus, and even the military, were caught trying to sneak out of the country.

X X X X X

It was difficult to sort out the various motives for each individual's involvement in the plot to make Omar Bahktar a martyr. Money seemed to be primary, while idealism ran a close second for most. There was at least one suicide per week as investigators probed deeper and deeper.

X X X X X

The opposing Party candidate, Howard Whitehorse, won the presidential election by default, which seemed a hollow victory until he announced that he had decided to appoint the former president to head up a special commission tasked with ferreting out the miscreants who had plotted his own destruction.

X X X X X

Omar Bahktar turned down an invitation from the Russian Prime Minister to hunt mountain goats in a rugged mountainous area. It was clear that the *he-man* Russian leader wanted a chance to redeem his *tough guy* spot as a person one should not *mess with*.

Adding another "off-camera" remark heard around the world, the former US President told the Russian, "I don't have to prove anything to anybody. To tell the truth, there were a bunch of times in Wyoming and Montana when I was scared shitless!" The late-night talk show comedians had a field day with that remark,

X X X X X

Acerbic left-wing comedians and pundits found that the American public was beginning to vote with their feet and their pocketbooks as divisive rhetoric became extremely unpopular when the *man on the street* began to see the results of extreme idealism.

X X X X X

Almost lost to the headlines was a back page news item of a sixteen-year-old kidnap victim plucked from a yacht in the Mediterranean by US Navy SEALS.

The girl said she had been working in an airport restaurant where an unidentified Middle Eastern-looking man began leaving her fifty- and hundred-dollar tips. One day the man's aide asked if she wanted to take a ride in his boss's private jet while they took it for a test flight. She was told to tell no one since it would be similar to a joy ride, which added to the excitement of the experience. The last thing she remembered after boarding the plane was being offered a soft drink. The next thing she remembered was waking up on a fancy boat with people speaking a foreign language.

She said her captor was continually being distracted by calls on his satellite phone, most of which seemed to cause more and more distress.

They were anchored at sea and the teenager was locked in her cabin as usual when she heard scuffling, several shots, and some shouting. Her door opened and an American in a wetsuit asked if she was okay. He had a backpack and held a black machine gun. He told her to stay quiet and he would be right back.

She heard one of the SEALS ask someone something about someone named Omega.

Then she heard another American voice call, "Found him!"

There was more scuffling, a couple of thumps, and everything was quiet.

The frightened girl said the SEAL came back and led her to the stern of the yacht, where he lowered her into a rubber boat. More SEALS got into the boat without saying anything and motored away from the yacht. One of the SEALS spoke quietly into a radio and soon she saw a shape rise from the sea that turned out to be an American submarine. As they were boarding the submarine, a brilliant explosion lit up the night sky where the yacht had been.

A doctor on the submarine checked her out, and she was allowed to call her parents. She told them that when she was old enough, she wanted to join the Navy.

Back in the USA, it was a winter of reaching across the aisle as both houses of government nervously exerted extraordinary effort to repair the rifts of years of partisan politics. By summer, some of the same ol' same ol' was sneaking back in.

X X X X X

The Little Big Horn Battlefield National Monument saw a whopping increase in visitors wanting to stand on the spot where the president held off the terrorists. Although the *terrorists* were merely hired criminals, the Left pushed the label so much that it stuck in the public's perception, and the Justice Department gave up trying to foist a different term upon the media.

X X X X X

The casino and Indian craft shop at Crow Agency did very well indeed because of the publicity. At Crow Fair that fall, the tribe was proud to point to the actions of an adopted member of the Black Eagle Family, Omar Bahktar. The former president was late for a ceremony honoring him and joked about operating on *Crow time*.

X X X X X

It was obvious that Omar had changed his demeanor that previous critics had labeled "arrogant" to something just short of humble. His speech was comparatively short.

"Let me be perfectly clear, heh, heh! This ceremony is not about me. It is about the office I once held and individual Americans who saw someone in need and came to the rescue. It is about the abuse of power and good and evil. You are all aware of the story by now. It was the office of the President of the United States that was under attack, and through that, it was an attack on all of us. Some Americans did not survive the attack. They will be remembered for their sacrifice and I am deeply humbled by that. Although I was urged not to mention the names of the people involved in last October's attack, there is one individual American who has, by tribal consent, earned the title of War Chief. I am proud to present to the world, Chief Black Stone!"

Billy Black Stone walked rather awkwardly onto the stage in full chief regalia.

The ex-president went on after the applause died. "Chief Black Stone fought and defeated the enemy on a field of battle. Although they had no horses, he took their ATV!" This drew a ripple of laughter. "He took their weapons. He counted coup on an enemy and gave an enemy his life. It is my honor to turn the stage over to my friend, Chief Black Stone." Omar thrust the microphone into Billy's hand and left the stage as a sign that he was now finished.

When the crowd finally grew silent, Billy nervously cleared his throat, startled as the amplified sound bounced back at him. "Um, I don't know what to say. This is pretty scary, you know. I guess all I can say is that I only did what my Grandfather did so many years ago in Europe. These things have changed the way I look at stuff, you know what I mean? Some of our young people have forgotten about honor. I hope this, here, today, helps to bring that honor and pride back. I want to thank the guys from the Relay Racers. They did a hell of a . . . , excuse me! A heck of a job. In fact they did all of the hard stuff up there." Billy nodded toward the battlefield.

Billy looked around for a place to put the microphone. Gene Plain Feather, the MC and sometimes auctioneer, came forward to take the microphone and prompt the crowd into another round of cheering while Billy hurried off the stage.

X X X X X

The local news had very little information on the deceased Sheriff Harper of Grant County, except to say that he had impeded rescuers and search efforts after Air Force One was shot down. How he had been implicated or who had compromised his office was never clearly established. Deputy Del Fulton was happy to spill his guts to anyone who would listen. He claimed to have been coerced by the former sheriff and then kidnapped by the *terrorists*.

X X X X X

The little Irishman, Kelly, somehow escaped custody and disappeared.

X X X X X

Brynulf's satellite phone and other items found in the big SUVs yielded a wealth of information that obviously led the Navy to Omega's yacht and the recovery of the teenaged kidnap victim.

X X X X X

By fall things were getting back to normal but with a lot less partisan bickering and a new sense of cooperation. How long would it last? Who knows?

Ace was back at Elephant Rock enjoying the peace and quiet. He and Jay Gee had set up hunting camp a week early, and now it was time to relax.

The Sims stove was ticking as the metal cooled, but the nearly full coffee cup on the edge still steamed. Ace was trying to read a book but kept nodding off. The muted sputter of an ATV down on the Swampy Creek Road caught his attention, and as he listened, he heard the engine stop. Ace put the book down and waited.

"Hello the tent!" Ace recognized Fred Fielding, Forest Ranger for the Boulder District.

"Go away. Whatever you're sellin', I don't want any!" Ace hollered in his best annoyed tone of voice.

There was a shuffle of feet, some murmuring and a stifled giggle, then Kasha thrust her head inside the tent flap. "Surprise!"

"Well now, look what the old tomcat dragged into my camp!" Ace said with a hearty laugh as he got to his feet. He was nearly bowled over by the enthusiastic hug he got from the excited young lady.

Fred held the flap back and Omar Bahktar stepped into the tent and stuck out his hand.

"I think about this place and you every day," he said.

Ace grinned and said, "Well, I don't have to wonder what you're up to. The papers, and the radio and the TV are keeping me pretty well up-to-date on the public stuff. So how are you holdin' up otherwise? You're lookin' good!"

"There is so much I'd like to say that I don't know where to begin," Omar said, "but I have been in touch with Ranger Fielding here for several months and we have something we feel we must have you participate in."

Fred was grinning behind the former president. "It's a pretty heavy thing, but I believe you'll like it, Ace."

Kasha was practically jumping up and down, "You have to come down to the quad to see it. Please!" The girl tugged on Ace's hand.

There on the road was a new side-by-side four-passenger ATV with a small utility box on the back. Fred reached in and pulled away the canvas cover on a large bronze plaque. Ace read the inscription.

IN MEMORY OF:
AIR FORCE PILOT, ELIEZAR WEINTHAL
SPECIAL AGENT, RICHARD MASON
WYOMING GAME WARDEN, JERRY "PAT" GARRETT
SPECIAL FRIEND, DOZER
Their lives were lost in the service of their country and
The protection of the President of the United States and his family.
Oct 2012

Ace stood silent for a minute while he thought of two close friends he had lost on the mountain.

"Yaz told me about Weinthal. She said he deliberately steered into the path of one of the missiles meant for your plane, sir," Ace commented.

Omar looked Ace in the eye. "Yes, I found out later he had just received his citizenship after moving here from Israel. He took being an American more seriously than many people I know. I would appreciate it if you would ride with us up to that spot where you showed me how to fire your shotgun. Ranger Fielding . . ."

"Fred." The old forest ranger interrupted.

"Fred," Omar continued, "has obtained the clearance to mount the plaque there and we'd like you to be present."

Ace looked back down the road toward the campground. "No Press, no secret service?"

Omar clapped Ace on the shoulder. "Who needs the secret service when we have you?" he grinned, then he added, "There are four other people at the campground, but its okay. You'll see."

It was a beautiful fall afternoon as two four-place ATVs rolled across the grassy park below the granite outcrop people were beginning to call Garrett Point.

It didn't take long to mount the plaque to a flat spot with explosive bolts.

Alden Spotted Horse performed a ceremony to bless the commemoration while Billy Black Stone, Melanie Yasulevicz, Ace, Fred, and the Bahktars; Omar, Elena, and Kasha looked on in respectful silence.

"Such a beautiful place!" Yaz said. "Its hard to believe what happed here only a year ago." Everyone agreed.

Billy spoke up, "I heard there will be another plaque on Bomber Mountain for the crew and staff who did not survive the crash of Air Force One."

"They are still putting that together, but I'm sure we'll get one up there next summer," Fred said.

"You know I've got plenty of elk steak in my cooler at camp and I also have some Kolts for afterward," Ace said with a twinkle in his eye.

"What's that?" Kasha wanted to know.

"Its firewater made by those crazy Pollack's down in Grant City," Billy told her, "and you're too young, so you'll have to settle for a Coke."

"I've waited for a year for one of those steaks!" Omar said as he climbed into the ATV.

"Just like old times, only better," Ace proclaimed.

The grownups were sipping the last of the Kolt beverage and feeling the effects. Kasha had climbed onto the top bunk to prop her chin in her hands, while Alden droned on about an old Crow legend. Fred said he would have to beg a sleeping bag from someone rather than drive down the mountain. Everyone else found excuses why they should stay and savor the moment and Ace clinched it by saying, "Okay, now you will all have to stay to hear this story, which will take all night to tell. It was fifty years ago, maybe more. I was a know-it-all young buck when I went to work for an old-time outfitter over in the Wind Rivers. I stumbled onto the secret of the payroll shipment of gold coins meant for the soldiers stationed in Yellowstone in the late 1880s or 90s. Some bandits held up the soldiers and disappeared. Some say it was Butch Cassidy, but I found out who got it in the end."

The light inside the canvas in the tent at Elephant Rock glowed late into the night.

The End
Of this story

CPSIA information can be obtained at www.ICGtesting.com
Printed in the USA
BVOW08*2006241113

336990BV00002BC/258/P